More pr Linda Grant and LETHAL GENES

25

By Linda Grant

LOVE NOR MONEY*
BLIND TRUST*
RANDOM ACCESS MURDER
A WOMAN'S PLACE*
LETHAL GENES*

*Published by Ivy Books

LETHAL GENES

Linda Grant

Linda Grant

IVY BOOKS • NEW YORK

Ivy Books
Published by Ballantine Books
Copyright © 1996 by Linda V. Williams

http://www.randomhouse.com

This book is a work of fiction. Names, characters, places, and incidents either are products of the author's imagination or are used fictitiously. Any resemblance to actual events or locales or persons, living or dead, is entirely coincidental.

Names of companies are also fictitious and any resemblance to actual corporate entities is entirely coincidental.

Library of Congress Catalog Card Number: 97-93585

ISBN 0-8041-1558-3

This edition published by arrangement with Scribner, an imprint of Simon and Schuster Inc.

Manufactured in the United States of America

First Ballantine Books Edition: November 1997

10 9 8 7 6 5 4 3 2 1

To Michael and Catherine Freeling

Acknowledgments

I am deeply grateful to Dr. Michael Freeling and the members of his lab at the University of California at Berkeley for their generous help with the research for this book. My particular thanks to Dr. Barbara Kloeckener, Barbara Lane, Assunta Chytry, Lisa Harper, Melissa Quilter, Denise Schichnes, and Randall Tyers. I would also like to express my appreciation to Michael Young of Heartland; Dr. Toby D. Gottfried of Calypte Biomedical; Al Holbert of Poseidon Systems; N. Tom Siebe, Chief Deputy Coroner, Sonoma County; and Elizabeth Lynn, Sensei, Eastshore Aikikai.

My thanks also to Susan Dunlap, Janet LaPierre, Barbara Dean, and Anne Jensen for their thoughtful and perceptive comments on the manuscript. And my great gratitude to Susanne Kirk, for being such a terrific editor, and for her support, encouragement, and friendship. Finally, a special thank you to my husband, Andrew, whose wisdom and support enrich my books and my life. And to my daughters, Erin and Megan, who provide so much pleasure and, occasionally, material.

1

"**C**ORN SEX, TEN o'clock," the note read. I picked up the phone and buzzed my secretary.

"Corn sex?" I asked.

"Oh, that's the guy from the University of California. He runs a genetics lab, corn genetics. He called late Friday afternoon, was really anxious to see you, so I fit him in this morning."

I considered pointing out that I spend enough time deciphering mysterious documents without adding my appointment book to the list, but I let it go. The investigation business can be grim at times; you've got to take your humor where you find it.

It wasn't corn sex that came to mind when Paul Raskin walked into my office, looking for all the world like James Dean, grown up and not quite so sulky. His hair was a shade darker and his chin a bit less sharp, but otherwise he looked as I imagined Dean would have if he'd had a chance to grow up.

I've got a soft spot for bad boys. Always have had. Maybe it comes from being the daughter of a cop. I can still remember the look on my dad's face when I was fifteen and Gary Marino picked me up on his motorcycle. Now that I have my own fifteen-year-old to deal with, I cringe at the memory. Back then, that moment was sweet indeed.

Raskin wore dark jeans, a denim shirt, and a black

leather jacket. His hair curled just over his collar, and his skin was tanned and weathered. My secretary, Amy, had said he was from a lab at the University of California, Berkeley, but he looked like a man more suited to the open road than the ivory tower.

I'm a private investigator, specializing in high-tech crime. It's not a Sam Spade world where the PI ogles the gorgeous client. I charge enough to keep my employers' minds on their wallets, and as a woman in a man's field, I work hard to keep sex out of the equation. Which is why my reaction to Paul Raskin unnerved me.

"Get a grip," I told myself as I offered him a chair. I could have suggested he sit on the couch and taken the comfortable chair next to it. I decided to put my desk between us instead.

He hesitated in the doorway, his eyes checking out the room. And as he walked across it, he seemed to be taking in everything from the Japanese calligraphy prints on the walls to the Bukhara carpet on the floor. He paused at the table beside the couch, and a smile came to his face, softening his features. "What a lovely suiseki," he said, indicating the foot-long, gray-green stone cut flat on the bottom and mounted on a carved wooden base.

I'm very fond of my suiseki. It's the top third of a rock that came from the bed of the Tuolumne River, and its smoothed surface reminds me of the parts of the High Sierras behind Yosemite. It has a tiny rounded peak at one end that dips down to a hollow, then flattens out like a rocky shelf.

Suiseki are a Japanese art form. Not many Americans are familiar with them, certainly not most of my clients. If they notice my suiseki at all, most wonder why I have a rock on my table. Paul Raskin was more than a pretty face.

"I like your office," he said as he sat down. Up close, he looked less like James Dean, but his smile had the same shy sensuality that had made the actor so appealing.

"Thank you," I said. I like my office, too. I've decorated it with things that give me pleasure. Many of my treasures, like the suiseki, have a personal connection as well. Most of my clients don't pay much attention to their surroundings, too intent on whatever problem has brought them here. A few seem actually uncomfortable to be in an office so distinctly individual.

"How can I help you?" I asked.

Paul Raskin's smile faded. He looked uncomfortable, unsure of how to start. Finally, he said, "Well, I have a problem, one that requires . . . discretion."

I could have told him that all the problems that walk through my door require discretion; that's why they're here, not downtown at the police department. But I said, "Anything you tell me is confidential. But not privileged. Since I'm not a lawyer, I can be subpoenaed to testify in court."

He looked surprised. "Oh, it's not that sort of thing. I wouldn't be asking you to do anything illegal. It's just that I'd like to solve my problem without getting the university involved."

"Why don't you tell me about it."

He leaned forward in his chair. "We're a maize lab, plant genetics. Around Cal they call us the bonsai lab because most of our research has to do with dwarfism. We study how plants regulate their shape: branching, height, leaf size, greenness.

"The trouble started a couple of weeks ago when someone broke into the greenhouse here, trashed some plants, and stole a whole batch of seed that was being dried. The cops thought it was vandals or maybe someone with a grudge against the students. They weren't too concerned. I should have paid more attention, but I didn't. Then Friday morning two students discovered someone had stolen vials with genetic material they were studying."

He shifted uneasily in his chair, and his features sharpened, becoming almost fierce. "Someone is way out of line. We've got to stop this before anything more happens." His voice was harsh with emotion.

I was startled by the strength of his reaction. "Do you have any suspects?" I asked.

He grimaced and shook his head. "I'm pretty sure it's someone in the lab. Probably a grad student or a postdoc."

His voice was even again, his posture relaxed, no trace of the intense emotion I'd seen flash moments before. Emotion so strong and so quickly suppressed can be a warning sign. I watched Raskin more closely.

"Who gains by sabotaging your work?" I asked.

He considered the question, then shook his head again. "No one. All the research is funded by government grants, so everyone has a stake in its success. That's the money that pays our salaries."

"How about someone outside? Anyone opposed to the research?"

"No. You say genetics and everyone thinks cancer cures or super tomatoes, but we're just doing basic research. No fancy products, no earth-shattering discoveries."

"But you're working with corn," I said. "Your work must have some application to agriculture. Didn't someone sabotage genetically altered strawberries several years ago?"

"Yeah, but that's not the kind of stuff we're doing. The corn isn't the product, it's the medium. What we're looking for is how specific genes affect growth. There'd be applications, sure. If we could isolate a gene that makes plants smaller and pop that gene into other kinds of plants, you could have two-foot fig trees, or three-foot palms. They'd love that in LA."

"So you're working on genetic engineering," I said.

Raskin pressed his lips together in an expression that wasn't quite a grimace. "Well, yes and no," he said. "We're not into making mini-palms, if that's what you mean. But we're doing the research that might enable someone else to make mini-palms.

"We may sell our work to the funding agencies as a boon to the horticultural industry, but what we're really interested in is getting the support to do the science. To poke around and figure out how things work. Any practical applications we happily leave to someone else."

It was hard to imagine anyone getting worked up enough over dwarf plants to sabotage a lab. "Okay," I said. "No financial gain. No political enemies. That leaves the people in the lab. Any grudges?"

"Oh, yes," he said with a smile. "At least as many as people. I guess I better tell you more about our not so happy little family."

He leaned back and crossed one leg over the other. He was probably around forty, but in good shape, a man used to physical labor. He wore his sexuality easily, like a touch of expensive cologne.

"Our lab's been very successful," he said, "because our PI, that's our principal investigator, Kendra Crawford, is very good at getting grant money. Kendra's not just a good scientist, she's great at PR and politics and all the other stuff you have to master to be a player in big science. She's a rising star at Cal. Grad students want to work for her, postdocs want to be part of the scene. Money's flowed easily, so she could bring a number of people on board. That's the problem really. She's been too successful too fast. She hasn't had time to keep close track of the lab."

"What's your role in this?" I asked.

"I'm Kendra's 'right hand.' It's my job to keep the lab running smoothly. I'm sort of a combination slave driver, ombudsman, and big brother. When someone messes with experiments, it's my job to get it stopped."

"You referred to a 'not so happy' family," I said. "What's the problem?"

"The problem is that the last guy who had my job was asleep at the switch. I hear he was fine for a while, then his girlfriend dumped him and his life sort of unraveled.

He just couldn't manage the lab anymore. With no one in charge, things got absolutely Darwinian. The students sound like a bunch of squabbling kids—'he stole my research,' 'she's pigging out on freezer space,' 'he changed the temperature of the water bath.' " He gave each complaint a different whiny voice and a facial expression to match. I laughed in spite of myself and he joined me.

"It's pretty funny really. I mean we're talking high-powered, very bright scientists here, and they sound like kindergartners on the playground. It's not a pretty sight."

"I'm curious why you're so adamant about not involving the university," I said.

This time his smile had a hint of apology. "We have a major grant coming up for renewal. In academia, the grapevine is very long and very gossipy. This is not the time to hang our dirty laundry on it. That's why Kendra will be paying you out of her own pocket."

Academia didn't sound much different from big business. You can catch a saboteur by going undercover, but it's frequently just as effective and much cheaper to call all the suspects in for interviews and scare them into better behavior. I explained the alternatives to Raskin.

As I expected, he preferred the cheaper option. I looked at my calendar. I'd blocked out most of the week to testify in an industrial espionage case, but the companies involved had struck a deal, so my calendar was open. I explained what I charged, and he didn't wince, so I gave him a contract.

"How soon can you start?" he asked.

"As early as this afternoon."

"Great," he said. "We need to move quickly before anything else happens." He rose to go and thanked me with a warm smile. A very warm smile.

I tried not to ogle as he walked out of the room.

Staff meetings at Sayler Investigations are over lunch on Monday. My assistant, Chris, claims that it's because no one dares to talk to me before noon, but the truth is that none of us wants to talk to anybody on Monday morning.

We're a small firm, just the four of us—my partner, Jesse, and I, Chris, and our secretary, Amy. We really could use another assistant, as Chris and Amy remind me regularly, but we haven't found the right person to fit into our feisty family.

Jesse had closed a case on Friday and landed a new one Saturday morning, so he was in unusually good spirits. "Catherine gets the corn and I get the chips," he announced as he unwrapped a Polish sausage sandwich. He wasn't referring to lunch. The corn was Paul Raskin's and the chips were a stolen shipment of microprocessors for medical imaging machines.

I knew why he was so pleased with the chip case. He loves high-tech stuff, especially when it involves the computer industry. Today he was wearing a suit, his young urban professional garb, but under the Brooks Brothers shirt beat a hacker's heart.

"You can go undercover and get double value for that bald fade," I said. He was still sporting the haircut he'd gotten for his last undercover job. The bottom two thirds of his head had been shaved to a five o'clock shadow so that the longer hair sat on top like a cap. It seriously undercut his cool professional image.

He ran his hand over what was left of his hair and laughed. "Claire really hates it," he said. "Says it makes me look like a twenty-year-old homeboy."

Claire is a manager in a commercial real estate firm and does not appreciate having a lover who periodically looks like a street kid. I sympathize with her. She's working hard to overcome the very stereotypes that Jesse uses to snare corporate crooks. Tall and lanky, he looks younger than his thirty years, and being young, black, and male are enough to make some people underestimate both his honesty and his intelligence.

"I bet she was just thrilled to take you to the office Christmas party," Chris said.

Chris takes grooming very seriously. The only time she's refused to do something I asked was when I suggested she dye her hair green for an undercover assignment. Just under six feet and slender as a model with a taste in clothes that makes me look shabby even when I'm well dressed, Chris is too striking to tail anyone. She's a woman both men and women notice and don't forget. She's great at doing just about everything else, and she has an uncanny ability to get people to talk to her.

Jesse reported on the missing microprocessors, and I gave a rundown on the Cal case.

"Genetics," Chris said sharply. "Before long they'll explain everything about us in terms of DNA."

"You suppose there's a hacker gene?" Amy asked, smiling at Jesse.

"No way," he said. "That takes years of practice. But if there's a danger gene, we all know who got that."

Everyone laughed and I rolled my eyes. "You think they'd be able to cure it with gene therapy?" I asked. Lately I seemed to have a knack for picking cases that turned ugly. Several doses of murder and mayhem had left me with almost chronic nightmares. I was beginning to feel jinxed.

"Check it out while you're over at Cal," Jesse said. "Even if they can't cure you, you'll at least get a great last meal. In Berkeley every kid who threw a rock in the sixties opened a restaurant in the eighties."

At Jesse's reference to a last meal, I heard Amy catch her breath. Chris shot him a dirty look.

"Hey," I told them. "Lighten up. It's just a joke. The biggest threat on this case is to my waistline."

If only that had been true.

2

FEBRUARY IN SAN FRANCISCO can bring anything from torrential rains to seventy-degree sunshine, sometimes within twenty-four hours of each other. We'd had the rain last week, and today was cool and breezy with banks of gray clouds sailing east across a sometimes blue sky.

As I drove onto the Bay Bridge, the sun was behind the clouds, turning the lower deck into a dark tunnel. Somewhere past Treasure Island, it became much brighter, and when I emerged at the Oakland end of the bridge, brighter sun poured down, making the tarmac sparkle. On my right, beyond the docks, the buildings of downtown Oakland stood out against the green hills beyond. The ugly scar left by the firestorm several years ago was covered by emerald rain grass and new houses sprouted like mushrooms on the hills.

To the left, Emeryville spread out across the flatlands and Berkeley climbed the hills beyond. At the base of the hills, the stone needle of the Campanile rose above the buildings around it to announce the location of the University of California at Berkeley.

I took the University Avenue off-ramp and drove up the wide street that ended at the western gate of the campus. The Indian restaurants and sari shops gave way to a scruffy assortment of marginal businesses that in turn were replaced by more prosperous shops and finally by the larger buildings of downtown Berkeley. Beyond the end of the street, the squat dome of the Cyclotron capped an intensely green hill.

At the top of University, I turned right and looped around the half-oval of grass in front of the entrance gate. Raskin had left a parking permit for me with the guard. I usually enter the campus at Sather Gate, where there's no guard and the plaza is full of students and ragged street people with a couple of frenzied preachers and maybe a mime or two. The university looked like a different school from the western gate. Here, the road curved uphill through gracious green lawns surrounding stately collegiate buildings, and students walked or cycled along the paths.

Koshland Hall, which was my destination, was on the northwestern corner of the campus about a block from the gate. I turned right at the end of the oval and drove to a wide driveway that seemed to lead directly under the buildings above it.

I don't like underground parking garages. Most of them could have been designed by muggers, and this one was a San Quentin special. Just waiting for the elevator made me uneasy.

Once upstairs, I crossed a wide walkway to the Genetics Building. As I stepped through the door, a subtle odor zapped my mind back to the college labs of my youth. I wondered which chemicals created the overwhelmingly familiar smell. Eau de lab. Curriculum and theory might change, ditto for books and projects, but the buildings still smelled the same. Nice to know there was one constant in this ever-shifting world.

Crawford's lab was on the second floor. I took the elevator and followed a hall that led to the back of the building, where a sign on the door read CRAWFORD LAB. I found the prof's office in a small room off the corridor just inside the door. The office door was open and inside a woman sat typing at a computer terminal.

I knocked and she turned toward me. "Kendra Crawford?" I asked.

She smiled and stood. "Please come in," she said.

Kendra Crawford had a Giacometti body, so lean she walked the fine line between fashion-model thin and malnourished. Her features were delicately chiseled, the bone structure clear beneath smooth pale skin. The thick dark hair that framed her face with waves was cut short.

She wore stonewashed jeans, ankle-high boots with medium heels, and a soft forest-green tunic accented with a silver necklace and earrings. She looked a whole lot more sophisticated and casually elegant than any professor I'd had in college. But, of course, there weren't many women at the podium back then.

I introduced myself and she offered me the only other chair in the office.

"I'm delighted you've agreed to help us," she said. Her voice had a touch of New York in it, maybe not the accent so much as the speed and energy behind it. Not a California voice.

"I think Paul may be overreacting a bit," she said, "but he's right that we need to do something quickly before the situation gets out of hand."

"Did Mr. Raskin explain what I propose to do?"

"Yes. We have our weekly lab meeting tomorrow at ten-thirty. I'll introduce you to the group then. You can begin interviewing them after the meeting."

"Sounds fine to me," I said. "I'd suggest you introduce me at the beginning of the meeting, so everyone knows who I am. That way, I can watch their responses, see if anyone looks particularly nervous."

"Good enough," she said. Her nod was curt. It wasn't hostile, but I had the feeling she wasn't long on patience. She crossed one knee over the other. The move was graceful but not relaxed. I wondered how much she really supported Raskin's proposal to hire me.

"I understand you don't want the university administration to be aware of the problem. Does that mean you don't plan to prosecute or take disciplinary action?" I asked.

"Nothing formal," she said. "But they'd have to leave the lab, and I certainly wouldn't recommend them to anyone else." The finality of her tone suggested that the culprit's career in science would be over.

"Do you have any idea who might be behind the sabotage?" I asked.

"If I did, I'd have dealt with them already."

I paused a moment to keep the irritation out of my voice, then asked, "Is there any reason for an individual or group of individuals to be angry?"

She gave a sharp, short laugh. "I suspect most of them think they have reason to be angry. The postdocs never think I give them enough time or credit, the doctoral students tend to feel downtrodden and abused by the postdocs, the lab technicians feel abused by everybody, and the undergraduates are miserable because no one remembers their names.

"The men think I discriminate against them because they're men. The women come here looking for a mentor and are upset when they find out I treat them just like the men.

"They come because this lab has a lot happening. It gives them a chance to do exciting science. That costs money, and someone has to go out and raise that money. They want the goodies the money brings, but they think I ought to be here all the time to hold their hands."

She sighed and gave an elaborate shrug. "So you see, just about everybody's angry." She picked up a pencil and bounced the eraser on the desk, staring at it absentmindedly. "I sometimes wonder if they'd feel differently if I were a man," she said. "I think subconsciously they expect a woman to be more nurturing."

She turned to me, and her voice grew sharp with irritation. "Well, damnit, I'm a scientist, not a den mother. I'm a much better researcher than I am a teacher, but the university expects teaching, so I do the best I can at it. And whether they're happy or miserable, I expect them to do their jobs."

I wondered if I'd find her abrasive manner less irritating if she were a man. Realized I might. Didn't feel too good about it.

She put the pencil down. Her voice softened slightly. "Years from now when they have their own labs at prestigious universities, they'll be damn glad I pushed them the way I did."

Maybe. But "for your own good" rarely plays well, even in retrospect.

The sound of shattering glass interrupted her. A male voice said, "Oh, shit."

Another male voice demanded, "Why don't you watch what you're doing?"

"Why don't you watch where you put stuff? You set the damn beaker right on the edge."

A third voice, which I recognized as Paul Raskin's, said, "Scott, just clean it up. It isn't radioactive, is it? Tony, let it go."

Moments later Raskin appeared at Crawford's door. He looked unperturbed by the disturbance in the lab. He gave us both his sensuous, lazy smile. "Hi," he said. "You want me to show Ms. Sayler around?" he asked Crawford.

"No, I want you to find those NSF forms, specifically the 98A's. We need to get them in. Have Raymond show her around."

Raskin shook his head. "Raymond's down at the Albany greenhouse," he said. "Why don't I ask Chuck or Julie to do it."

"Get Julie," Crawford said. "I want Chuck working on his paper for the grant."

Raskin nodded and turned to go. If Crawford's abrupt manner bothered him, he didn't show it.

As we waited, I asked, "Can you think of any reason why this might be happening now? A possible trigger?"

"Not really," she said. "There's a lot of pressure right now because we're finishing up an NIH grant renewal application. But that's just normal stress. No excuse for sabotage."

I asked a few more questions and studied the woman who had hired me. She wasn't long on people skills, that was for sure. Her manner was abrupt and cool. She reminded me of another client I'd had, an auditor, who'd announced that he was hired to be smart, not nice.

RASKIN WAS BACK in a couple of minutes with Julie Chun. She was about five four, fine-boned and slender, wearing jeans and a cranberry-colored tee shirt with a baby seal on it. She was an attractive young woman, probably in her late twenties, with almost flawless skin the color of old ivory and thick black hair pulled back and held in place with a blue scrunchie. Her left eyebrow was interrupted midway by a small scar, making it appear permanently arched.

Raskin introduced us and she gave me a warm smile that had an amused, almost mischievous quality. When he told her who I was and why I was at the lab, her smile faltered and she grew serious. I could hear relief in her voice as she said, "Oh, thank goodness. I hope you can put a stop to this."

"That's the plan," Raskin said, then, turning to me, he explained, "Julie's been a victim of sabotage twice. She can tell you about it while she shows you the labs."

Julie led the way out of Crawford's office into a short corridor that extended from the outside hall to the labs. It was lined on one side with dingy white refrigerators and on the other with a counter covered with equipment. Yellow tape and stickers warned: DANGER—RADIO-ACTIVE MATERIAL.

"I'm so glad you're here," Julie said as soon as we were out of the office. "It's been awful, knowing someone wanted to hurt me and having no idea who or why." She kept her voice low, just above a whisper.

Past the refrigerators, we stepped into the large open space of a lab. The wall ahead of us was mostly windows, so the room was bright with both natural and fluorescent light. Long lab benches extended from the windows along both walls, and a third, parallel bench projected into the room, dividing it in half. We stepped around a guy on his hands and knees sweeping up broken glass at the end of that bench. At his feet a Geiger counter clicked softly, searching for radioactivity.

Each of the lab benches ended in a lower desk beneath the windows. The work surfaces were littered with equipment and papers, and the shelves above the side benches and running down the center of the middle bench were packed with glass bottles of various shapes and sizes bearing labels in a range of pastel colors. It was a scene of orderly chaos.

"The library's there," Julie said, pointing back to the left, "the other lab's over here, and we have one more lab down the hall." She led me to the right, past the lab bench where a woman with blond hair in a braid that reached almost to her waist was using a large syringe to inject something into tiny vials that looked like plastic bullets.

A passageway with small rooms on either side connected the two labs. The second lab was similar to the first in layout, but had twice as much space. At one of the benches in the middle a blond man and woman who looked enough alike to be related were studying black-and-white photographs. "They're still not clear enough," the man complained. "It's the damn developer; it was too old."

"So we'll do them again," the woman said. "Like Kendra says, it doesn't matter what we know they show, they've gotta be so clear no one can argue with it."

The man groaned. "Damn, I was hoping to go home tonight."

Behind him, a red-haired woman said, "Lots of luck. I heard Kendra tell Chuck he should consider giving up sleeping. And I don't think she was kidding."

"This is my bench," Julie said, patting the one we were now standing next to. Bottles and papers covered most of the surface. Two trays of three-inch-high corn plants were shoved to the back.

I took a few steps toward her desk. To the wall behind it, she'd taped several snapshots—two of herself with what I assumed was her family, one of a hilly rural landscape with cultivated fields, and another of two elderly women standing in front of a tiny house that was little more than a mud hut.

"That's my great-aunt and my grandmother," she said, "in China. And that's one of their fields. I visited them last year."

"Was it your first trip back?" I asked.

She nodded. "I wasn't so keen on it, but my parents insisted. I'm really glad I went. It gave me a new perspective on a lot of things."

Just then the door banged as a small woman with dark, wildly curly hair hurried in. "Shit, who's got a key to the greenhouse? I lost mine," she called from the middle of the room. No one jumped to help her.

Julie sighed and reached into her pocket. "You can use mine, but I have to have it back by tomorrow morning," she said.

"Thanks, Julie," the other woman said, coming over to us to claim the key.

"Catherine, this is Raisa Strom. Some of her plants were destroyed when my seed was stolen," Julie said. "Raisa, this is Catherine Sayler. She's going to investigate the sabotage."

"Great," Raisa said. "It's about time somebody did something about it. I've got to rush. I've got an appointment in the city, and I have some crosses to do before I leave." With that she hurried off, leaving me feeling I'd just shaken hands with a small whirlwind.

"Crosses are cross-pollinations," Julie explained, "when you take pollen from one plant and use it to fertilize another."

"Tell me about the sabotage," I said.

At the mention of the sabotage, her face became serious, even sad. "Well, I had seed drying in the greenhouse. After we harvest the ears, we leave them on a rack there for several weeks. I'd planted off schedule, so I was the only one who had seed then. But lots of people had plants. Someone broke in and stole all my seed and snapped about a dozen of Raisa's plants.

"It probably doesn't sound like such a big deal, some corn and a few plants, but losing that seed set me back four months; that's how long it'll take me to grow another batch, and Raisa lost one plant she won't be able to replace. It came from an ear with an unusual mutation and that ear only produced a few kernels, so Raisa might not ever get a chance to see how that mutant gene affects the plant.

"See, the corn we grow here isn't like what you get in an Iowa field. We're working with mutants, and some of

them aren't very hardy. We hand-pollinate, but sometimes we get ears with only a few fully developed kernels. Losing a plant from one of those is a big blow."

"Paul said you lost some vials of genetic material as
well," I said.

She nodded. "Not at the same time, though. The vials
were stolen last Thursday. Let me show you." She led the
way back toward the refrigerators outside Crawford's
office.

They were just like the appliances you find in a kitch-
en, the large-size, plain-vanilla kind, but when Julie
opened the first one, there was nothing inside you'd consider for a midnight snack. The metal shelves were full of
trays of small plastic vials about an inch long and tapered
at the bottom. She took out a tray labeled "Chun" and
held up one vial so that I could see the contents. It wasn't
much, just an opaque drop of liquid in the bottom of
the vial.

"These are eppendorf tubes," she said. "The drop in
the bottom is buffer and it contains the DNA molecules
with the genes we're studying." She replaced the vial and
returned the tray to the refrigerator, closing the door
carefully. "Each of those molecules represents months of
work, at least. Six of my vials and six of Chuck Nishimura's disappeared Thursday night. It couldn't be an accident. Somebody stole them."

"Are those vials worth anything to anyone?" I asked.

"Not to anyone but the person studying them," she said.
"It's like the corn. Its only value is to the researcher. We're
not doing anything super-secret here. And besides, Chuck,
Raisa, and I are all working on different projects."

The middle of the lab wasn't the best place to get Julie
to talk freely, so I said, "Is there somewhere around here
where we can get coffee?"

"In the building across the courtyard," she said. "I can
show you the other lab on the way."

She led us down the hall to a double room just like the

one we'd left except that it faced west instead of north. "We have the room on this side," she said. "The Drake lab has the other half." From the Drake lab I could hear soft jazz playing and the murmur of voices. In the Crawford lab, I heard two women arguing over how long they should run the "sequencing gel" and a guy complaining about the jazz.

We rode the elevator down and crossed a narrow courtyard to a smaller one-story building that mirrored the architecture of the larger one we'd just left. Inside was a trendy little café with sleek lines and a counter at one end with PAT BROWN'S GRILL in neon above it. A reminder of how much things had changed since my college days.

The muffins, Danish, and croissants at the counter were another reminder. They were plump and fresh, a far cry from the cardboard Danish of my youth. I ordered a croissant.

"Plain, almond, or chocolate?" the girl behind the counter asked.

"Plain," I said, "and coffee."

"Decaf or regular, flavored, espresso, or latte?"

"Decaf will be fine," I said. Jesse was right. Passions in Berkeley had turned from revolution to food.

When we were seated, I said to Julie, "You were a victim of sabotage twice. Any idea who or why?"

"None," she said. "I've really tried to stay out of the vendettas and turf wars in this place. I thought I'd succeeded." She put her index finger in her mouth and chewed on the nail, then pulled her hand away as if she'd just realized what she was doing. All the nails on her hand were bitten down to the quick.

I could feel her tension as I sat across from her. Yet her face revealed none of it. On the surface she was poised and self-possessed. It's harder to read emotions across a culture gap. I wondered if an Asian might see things I was missing.

"Have you broken any hearts?" I asked.

"Not me," she said with a dry laugh. "Oh, several guys have sort of come on to me, but none of them were devastated when I didn't respond."

"Which guys?"

"Well, I went out with Scott several times. And Dorian's asked me out once or twice. I guess you could say Chuck and I are dating since we hang out a lot together, but that's more friendship than romance. The guys'll all tell you I'm a real drudge, more interested in corn than men."

"And are you?"

"For now, I am," she said. "Especially here, where the mood is fratricidal." The hand went to her mouth again. This time she pulled it away and covered it with the other hand. The nails on that hand were also bitten to the quick.

"Is there any reason someone would want to interfere with your research? Would the seed you lost be useful to anyone else?"

She shook her head again. The frown deepened. "I'm not even working on the same thing as the others. They're mostly studying the *Bonsai 4* gene and other dwarf genes. But I'm working on what you might call an anti-Bonsai gene. When my mutant is in the same plant as *Bonsai 4*, the plant isn't dwarfed; it's normal. And I haven't cloned it yet. I'm just trying to understand how it works." She stopped and shrugged.

"So there's no way your work is related to the others'? No way it might threaten or seem to compete with theirs?"

She shook her head emphatically. "That's what's so damn stupid about this. I'm not a threat to anyone, but someone out there is trying to destroy my career."

She must have feared I'd think her overdramatic because she added, "That's really what they're doing. I only have a year to go on this postdoc. The stolen corn sets me back by four months. The clones that were stolen could take another month to replace. If I don't finish the research, I don't publish a paper, and without a paper, I won't have a shot at a decent job. I'll end up teaching at a junior college and never get a chance to do real research."

She looked near tears. The muscles around her mouth twitched as she struggled to control them. Gone was the calm, self-possessed image she'd projected earlier, revealing all too clearly the pain and fear beneath it.

"Please," she said. "Please, find out who's doing this and make them stop."

I put my hand on top of hers and held it for a minute while she fought down the tears that were pooling in her eyes. My own chest was tight as I watched her struggle. She blinked several times and took a couple of deep breaths, then wiped the corners of her eyes.

"I'm sorry," she said. "I didn't mean to get so emotional. I just don't understand what's going on and it scares me. Someone here really seems to hate me, and I don't even know why."

We talked for a few minutes more but didn't come up with any reason someone would want to sabotage her career. She was so concerned with the threat to her research that she hadn't even considered that she herself might be in danger.

"No reason to assume that," I told myself as we walked back. But I still felt a band of tension across my chest.

I wanted to check in with Paul Raskin before I left. I found him with another man in one of the small side rooms between the two labs. Both men were wearing goggles and gloves, and they were standing in a corner with a piece of apparatus marked DANGER—HIGH VOLTAGE. Tape with radioactivity symbols was stuck to almost every open surface.

"Make sure the damn thing's off," Raskin was saying. "I don't want to end up as toast."

"It's off," the other guy said. He was tallish with a straw-blond buzz cut, and was wearing a red 49ers tee shirt and cutoff Levi's. In one gloved hand he held a test tube, in the other a large plastic syringelike implement.

Raskin noticed me at the door. "Oh, hi," he said. "Can you wait for just a couple of minutes? I'd like to finish loading the gel."

"Sure," I said.

Julie was at my elbow. "That's the sequencing rig. They're using it to run a high-resolution separation of small DNA fragments," she explained, then realizing she might as well be speaking Greek, she added, "The stuff in the tubes is strands of DNA of different lengths. The gel separates them. In this case, some of the fragments are really hot."

"Hot?"

"Really radioactive."

The blond man drew some liquid from one test tube with the syringelike tool and deposited it in a column behind a large vertical sheet of clear plastic. I guessed that the gel must be behind the sheet. How you'd cut anything with it I had no idea.

"How does he cut it?" I asked.

"With enzymes," she said. "They're like chemical scissors designed to cut DNA at certain sequences. We get them from bacteria and fungi. They evolved the enzymes as a kind of weapon against viruses."

When he'd finished with the first tube, the man popped the tip of his syringe into a box marked RADIOACTIVE WASTE and replaced it with a new cap, then reached for a second test tube.

Raskin picked up on Julie's explanation. "Critters are always looking for ways to kill off the competition or at least get a leg up on it," he said. "Every critter has its own DNA sequences. If you have something that cuts the other guy's DNA but not your own, that's a terrific weapon. So the bacteria evolve an enzyme that cuts specific sequences they don't have. It's all trial and error, of course. Develop an enzyme that cuts your own DNA and you're out of the gene pool."

I looked at the high-voltage warning and the radio-activity stickers and felt an unpleasant chill. Raskin was talking about bacteria, but the urge to kill isn't limited to lower life forms. This lab with its high-tech equipment and multitude of chemicals contained as dangerous an arsenal of weapons as an NRA convention.

4

CRAWFORD'S OFFICE WAS empty, so Paul Raskin and I went there when he finished with the sequencing rig. "I think it'd be a good idea if I checked out the lab and suggested security precautions," I said.

A frown creased his brow. "That could be tough. Anything we do to restrict access to the lab would slow things down too much," he said. "We've got people coming and going at all hours. Some students really prefer to work at night, and others have to be there to meet the grant deadline."

"Do you have much dangerous equipment like the machine you were working with in the other room?"

Raskin sucked in his breath, but he didn't look surprised by my question. "Some," he said tightly. "And plenty of serious chemicals."

"So you've thought about the possibility that people in the lab could be at risk."

"I've considered it, sure. But that's just my garden-variety paranoia. I don't think there's any real danger here." He didn't quite convince me that he believed it.

I left the lab just before five. A band of gray clouds hovered over the hills of San Francisco, and above them the sky was a delicate blue-gold. But neither the beauty before me nor the Mozart flute concertos on my car stereo could lighten the sense of foreboding I felt.

The thing I hated most about the aftermath of dealing with violent cases was its effect on my judgment. I have to be able to rely on my instincts, play my hunches. Having my jittery psyche sounding alarm bells was a real drag.

On the other hand, I couldn't dismiss my uneasy feelings completely. Paul Raskin knew the people in the lab. If he was worried, it was a bad sign.

My reaction to Raskin himself was another bad sign. Every time the man walked into a room I was aware that I'd been sleeping alone too long. My lover, Peter, had only been gone for two weeks. It galled me that I couldn't keep a tighter check on my libido.

By the time I got home, the sky was deep blue on its way to black, and the neon lights of the shops and restaurants along Divisadero Street glowed with the intensity of an Arthur Ollman photograph.

I passed my office and saw no lights inside. It's small as Victorian houses go, but it's just three blocks from my flat, and though at this point it's more the bank's than mine, I still get a thrill when I look at it.

If my office was dark, my flat made up the difference in the electric bill. Every light was on, and as I opened the front door, "Friend of the Devil" blared from the stereo in the living room. My niece, Molly, had the volume just below the levels I remembered from the old Fillmore Auditorium. There must be something about the teenage nervous system that requires a heavy bass beat. Maybe it's soothing, like the rhythm of a mother's heart for a newborn.

Fortunately, Molly is a Dead Head. I don't know if our relationship could have survived if she were into heavy metal or rap. It'd been almost a year since the ongoing battle with her mother had flared into full-scale war and she'd decided to come live with me. By now, I was so used to the loud music that I almost didn't hear it anymore. In fact, the house seemed too quiet when she was away.

"Mom called," Molly announced. "She wants to take me shopping on Saturday." Her tone made it sound like a truly disgusting social perversion.

"Could it be that she doesn't like the holey-jeans-and-grungy-tee-shirt look?" I asked.

"She says she's seen better-dressed kids at homeless shelters."

"It's probably true," I said. "*I've* seen better-dressed kids at homeless shelters." Molly favors gutter-punk fashion with its oversized baggy pants, heavy boots, and tight tee shirts. I hate the pants and boots, but I'm quite partial to the tee shirts. Today's choice was kelly green with a knockoff of the McDonald's logo that read "McVegan."

I don't hassle Molly about her attire. I save my energy for the weekly battle over her desire to pierce various parts of her anatomy.

"Don't *you* start," Molly growled. "You know Mom's just afraid her society friends'll see me."

I figured embarrassing her parents was a big part of the appeal of those baggy pants, but I wasn't dumb enough to say it. Especially since I realized that I rather enjoyed the effect they had on my uptight little sister.

"Hey, life is tough in the fast lane," I said. "You should be more compassionate." Of course, it was I who should have been more compassionate. I knew what a tough time my sister Marion had had when Molly's father decided that being a parent was too much work and exited their life. I didn't begrudge her the big house she'd acquired with her second marriage, just the attitudes that came with it.

I went to the kitchen to get a Sierra Nevada Pale Ale, then came back to join Molly in the living room. "I hope you were reasonably civil," I said as I sank into my favorite chair. "You know that every time you make her mad, she calls and chews me out."

"Well, if you were a fit guardian, I'd be decently dressed and well behaved," Molly said, doing an uncanny impersonation of Marion's voice.

"Be careful. You could live in Palo Alto." It was my stock warning, used only in jest since I'd never have sent her home. "Are you going shopping?"

"I told her that you were taking me to Marin."

"Oh, great, now you're going to make a liar out of me."

"Like you don't do it for a living," she said. "Of course, if you wanted to go to Marin . . ."

"You are a bad kid," I said. "If you weren't so funny, I'd have drowned you long ago. I'm going to aikido on Saturday. You're on your own with Marion."

Molly groaned.

Dinner was a simple affair, leftovers of the chicken salad I'd made over the weekend. Molly didn't complain. In my house, people who complain get to cook.

As we were finishing up, Molly said a bit too casually, "Mom asked when Peter was coming back."

"Probably a month or so. Depends on what they find in Guatemala," I said. Peter Harman was my lover. He was in Guatemala with a forensic anthropologist who'd invited him to study skeletons from a mass grave outside a rural village. Peter's an unrepentant leftie. An invitation to stir up trouble for a repressive dictatorship had the same appeal for him that a red sports car has for other men in their forties. The anthropologist hadn't had to ask twice.

"But he is coming back," Molly said.

"Sure," I said. "Of course he's coming back. What's going on here?"

"Well, Mom seems to think that maybe you're breaking up. She said Peter didn't have to go to Guatemala without you."

I looked across the table at her and tried to frame an answer. The truth was, I didn't know what would happen when Peter came back. He'd urged me to go with him. I'd refused, saying I didn't want to trade old nightmares for new ones, but his desire to go and my choice to stay were more complicated than that.

I'd spent the past November and December with a fractured shoulder that rendered my right arm useless, stalked by a psychopath who sent frequent reminders that I was his current obsession. The psychopath was dead, but I hadn't been able to shake the unsettling sense of vulnerability he'd created. He haunted my dreams and unfamiliar sounds still set my heart pounding.

Peter's presence was a solace but it hadn't helped me get over my fear. That was something I needed to do on my own, and my stubborn insistence on that had driven a wedge between us. The more he tried to reach out to me, the more I edged away. The offer to visit Guatemala had come as a relief to both of us.

Molly was watching me expectantly, the skin between her eyes creasing exactly the way her mother's did when she was worried. "No, we're not breaking up," I said. "Sometimes people just need some time apart so they can come back together."

I hoped it was true.

5

THERE'D BEEN WIND during the night, and the next morning the sky was cloudless and the air clear and clean. The city sparkled in the hard, winter-white light. It was a day to go walking on Mount Tam. Instead, I went to the Crawford Lab.

I got there about half an hour before the meeting and went looking for Julie. I didn't find her, but I met Paul Raskin in the hall outside the lab. He still reminded me of James Dean. Damn.

"Is Julie here?" I asked.

"She's out today. Stomach trouble."

My own stomach knotted up. "What kind of stomach trouble?"

"Probably a touch of food poisoning. Nothing serious, though," he said.

"Has she been seen by a doctor?"

Raskin knew where I was leading. I could see it in his eyes. "No," he said, "but one of the women she lives with is a med student. Really, it's nothing serious."

"It still might be a good idea for her to get some lab tests. As you said yesterday, there are a lot of nasty chemicals in this lab."

He considered it, then shook his head. "I don't think she'd do it even if I suggested it, and I'm not going to suggest it. It'd just scare her."

There are a lot worse things than being scared, I thought, but I didn't say it to Raskin. I thought of Julie's fingernails bitten to the quick and realized why he might be anxious not to add to the stress she was already under. "Would you mind if I called her, just to check?"

He shrugged and led the way to his desk. A lab roster was taped to the wall next to it. "Go ahead," he said, pointing to her number.

I called Julie from the phone on his desk. She sounded weak but she assured me that she was feeling better and had been able to keep down some tea and crackers.

"Any idea of what caused it?" I asked.

"Probably salmonella," she said. "I share a house with a bunch of people. We've gotten sort of sloppy about the kitchen."

"Oh, so a bunch of you got sick."

"No, just me. But I made a salad last night. I figure the chopping board was probably contaminated."

"Oh," I said. "Well, I hope you feel better soon."

She thanked me for calling, and I hung up, still feeling uneasy.

"Satisfied?" Raskin asked.

"Not completely. It could be just coincidence, but when someone's already deliberately sabotaged her work twice, I wouldn't be too quick to assume that."

Raskin nodded soberly.

I turned around to discover that the lab was deserted. Raskin checked his watch. "Almost time for the lab meeting," he said. "You better check in with Kendra. She's in her office."

Crawford was on the phone. I knocked and she motioned me to a chair.

It's hard not to eavesdrop on someone on the phone. Not that it would occur to me to try. I could claim that my nosiness is a result of my profession, but I suspect it's the cause rather than the effect.

Crawford's voice was sharp with irritation. "Look, Arthur, we're not working on leaf curl here. This is a genetics lab, not a subsidiary of Monsanto. Let them work on it at Davis." She listened for a minute and her face clouded. "If that's a joke, it's not funny, and if it's a threat, it's extremely inappropriate."

Her frown only deepened as she listened to the response. "Yes, I understand you. Yes, I will think about it." She put the receiver back on the hook a shade harder than necessary.

"Damn," she said. "Between the legislature and the lobbyists, the university and the funding agencies, it's amazing we get anything done. If the farmers have their way I'll spend the rest of my life on leaf curl and square tomatoes."

"Where do the farmers come into it?" I asked.

"It's complicated," she said. "And archaic. Plant biology is part of the school of agriculture rather than science. The farmers and the agribusiness companies want us working on whatever is costing them the most money at the moment. They couldn't care less about fundamental research. They're not even interested in trying to solve the problems that are coming down the road."

She looked up at the clock and rose from her chair. "We better get to the conference room." As we walked down the hall, she continued, "The fools are always asking, 'What's this going to do for us?' They don't see that the really big breakthroughs come from places you can't predict. Research that has no practical application today could solve a problem we don't even recognize yet."

The conference room was just down the hall. Though there were lots of people in the room and the door was open, there was no buzz of conversation as we approached.

Inside, about fifteen people sat around a large table and on chairs along the wall behind it. Paul Raskin sat next to a smaller table in the back of the room, leafing through some papers. He looked up and smiled at me when we came in.

The rest of the people were young, mostly in their twenties, casually dressed in jeans and tee shirts. Just over half were women, and most of them wore their hair either long or very short in styles that required little attention.

Despite their casual attire, there was a sense of tension. No smiles, no jokes, not even any whispered conversation. Many of the students read or made notes, one seemed to sleep, and the rest sat stonily waiting.

I tried to sense whether they were hostile, scared, or just apathetic. I got hints of all three.

Crawford took the seat at the head of the table. I sat next to her. She introduced me and explained why I was there, then turned to me. "Catherine, would you like to say anything to the group?"

I took a minute to let my gaze travel around the table. Everyone, even the sleeper, was paying attention now. "I'd like to interview each of you separately," I said. "And I'm asking you not to discuss the meetings with each other. What's said in the interview room is completely private. It's not to be repeated. Do you understand?"

Nods all around. I didn't believe for a second that they wouldn't discuss the interviews. There was more theater than substance to this phase of the investigation. Setting the stage. Getting everyone a bit edgy. From the serious faces around the table, I could see it was working.

I had them introduce themselves and state their positions in the lab, so I could put names to faces, then Crawford took charge of the meeting again.

"Any general announcements?" she asked.

A chunky young man with shoulder-length dark hair spoke up. "I don't know who the hell's eating in the darkroom, but it's gotta stop. There were crumbs in the developer last night." Murmurs of assent and dark looks from several others around the table indicated he wasn't alone in his irritation.

"Yeah, and when you use the last of the developer, you can damn well mix up more," said the man next to him. "Every time I go in there, the developer's gone, and no one ever bothers to replace it."

The woman I'd seen in the lab chimed in. "It's the same with the lab supplies. Someone's going through Taq polymerase like water. Doesn't it ever occur to you guys to order more?"

From the looks on people's faces, the room was about to erupt into a litany of complaints. Crawford squelched them with "Everyone's under a lot of stress right now, especially those of you with papers due. Try to cut each other a little slack."

Frowns and glowers suggested that slack was in short supply just now. Crawford herself didn't seem to have any extra when she lit into several students whose papers were to be included with the grant. "Lois, Chuck, Dorian, Margot, and Tony, a reminder," she said, "I need *everything* for the grant by the first. I've okayed your drafts, let's see the figures. It won't do me a bit of good if you submit on the second or the third, so get your priorities straight. Until those papers are mailed, I want you here, working. You're excused from Scott's presentation."

The five beleaguered students got up and shuffled out of the room. I've seen prisoners being led off to jail who looked happier.

Raskin spoke up next. "Rick is sick again. He needs someone to do his crosses. Any volunteers?"

A sleepy-looking guy just down from me whispered to his companion. "Ever notice how Rick is always sick when his pollen sheds?"

Crawford frowned and Raskin shrugged and sat down. "Any more announcements?" Crawford asked. When no one spoke, she said, "Scott, you're on."

The guy I'd seen with Raskin the day before stepped forward. He was wearing a different 49ers tee shirt and the same cutoff Levi's. His broad smile spread over prominent teeth, and his nose canted a bit to one side as if it had been broken. Paul moved a slide projector into position near him.

As they were setting up, I looked around the table. Several students were studying me with some interest, but they each looked away as soon as our eyes met.

"For the benefit of newcomers," Scott said, "I'll begin by briefly outlining the goal and strategies of our Bonsai project. Raisa, will you turn off . . . thanks, and the mood lights . . . perfect. May I see the first slide, please."

A slide of two corn plants flashed on the screen. Judging from a measuring stick standing between them, the first plant was just over five feet tall; the second was under three feet. Its thick leaves were much closer together, giving it the appearance of a bush.

"Here you see two sibling plants, one of normal genotype and the other carrying a single copy of the dominant dwarfism allele called *D8-1377*. As you should all know, we have cloned the DNA that encodes *D8-1377* by transposon-tagging, and the DNA sequence suggests that D8 protein encodes the extracellular receptor for the plant growth hormone gibberellic acid.

"The next slide, focus please, shows the sequence. As you can see . . ."

I couldn't see anything except rows of dark smudges arranged in vertical columns. Scott spoke with excitement about "six extra base pairs in the receptor domain." It's hard to pay attention when you only understand two percent of what's going on, so I spent the rest of the time studying the suspects, conveniently arranged around the table. Even in the dim light I was able to see enough to put names to faces.

I must have dozed off, because I was startled when Scott called, "Lights up! Questions?"

An undergrad named Carrie asked a question and the young woman next to her, also an undergrad, followed up on it. Then Joellen, a doctoral student, made a suggestion that Scott didn't seem to take as seriously as she thought he should, and they exchanged sharp words. It was mostly downhill from there as other students either criticized Scott's work or jumped on Joellen.

The argument had an angry stridency. The classroom debates I remembered from college were sparring matches, verbal fencing contests. This was downright nasty, and a good deal more personal than was appropriate. I studied the response of the students not actively involved. A few looked disgusted or bored, some watched with amusement, several exchanged whispered comments.

My stomach knotted. I knew too well how easily a seemingly harmless situation could turn deadly. How anger too freely expressed can lead to violence. I struggled to shake the sense of foreboding that the hostility in the room evoked in me, and only partially succeeded.

Crawford's voice interrupted the argument and cut it off. "Good work, Scott. We'll hear from you again when you have a presumptive protein. A final announcement, Carrie's been accepted to MIT. I understand they were very impressed by her work on defective *MuDR* in our revertant *D8-1377*." Turning to Carrie, she said, "Congratulations, Carrie. Congratulations from all of us."

Around the table, only a few people looked pleased by Crawford's praise. Paul Raskin smiled and made a thumbs-up signal to Carrie. The rest of the crew looked sullen or disinterested. Raskin had been generous when he described the Crawford lab as a bunch of "squabbling kids."

6

PAUL RASKIN HAD cleared off a table for me in one of the small rooms the Plant Biology Department used for storage. It was on the window side of the building, which made it brighter and more pleasant than its twin across the hall.

I interviewed three students before lunch, all postdocs. The first was a dour young woman; the second, a guy with a sweet smile and a shaved head; the third, Raisa Strom.

I got the same story from all three. They had come to Cal after getting their doctorates at prestigious schools. They had less than three years to do research and publish papers before seeking their first academic job. They were stressed and terrified by the threat of delay.

Having already been a victim, Raisa was particularly upset. She told me several times that she was "up to her eyeballs" in debt with student loans and had to be ready to go on the market when her fellowship ran out.

"You know, just 'cause you have a Ph.D. doesn't mean you've got a job," she said. "Berkeley's full of plumbers and painters with Ph.D.s. And maize genetics isn't exactly a growth industry. There're only a limited number of places."

I tried to get her to tell me who might have a grudge against her. The only candidate was Chuck Nishimura, another sabotage victim.

"He's had it in for me since last year," she said. "He

thinks I stole his research. He's been bitching and moaning about it ever since. Does everything he can to turn people in the lab against me." There was a harsh, aggrieved quality to her manner. If her colleagues didn't like her, it might not be all Chuck's fault.

"Did you steal his research?" I asked.

"Of course not. We were working on similar things and I got lucky," she said. "I drew on his findings, but I certainly didn't steal anything from him."

That was all I got out of her, and by the time I was finished with the interview, we were both glad it was over.

I realized when I checked my watch that some of my irritation was probably the result of an empty stomach. It was one o'clock, time to check out Jesse's judgment on Berkeley food.

Paul Raskin and I must have turned the doorknob at exactly the same moment, because as I pulled the door toward me, he nearly fell into the room. He recovered quickly and laughed. "I was about to ask if you'd like to go to lunch," he said.

"Absolutely," I said, almost as aware of my empty stomach as I was of his blue eyes. "I'm starved."

"You like Thai?"

"Sounds great." Truth is, I like almost anything I don't have to cook.

"It's a bit of a walk. That okay?"

A bit of a walk can be anything from three blocks to three miles, depending on who's measuring. And men in running shoes tend to judge differently from women in heels. I asked for specifics.

"Five blocks, maybe six. We could drive if you'd like."

"Five blocks I can walk."

We headed for the door, only to stop at the sound of loud, angry voices from the lab behind us. We walked back to check and found two men arguing. Chuck Nishimura, one of the sabotage victims, stood facing a very intense young man named Dorian Barker.

"Don't be such an obsessive-compulsive," Chuck said.

"Oh, sure, make it my problem. Like it's my fault you're a slob. You just keep your hands off my pipettman, you hear. I don't want to see you anywhere near my bench." Dorian's voice was shrill with anger.

Chuck shook his head dismissively. "Jeez, Barker. Calm down, you'll have a heart attack."

Raskin rolled his eyes and stepped into the fray. I watched as Dorian stated his complaint in nasal, aggrieved tones.

He was a skinny guy with a long nose and prominent Adam's apple. Though he was probably in his late twenties, frown lines already ate deeply into his forehead. His name brought to mind Oscar Wilde's Dorian Gray, but *this* Dorian wore his trials engraved on his face and wasn't aging any more gracefully than the portrait in his namesake's attic.

Raskin interrupted when Dorian expanded his complaint to include events the week before. It didn't help matters that Chuck delivered his side of the story in a voice that was a parody of Dorian's. Raskin smacked Chuck down and got them to break off the fight, but he clearly hadn't healed the rift.

"Poor Dorian," Raskin said as we walked away from the lab. "He's too high-strung for this place. It's eating him alive."

"He seems awfully angry at Chuck," I said.

"He's like our lightning rod," Raskin said. "He picks up all the negative energy in this place and broadcasts it back. And Chuck's teasing makes it worse. They shouldn't work so close to each other. I've got to move them before one tosses the other through a window."

Outside, the sky was a bright blue. Across a spring-green lawn, pink-tinted blossoms sat like cups on the bare branches of a tulip tree. Students with backpacks walked between buildings or stood chatting in small groups. The groves of academe looked sweet.

We headed along the front of the campus back to University Avenue and turned to walk down it. At the end of the broad street the bay stretched like a blue band topped by the mountains of Marin County.

We walked for a couple of blocks, past small shops and a number of restaurants. The street was tougher than I remembered. Not college scruffy. Urban gritty. We were panhandled four times before we reached the restaurant.

It was a light and airy place with high ceilings and large display windows along the front wall.

"So, how'd you like the lab meeting?" Paul asked after we were seated. "I'm afraid the presentation must have been incredibly boring for you."

"Well, it's true that I couldn't understand ninety percent of what was said," I replied. "What's a transposon anyway?"

"They're mutant makers, little bits of DNA that jump around from place to place. We call them jumping genes. Sometimes they wreck a gene when they land inside the DNA. And depending on the piece, you get different effects on the plant. We're interested in the wrecked genes, mutants, that cause dwarfs." He paused. "You really want to know this stuff?"

Not too many people have the sensitivity to realize that others may not be as interested in their favorite subject as they are. I found his concern endearing.

"Yes," I said. "Please go on."

"Okay, here goes." He leaned forward and I was aware of the warm intensity of his gaze. "We spray our plants with GA3, short for gibberellic acid. It's one of the five plant growth hormones. You put it on a plant, and the plant gets taller, skinnier, its leaves narrow and get less green. When we get a dwarf, it means that someplace there's a transposon that did something to counteract the effects of the GA3. Maybe it messed up the GA3 receptor so the plant couldn't use it, or maybe it cut up the GA3 before it could affect the plant. Could be any number of things.

"In fact, in our first batch of plants there're six different kinds of mutants; we call them *Bonsai 1, 2, 3*; you get the idea. *Bonsai 4* produces the best plants, so Kendra decided that's the one to go after. We cross the Bonsai 4 plants with normal ones, and get dwarfs. Now we know it's dominant, and that's essential. We've got the plants with the gene, but we don't know where or what it is. To clone it, you have to find it.

"That's where the jumping genes come in. You cross the Bonsai 4s with a strain that's known to have lots of jumping genes, and you look for the offspring that are normal. Because if they're normal, that means a transposon has jumped into the gene that was already mutated and wrecked it. Since we have the exact DNA sequence of the transposon, we can find it in a larger piece of DNA.

"That's getting pretty technical, but the point is, we've identified the gene. Now we're working on getting it in the tube."

"Which means?" I asked.

" 'In the tube' means you've cloned the DNA that's the *Bonsai 4* gene. Then you can make an infinite supply of this single gene that can make any plant a dwarf."

"And that's worth big bucks, I assume."

"Medium bucks," Paul corrected. "There's money in ornamentals but it's not big bucks. Still, our goal is to get the gene in the tube before anyone else."

I started to ask who the competition was when the waitress arrived to take our order. We'd been so busy talking, we hadn't gotten to the menu, so we took a couple of minutes to study it.

"Are you a loner or a sharer?" Raskin asked. The question obviously referred to the food, but his eyes held mine a moment longer than necessary and there was a warm playfulness in the way he said it that suggested another layer of meaning.

"Depends on what I'm offered," I said.

"How about stuffed chicken wings?"

"For stuffed chicken wings, I'm definitely a sharer," I said. "And how do you feel about Silver Noodle Prawns?"

"Ah, I sense a kindred spirit," he said, giving me his crooked grin, which somehow managed to be both shy and sensual. I smiled back, and realized as I did that my smile had layers, too.

"A couple of weeks of sleeping alone and my hormones run wild," I thought. Flirting can be dangerous when your lover is a thousand miles away. I tried to get my mind back on business.

We ordered two Tsingtao beers, and as the waitress left, I said, "Tell me more about the competition to find the gene."

"Well, in science, there are usually a number of labs working on the same problem, and they both cooperate and compete. It's really not a factor in the sabotage, if that's what you're thinking."

"I suspect we don't need to look much further than the anger and tension in the lab to find the cause of the sabotage," I said. "People really seem to be at each other's throats."

"A lot of that's the pressure to finish the grant proposal. It affects everyone, even people not working on that project."

"What happens if you don't get the grant?" I asked.

"We can apply a couple of other places, but ultimately, if we don't get it, people get laid off. The two postdocs would be the first to go," he said. "See, the university only pays for Kendra, Raymond, and me. Everything else—equipment, research expenses, student salaries, secretarial, phones, even xeroxing—comes from grant money. You can't do research if you don't get grants, it's as simple as that."

"But none of the people who were sabotaged would be directly affected?"

"Chuck could be. He's on the grant. Not Raisa or Julie. They're both on other grants."

"But Julie and Raisa still feel threatened," I said. "Both are worried about how this will affect their research and Julie seems actually afraid."

Raskin nodded. His features sharpened as his forehead contracted into a frown. "Yeah, I know," he said. "I don't think her stomach trouble has anything to do with this, but I don't like that she's been a target twice. Kendra thinks I'm overreacting. But these days you never can tell what something like this might lead to."

I knew. He did, too. That's why we were worried.

The waitress arrived with our food, a welcome distraction from our dark thoughts. Raskin smiled approvingly as he surveyed the two dishes. "Looks good enough to eat, doesn't it?" he said, taking his half of the chicken wings and passing me the rest.

The tiny wings were wonderfully succulent. Raskin dipped his in sauce hot enough to start an oral bonfire. "This sauce is great," he said.

"A bit hot for me."

"I'm surprised. You strike me as a woman who'd enjoy hot stuff." His smile had a teasing quality, and the layers were back.

"I don't like to get burned."

"I figure you have to risk getting burned to get the full flavor out of life," he said.

I was feeling a heat that had nothing to do with hot sauce. I steered us back to safer ground.

"What did you do before you became a right hand?" I asked.

"I was a left hand," Raskin said with his sexy grin. "What did you do before you became a private eye?"

"I've always been a private eye," I said. "Pay's better

than for a public eye. But you don't get off so easily. Were you always a scientist?"

"I studied biochemistry," he said. "Started on a doctorate but dropped out before I got my degree. I've kicked around, done a bunch of different stuff."

He was still smiling and his tone was light, but the smile had become a bit forced. "Is it exciting being a private eye?" he asked. "You ever get into the kind of stuff you see on TV?"

I've been asked that question dozens of times, usually by people who watch too much television. But I sensed that what lay behind Raskin's question was not naiveté but a desire to distract me from my curiosity about his past.

7

AFTER LUNCH WE walked slowly back to campus, enjoying the sun and the soft springlike air. On the lawn in front of Koshland Hall, two girls in shorts and a shirtless boy lay stretched out on their stomachs.

"Easterners," Raskin said. "They can't quite believe the sun's shining in February. The natives are still wearing sweaters."

I knew what he meant. The weather was nowhere near warm enough to run around in shorts, unless you were used to winters where the ground froze six inches deep. Then California in February seemed like a tropical paradise.

"This is the time the university does its recruiting back

East," Raskin said. "They wait till it's been snowing for months and the ice is still an inch thick on the sidewalks, then they fly the hot prospects out and let them stroll under the flowering trees and soak up the sunshine. Poor bastards are so blinded by all that sun that they can't wait to sign on the dotted line. No one ever tells them that it's foggy most of the summer."

"Looks pretty good to me," I said. "Almost enough to make me want to go back to school."

Raskin laughed. "Me, too. But only if I could be an undergrad. We'd like to go back; they can't wait to get out. Isn't that just the way of the world?"

"You want to see the greenhouse today or tomorrow?" Raskin asked as we were walking upstairs.

"Today," I said. "Putting off the bulk of the interviews until tomorrow will give the students time to think and might make your saboteur more nervous."

"Okay," he said. "I can rearrange the interviews. Our lab tech, Raymond, can take you over there. There's one student you'll want to see who won't be around tomorrow, so I'll send her to you now."

I knew within minutes why Raskin wanted me to interview Margot Crowe. She was the lab gossip. She was a grad student, a large girl, not fat but tall and fairly large-boned, who wore her auburn hair in a stylish short cut that was long on top and cut close on the bottom. Her gray tee shirt proclaimed, "File Not Found. Fake it (Y/N)?"

She gazed at me expectantly across the table, like a patron with a front-row seat, but it only took a couple of questions to get her to move to center stage.

I started by asking about Raisa. Did she know of anyone who had a grudge against her?

"Well, Chuck certainly does," Margot said. "I mean, he'll tell you himself. He's told everybody. He thinks she stole his research idea, and he's still pissed about it. Actually, I'd probably feel the same way if it was me.

"And there're several of his friends who're down on her. I call them 'the boys' club' because they hang out together and whenever one of them has a problem, they're sure it's because they're men."

"Who's that?"

"Chuck, Scott, and Miles. Sometimes Rick."

"Anyone else who might have it in for Raisa?"

"No one in particular. She's not real popular. I mean, she can be impatient and she's not too tactful a lot of times, so she pisses people off. But she's also helped a couple of people out of jams, which not everyone here would do. She stayed up all night to help me finish the tables for a paper so I could submit on time."

Margot talked so fast that I wondered how she kept her breath. But if she made everyone's business her own, she didn't seem to do it with any malice. There was no undertone of insinuation or unpleasantness in her talk.

"How about Julie? How do people feel about her?" I asked.

"She's pretty much a loner. Some people think she's sort of stuck-up because she comes from a microbiology background. I think it's partly cultural. You know, she's Chinese, and doing well is really important to her. Well, it's important to all of us. But, like her parents didn't want her to be a scientist, so she's sort of got something to prove, I think."

"Chuck and Julie are both Asian," I said. "Is there any anti-Asian feeling in the lab?"

"No," she said, shaking her head. "Well, I mean, sometimes you hear someone make a comment about how they're going to have to work extra hard in a class because there are so many 'rice eaters' in it. But that's mostly undergrads, and it's not really malice, just nervousness. And it's more a general thing, doesn't seem to affect people at a one-to-one level. It's not a race thing, the sabotage."

I hoped she was right. I'd asked Paul Raskin about the possibility and he'd dismissed it almost immediately. With the kind of tension I sensed in the lab, racial animosity would find a fertile field.

"Teri's probably not too fond of Julie right now," Margot said.

"Teri?" I said, looking down at my list of students.

"Teri Shaw. She's an undergrad, a senior, I think."

"What's she got against Julie?"

"Well, Teri and Chuck have been an item since September, but a couple of weeks ago they broke up and he's been spending lots of time with Julie."

"Did they break up before or after the plants were trashed at the greenhouse?"

She thought for a moment. "Before, maybe a week before, just after Christmas."

The time was right, and jealousy was certainly a powerful motive for mischief.

"How about Chuck?" I asked.

"Teri still seems friendly with him. He's kind of a cutup, gets along pretty well with everybody, except, of course, Raisa. She blames him for making other people mad at her." She paused, then added, "And maybe Scott. Scott had the hots for Julie before Chuck moved in on her."

For a woman not interested in romance Julie attracted a lot of attention from the opposite sex. "What about Dorian?" I asked. "I heard him arguing with Chuck."

"Oh, Dorian," she said. "Yeah, he and Chuck work right next to each other. It's not that Chuck's really a slob, but Dorian is a fanatic. If one person could be both anal-retentive and obsessive-compulsive, that'd be Dorian. And he's truly tweaked. To tell the truth, he makes me a bit nervous."

"Why?"

"Well, beyond his bizarre neatness fetish, he's a gun nut. He's always bringing in gun magazines." She shivered.

That set off the alarm bells. "Has he ever brought a gun in here?"

"Oh, no. Well, not that I've heard about. But he likes to talk about them."

"You think he's dangerous?"

She shrugged. "Probably not, but you never know, do you?"

You don't. I should. I'm paid to know, and I don't. It bothers me—especially when guns are involved.

THE BRIGHT SUN I'd enjoyed outside was rapidly turning the small room into a solar oven. I was grateful when a tap on the door announced that it was time to see the greenhouse.

The man standing in the hall was beyond overweight. In Berkeley, he may have been gravity-challenged, but anywhere else he was fat. He was a fireplug of a man, carrying at least two hundred and fifty pounds on his five-foot-five frame. His tan pants and short-sleeved, dark plaid shirt were cut large enough to fit comfortably. The skin on his arms was heavily freckled.

"Hi, I'm Raymond Zak," he said. His voice was soft and low. He had a nice smile. I tried to guess his age, but his weight made it difficult. His face was unlined, but his brown hair was thinning on top and receding at the temples. Early forties maybe. "Paul said you'd like to see the greenhouse."

"I would, but I'd really like coffee first," I said. The warm room had made me sleepy, and I stifled a yawn as I stood up.

"A woman after my own heart," he said as we headed for the elevator. "I sure hope the FDA doesn't decide to regulate caffeine. They'd probably jail me as an addict."

"You and half the Bay Area," I said.

At Pat Brown's Grill, I ordered an espresso and Raymond got regular coffee. "You should try the scones," he suggested. "The ones here are really good."

"I'm still full from lunch," I said. "College food sure has improved since I was in school."

"It has here," he said, "but it's a mixed blessing for a guy like me."

"It must take a lot of self-control to stick with coffee," I said.

He laughed. "More than I used to have. But not lately. It's the weirdest thing, but lately I just have no appetite at all. It's terrific, really. I mean I've lost seven pounds in just over a week. I have to remember to eat most of the time."

I started to say that I'd love to have that problem, but it seemed insensitive to worry over an extra five pounds with someone who had a real weight problem.

We walked out of the building and down to the corner. The greenhouse was just across the street, in the middle of a long block that seemed completely out of character with both the campus and the town. With its low wooden buildings, greenhouses, and open field, it looked as if it belonged at an agricultural field station.

"You guys must have a lot of power to keep your greenhouses on such prime real estate," I said as we waited for the light to change. "I'm surprised the university hasn't tried to stick a ten-story building on that lot."

"Oh, they'd love to, of course," Raymond said. "But

the land was given with the proviso that it be used for agricultural purposes. If they could figure a way to get around the will, we'd be driving an hour and a half to Brentwood to do every little thing."

We crossed the street and began walking up the block. It was about twice as long as a normal block, and the entry gate was in the middle. Not a long distance, but I noticed that Raymond was breathing hard by the time we turned in at the open gate. I slowed my steps to make the walk easier.

The gate opened onto a paved area with a row of greenhouses on our right and a low building in front of older greenhouses on our left. Large grow lights glowed in the glass houses, and ventilation fans hummed.

The building was late fifties vintage, and it hadn't aged particularly well. Raymond unlocked a door and led the way into a dusty room. The wall next to the door was lined with what looked like carpenters' aprons and beneath it a bench was covered with gardening implements. Ahead of us black plastic garbage bags hung from the ceiling.

"The bags are full of dead moths, from another lab," Raymond said. "We share the space."

"Who has keys to the door?" I asked.

"Our students, students in a couple of other labs. Lots of people."

Raymond took an apron from the wall and tied it around his ample waist. "This is a planting apron," he explained. "Holds everything a farmer-geneticist needs."

He led the way through to a room with the rich earthy smell of a greenhouse. Bins of soil lined one side and worktables the other.

From there we stepped out into a little piece of Iowa enclosed in glass. Cornstalks filled the room and the heat from the sun on the roof and the grow lights made it like a steamy day in August. The floor was concrete, and the plants rose out of five-gallon plastic pots instead of earthen beds.

As we walked down the path through the center, we passed plants of different sizes and shapes. Some were robust and healthy, others looked as if their slender stalks could barely support a single ear. At the end a set of plants sprawled horizontally on the floor.

"Oops," I said. "I didn't know corn did that."

"Those are lazy corn plants. They're antigravitropic mutants. Grow straight up for a bit, then straight down. Those are doing their damnedest to head for the center of the earth."

"Is this where Raisa's plants were destroyed?"

"Yeah, they were over there on the left," he said, pointing. "Third row from the back."

"And the seed that was stolen?"

"It was drying on a rack back in that same corner," he said. "Those were the only ears in any of these green-houses. There's nothing left to dry now. You want to see what we do here?"

"Sure."

"I have to do some crosses for Rick. He's a postdoc who's really allergic to corn pollen."

"Why on earth did he choose to study something that made him sick?" I asked.

"He didn't. But all the exposure to corn made him hypersensitive. It's an occupational hazard. And not all that unusual. Chuck is so allergic he has to take medicine and wear a special mask whenever he comes in the green-house. And Kendra doesn't have trouble with pollen but for the last couple of years she's had to give up eating corn on the cob."

Raymond pulled a set of cards from one of the big front pockets of the apron. I followed him as he searched for a specific plant. "It must be really tough working with something that makes you ill," I said.

"I wouldn't do it," he replied, stopping to study the tag

on one stalk. "But for someone like Rick or Chuck who's already invested years in corn genetics, switching to another organism would practically mean starting over. Chuck's super-careful, so I don't worry about him, but Rick's rather immature. He doesn't take the right precautions, and he's sick a lot. He's lucky it hasn't been worse."

He stopped in front of a tall plant. A brown paper bag covered the tassel and a smaller, waxed-paper sack shrouded its single ear. "How much do you know about the sex life of a corn plant?" he asked.

"Hadn't occurred to me that they had one," I said.

"Most everything has a sex life," he said with a smile, then flushed slightly with embarrassment. "The tassels up on top are the male part of the plant. They produce the pollen. The ears are the female part. Each kernel on the cob starts as an embryo sac surrounded by tissue that grows out to be a long silk. The pollen falls on the silks, makes its way to the embryo sacs, and three weeks later, you can boil the water for corn on the cob."

"So each kernel is the result of a separate mating," I said, "even though they're all on the same cob."

"That's right," Raymond said. He reached up for the bag covering the tassel, held the bottom shut, and bent the stalk very gently until it was almost horizontal. Then he shook it vigorously. Finally, he eased the bag off, holding it carefully so that no pollen escaped. "That's what makes corn so great for studying genetics. You get a nice big family with each ear.

"But just like jealous daddies, we don't want our girls making it with the wrong boys. Hence the paper condom." He pointed at the waxed-paper sack that covered the ear.

With his free hand he pulled off the sack, revealing an immature ear with its tiny silks extending about a half inch. He gently shook the pollen from the bag onto the silks, replaced the sack over the ear, covered it with the bag, and secured it with a staple. Then, he took out a marker and wrote on the bag and the card. "Keeping good records, who begot who, is the heart of this business," he said. "We're following generations of development here. You have to know the full lineage of each ear."

He showed me the card with initials and a three-digit number in the right-hand corner. "This is the card for the family, the kernels on one ear. The parents are on the front." He flipped it over to reveal a row of numbers, "and the offspring are on the back. The top row had this family as mom, and bottom row as dad."

"So there're a lot of ways to sabotage work besides destroying the plants," I said.

Raymond nodded glumly. "Switching bags or just removing them at the wrong time, stealing the records, messing with the tags that identify the plants. Any of those would do it. And at every step there are different problems. This is one of two greenhouses. We can't afford guards; I can't watch every student who comes in here."

"Still, I can probably come up with some measures to make it a little more secure," I said.

"I hope so," he said. "You mind if I do a few more crosses before we go? It'll only take a couple of minutes."

I rather enjoyed the moist warmth of the greenhouse and was in no hurry to get back to the lab. I watched as the technician gathered pollen and distributed it to different ears, carefully covering each with its own sack as he finished.

As I followed Raymond, I almost tripped over a large gray cat sitting at the end of one row. The cat darted away.

"That's General Mosby," Raymond said. "Our rodent-control expert. Or he used to be before he got old and blind. There's a joke that Mosby's food and vet bills were once paid by NIH under 'mousetraps.' He still catches the occasional mouse and his scent scares off others, but we have to rely on trapping the rest. He'd probably be a bit more motivated if some of the students didn't slip him treats."

Mosby seated himself at the opposite end of the greenhouse and ignored us. He wasn't as fat as my cat, but he was a long way from skinny. "He doesn't look as if he's going hungry," I said.

"That's because of Teri," Raymond said with a chuckle. "I know she's feeding him. She's worried about him because the mice in here have gotten so skinny they don't make a decent meal. Teri's a real animal lover."

"Teri Shaw?" I said. "Someone said she was Chuck's girlfriend for a while."

Raymond nodded. "Since the term started. They hit it off right away. But they broke up not too long ago."

"Shortly before Julie's seed was stolen, and Chuck's epi tubes were destroyed," I said.

Raymond stopped what he was doing. "You suggesting Teri might be behind the trouble?"

"It's a possibility. What do you think?"

He shook his head slowly. "I don't think so. Teri's not your typical undergrad. She's very serious about her work. A lot like Kendra herself. Very bright and ambitious. Not really a people person. I don't honestly think she cared that much about Chuck. Not enough to risk trouble with Kendra."

He walked to the end of a row and checked the number on a plant, then continued talking as he shook the pollen from its tassel into a bag. "The older students tend to underestimate Teri's intelligence. She's so cute and tiny, that's all they see. They don't look beyond the surface to see what she's really like."

I looked at Raymond Zak's ample body and thought that he must understand too well how it felt when people didn't look beyond the surface.

"How about Scott?" I asked. "I understand he was interested in Julie before she started dating Chuck."

Raymond considered my question for a moment, then shook his head. "No, Scott's like Teri that way. He's incredibly ambitious and very calculating. I wouldn't count too much on his ethics if someone stood between him and his career interests, but he's not the type to brood over a woman."

"Is there anyone else who's smarting over an affair gone sour or a romantic rebuff?"

He didn't answer for a moment, then he said, "Hard to say. We're not running a monastery, and even the most obsessed students still have hormones. You throw a bunch of people together in an intense situation where they don't have much time for relationships outside the lab, and you get quite a few pairwise combinations."

Raymond finished his work with the corn plants and showed me the rest of the greenhouse building. The lot sloped, so that there was another floor of rooms underneath the greenhouse. Despite the windows at the end, the lower floor felt like a basement. Exposed pipes ran along the ceiling, and bare bulbs dropped pools of anemic light. The whole place was as dusty as any farm building.

"This is where Kendra had her lab before Koshland was built," Raymond said. The contrast between the gleaming new lab and this dusty hole was striking.

"I'll bet she was glad to get out of here," I said.

"The new lab's nice," he agreed, "but none of us minded this place too much. People see Kendra all decked out at lectures and meetings, and they don't realize that she spends so much of her time calf-deep in mud. You got to like to muck with plants to be a maize geneticist."

"Is any of this space in use?" I asked.

"Oh, sure. Some students in other departments have offices here, we store stuff, and then there's the corn room."

"Which is?"

"Oh, sorry. It's where we store the seed. The corn

dries upstairs in the greenhouse, then it's brought down here to the corn room. It's just a windowless room where we can control temperature and humidity and fumigate to keep out the critters. It's important because that's where we keep the family trees for everything we plant."

I made a mental note to tell Crawford to change the lock on that door.

AFTER THE DARK halls under the greenhouse, the sun was blindingly bright. It bleached the buildings across from me of color, turning the scene into an over-exposed photo. "Do you use those, too?" I asked Raymond, indicating the newer set of greenhouses.

"Not at the moment," he said. "Our other greenhouse is down in Albany, near the freeway."

As we walked back to the lab, I asked, "How long have you been at the lab?"

"Six years. That makes me the old-timer. I've been there longer than anyone but Kendra," he said. "I'm what the university calls a senior research associate. Students come and go, even professors come and go, but I'm here for the long haul. I've worked in a rodent lab and a fly lab; this is my first plant lab."

"Were you trained as a scientist?"

"Me? No. I'm an artist. I did botanical illustration for a couple of years, but I've got health problems, and I wanted a job with medical benefits, so I applied to work for the university. It's a good job, and it leaves me time to do my art."

"Art and science, a nice combination," I said, thinking that Raymond Zak was both calmer and more balanced than anyone else I'd met at the lab.

"Could the vandalism be an attack on Kendra?" I asked. "An effort to embarrass her or damage her reputation?"

He started walking again. "I suppose that's possible. She evokes strong responses in a lot of people. Some of the women, undergraduates in particular, almost idolize her. She's their role model for success. Grad students are a bit less starry-eyed, but generally they identify with her. Postdocs don't feel so good about her. I've heard them complain that she likes being one of the few women at the top, and she's not about to help another woman join her.

"Of course, postdocs are the most stressed-out people in the lab, so I don't know how seriously to take their complaints. The guys vary in their responses. Some feel she favors the women; I think some maybe resent taking orders from her."

"Any conflicts with particular individuals?" I asked.

"Plenty of conflicts, not with anyone in particular."

"Any emotional or romantic entanglements?" I was on soft ground here. It's tough to get information about the boss. Even if everyone talks behind their back, they'll rarely tell an investigator.

"Not within the lab," Raymond said. "Sexual harassment rules apply to women as well as men, and the feds can tie up a lab for years. Kendra'd never risk giving anyone that kind of power over her."

We reached the corner and started across the street. I took a chance and pressed Raymond a bit harder. "Sometimes clients don't tell me things I need to know," I said. "Makes it harder to do my job. Is there anything I should know about Paul or Kendra? Anything that might be relevant to the sabotage?"

His sharp intake of breath made me turn and watch him more closely. I was almost certain he was debating whether or not to tell me something. Finally, as the pause became uncomfortably long, he said, "No, I don't think so."

"Anything you tell me would be completely confidential," I said.

He nodded but didn't respond. As we reached the curb, he said, "Paul's an excellent right hand; he's really turned the lab around, but I think maybe he's not so aware of how he affects people. Maybe he's a little irresponsible."

"What do you mean?"

Raymond chewed on his lower lip. "Well, a number of the women are attracted to him. He flirts a lot. He hasn't actually gotten involved with anyone—Kendra'd never permit that—but he could be stirring up jealousies."

I tried to get Raymond to elaborate. He claimed he didn't know anything more. He wasn't a good liar.

It took me an hour and a half to get home. It used to be that westbound was the light direction for five o'clock traffic, but lately there doesn't seem to be a light time or direction.

The situation was made a great deal worse by the fact that Caltrans has never gotten around to replacing the Cypress Freeway that collapsed in the quake of '89. LA freeways that came down in '92 were back in service long ago, but in northern California, we're still waiting. And we'll probably get to wait a good deal longer.

Caltrans is exacting penance for all the hassle we've given them about their desire to pave the state. Their favoritism toward the southland is understandable when you consider that in LA freeways are regarded as right up there with food and shelter as necessities of life while here they're at best a necessary evil.

By the time I finally got to Divisadero Street, I was debating between getting take-out or going to a restaurant. I was under no illusion that Molly would have thought of starting dinner.

One of the advantages of our neighborhood, of many neighborhoods in San Francisco, is the rich variety of ethnic restaurants. Little places started by families fleeing war or famine, dictatorships, or just grinding poverty at home. San Franciscans won't eat nearly as well if the immigration zealots have their way.

I made a detour to a nearby Mandarin restaurant. The rich, spicy fragrance from the kitchen made my one o'clock lunch seem pretty distant.

Molly had the coffee table covered with books and papers and the music up full blast. She's been spreading out from her room of late. Candy wrappers, grubby sneakers, and empty soda cans marked her expanded territory.

"Food," I announced. A heavy mass of fur hit my legs and tried to insert itself between my ankles. Piteous cat sounds competed with a rock group I didn't recognize.

"Don't listen to him," Molly called. "I fed him at five."

I stepped over Touchstone, who continued to do his starving-cat routine. At least five pounds overweight, he doesn't get nearly the sympathy he thinks he deserves. "Come eat while it's hot," I told Molly.

I didn't need to call her twice. She's fifteen and still growing, with an appetite that can empty a refrigerator in under an hour.

As she heaped broccoli beef on her plate, I asked, "How was school?"

Molly shrugged, the usual answer to questions about school. She pulled the second carton of food toward her and peered in, then drew back and wrinkled her nose. "Why'd you get prawns? You know I hate prawns."

"I didn't know you hated prawns," I said.

"Well, I do. And I hate the way they always leave the little tails on, so they crunch in your mouth. It's like eating bugs."

I could have suggested that she remove the tails but I was delighted to have found a dish I could eat without having to race Molly for the last helping.

She took the rest of the broccoli beef and asked, "What's the new case?"

Knowing my meal would not disappear if I made the mistake of talking instead of eating, I told her about the lab.

"Sounds as if they're all obsessed," she said, taking more rice. "Half the kids at school are like that. All they can think about is college. They spend all their time studying so they can get in some big-name school. It's so dumb."

I was about to agree with her when I saw where this was heading. "Oh, no, not so fast," I said. "You're not suckering me into condemning homework. There's lots of room between obsession and sloth."

"What's sloth?" Molly asked.

"Sloth is three hours of TV a day, not doing homework, and generally chilling."

"Sounds good to me," she said.

We ate in silence while I considered the issue of obsession. The lab ran on it, but then so do most successful enterprises. Including Sayler Investigations. I was certainly in no position to be too critical of obsession as a motivating force, but I also knew that it could have a dark side.

10

T HE LURID IMAGES and dark sense of terror were
back that night. I woke several times with my heart
pounding and my body damp with sweat. As I was trying
to go back to sleep, I realized that this time there was a
new character in the dreams. A slight, dark-haired woman
in a hospital gown. Julie? Evidently, my subconscious
hadn't bought the argument that she wasn't in any real
danger.

When the alarm went off the next morning, I was
finally sleeping soundly. I might have ignored it if I
hadn't known that in exactly fifteen minutes Molly's
clock radio would blast rock music at several decibels
above my pain threshold. It seems to be the only way to
rouse a fifteen-year-old, but my old body needs to wake
up before I can face the din.

The kitchen was bright with sunlight, and it lifted my
mood immediately. I don't know why February sunshine
is so much more potent than July sunshine. Though it
comes every year, it still feels like a surprise gift.

The sun even coaxed a smile from Molly, but not
much more. We had our usual almost-silent breakfast.
We don't attempt conversation in the morning, but no
one has ever been able to train Touchstone to cooperate.
The moment the refrigerator opens and a milk carton
appears, he starts in with cute purring sounds that esca-
late to mournful howls until we've both surrendered our
empty bowls.

* * *

Traffic in the city was heavy, but on the Bay Bridge it was surprisingly light. I put on a tape of Vivaldi guitar concertos to match the sunshine and thoroughly enjoyed the ride.

I started the morning by interviewing Chuck Nishimura, the student whose epi tubes had been stolen. He was a stocky young man, about medium height, with a broad, pleasant face and a wide grin. His thick black hair was cut short, forming a soft brush on the top of his head. His gray tee shirt read, "Subvert the Dominant Paradigm."

His manner matched the shirt: easy, funny, friendly. He was less upset by the loss of the genetic material than by the malice he sensed behind it. "It's as if we've got our own private terrorist," he said.

I asked about his run-in with Raisa the year before.

"More a run-over than a run-in," he said. "She stole my research idea." He described how they'd been working on the same project and he'd gone to her with an idea for research for his dissertation. She'd discouraged him, then gone ahead and done the research herself.

"So now she's got a paper and I've got zip," he said bitterly. "It was really unethical. Postdocs aren't supposed to steal from grad students. It'd be like me ripping off an undergrad. You just don't pull stuff like that."

"Seems as if there's a lot of destructive behavior here."

"It's like the greenroom for hell," Chuck said.

When I asked if Raisa might have stolen his epis, he looked as if he really wanted to say yes, but then he shook his head. "I don't know," he said. "Hard to imagine even her being so low."

He hesitated longer when I asked about Dorian Barker. "He's a strange guy," Chuck said. "I don't know about him."

* * *

My morning of interviews didn't give me much more than I had the day before. Several people mentioned the conflict between Chuck and Raisa; most of them sided with Chuck. Failed liaisons were common enough that no one seemed to think much about Chuck and Teri's breakup. Everyone, including the Asian students, dismissed the possibility that the sabotage was racially motivated.

When I mentioned Kendra, they were all full of praise and admiration, but a bit of probing revealed the splits Raymond had suggested. The undergrad women were nothing short of worshipful; the postdocs were considerably less enthusiastic. It didn't take much encouragement to get them to tell me that Kendra had given Chuck first authorship on a paper when they thought he'd done less work than the two women on the project. The men were no happier. The ones Margot referred to as "the boys' club" complained that women had the edge.

I paid particular attention to Dorian Barker. He was so tense he had trouble sitting still in the chair, and his constant shifting and fidgeting got on my nerves. His nasal voice was pitched to complaint, and he told me several times that he had to finish his paper for the grant proposal.

With his hostility to Chuck, he was a good candidate for saboteur, and he didn't have much good to say about Raisa either, but when I asked about Julie, his whole manner changed.

"She's a really sweet person," he said. "She never gets involved in the kind of shit other people here dish out."

"Yet someone has sabotaged her work twice."

"That really sucks," he growled. "Whoever did that is just slime."

Chuck's former girlfriend, Teri Shaw, didn't come into the lab until three-thirty, so she was last on my schedule. She reminded me immediately of Kendra Crawford. She was shorter, and with blond straight hair instead of dark waves, but in dress and bearing Shaw was a miniature of the professor. Her green designer jeans, black jersey, and tan jacket could have come from Crawford's closet. I wondered if her choice of clothes was an unconscious form of hero worship or if she'd intentionally modeled herself after the professor.

She was petite, no more than five three, with a gymnast's trim body. With her wide blue eyes, ski-jump nose, and ash-blond hair, she was an attractive young woman. There was a seriousness in her eyes and in the set of her mouth that made her seem older than the other undergraduates.

I asked my standard questions. She gave the standard responses. Finally, I said, "I understand that you and Chuck Nishimura were going together for a while."

"Boy, this is really gossip central," she said with more irony than irritation. "Yes, we were 'going together,' but we broke up."

"What happened?"

She shrugged. "We didn't have time for a relationship," she said matter-of-factly. "It was fun at first, but it takes a lot of energy to have a serious relationship. We're both working really hard in school. There just wasn't time."

She said it without any visible emotion. I was inclined to accept Raymond's assessment that she really didn't care that much.

Too bad. My job would have been a lot easier with a good solid suspect.

I found Crawford in her office when I finished just before four. "So what have you got?" she asked as I shut the door and before I'd had a chance to sit down.

"Not a lot," I said. "Possible suspects, nothing firm. At this point, the main thing I'd recommend is that you tighten security."

"You've seen the setup here. You can see how impossible that is," she objected. "It's just not compatible with being on a college campus." Her tone was sharp. I wondered how Raskin managed to work with her.

"Not complete security, no. But you're not dealing with Libyan terrorists," I said. "I can suggest several things that will reduce the likelihood of sabotage and minimize the damage."

"And those are . . . ?" She looked more skeptical than pleased.

"First, you need to protect your data. Multiple backups of every computer file, at least one set stored outside the lab. And you update those daily. Next, re-key your office and the corn room so only you have access. Make multiple copies of any documents, diagrams, or slides of importance. I can install surveillance cameras. I'd put one on the refrigerators, a couple in the greenhouse, here and in Albany. They're small and we'll put them where no one will notice them."

She nodded, but her expression remained cool. "I'm not sure about the cameras. I'll need to think about that. The other things make sense."

It all made sense, but I didn't say that. "Finally, we keep your saboteur nervous, increase the risk of discovery. Put sign-in sheets in the labs, greenhouses, all the rooms you use, and make a big deal out of requiring people to sign in and out. Check the lists and—"

"I can't do that," she interrupted. "This isn't IBM. I can't force people to sign in and out. We've tried a sign-up sheet in the radioactive area to make people be more responsible for cleaning up their mess. It never worked. Besides, it'd be terrible for morale."

"This is considerably more serious than a cleanup problem," I said. "And morale is already terrible. Between the hostility level and the anxiety level, it'd be a close race to see which was highest."

She glowered at me, and I realized I'd let my irritation get the best of me. "It's your call, of course," I said.

She tapped her index finger against the desk, the nail rapped out a ragged rhythm, but she seemed unaware of the sound.

"The other thing you can do is to drop in at times when you're not expected," I said. "You and Paul, maybe Raymond. I can arrange to come by every day or so at different times if you'd like. We come in, check the sign-in sheet, look around, maybe chat with whoever's here. Just to make sure that everyone knows we're watching, that one of us could appear at any time."

She nodded. "I like that," she said. "It'll keep people on their toes."

"It's something you can do without me," I said. "That reduces the cost."

The nail continued to tap. She seemed completely unaware of it. I had a terrific urge to put my hand on top of hers to stop the drumming.

"I think it's worth it to have you involved," she said. "It'll make the students take things more seriously."

"Fine," I said, wondering if she was one of those people who always do the opposite of what you suggest.

"I'll have Paul call a lab meeting for tomorrow at eleven," she said. "You can check out the Albany greenhouse afterward."

I was on my way out when Raymond Zak motioned to me from the lab bench in the far corner. I went over to him.

He looked uncomfortable; there was no sign of humor in his usually smiling face. "I have something that I think you should know," he said, his voice low. "About the lab, and maybe about the sabotage."

"Great, let's go to the interview room."

Raymond hesitated, then nodded and started toward

the room but stopped. I moved so that I could see around him. Paul Raskin, Scott, and Dorian were coming down the corridor from the other lab. Dorian was talking, Scott was shaking his head, and Raskin was listening intently, his face serious, so that his sharp features seemed almost fierce. They stopped in the doorway and looked up at us.

The lab technician took a step backward. I could feel his tension. "I think those papers are in the library," he said. "I'll get them for you."

He hurried off before I could say anything. Raskin and the two students went back to their conversation.

Raymond was back in a minute. He handed me a folded sheet of yellow lined paper. "If you don't need anything more, I should get back to work," he said, and turned back to his bench.

"Thank you," I said.

"I'll see you tomorrow morning," he replied.

He was back at his desk by the time I opened the paper. On it, he had written, "I can't talk here. Meet me for breakfast at eight tomorrow. The Royal Café on San Pablo in Albany."

11

I'D HAVE LIKED to suggest that I meet Raymond after work instead of waiting till the next day, but I didn't get the chance. He never met my eyes, and he stayed as far from me as possible. It was as if he'd built an invisible wall around himself.

After almost an hour of waiting for people to leave so that I could talk with Raymond, I gave up and went home. But as I sat in line at the Bay Bridge toll plaza and studied the taillights of the car in front of me, I couldn't get him out of my thoughts. He seemed almost afraid when Paul, Dorian, and Scott came into the room. Strange behavior for a man who'd seemed so at ease only hours before.

Once on the bridge, traffic thinned out and then clotted up again just past Yerba Buena Island. I rarely mind slow traffic there. It gives me more time to savor the view. With the North Bay on the right, the South Bay on the left, and the light-studded office towers of downtown San Francisco in the near distance, it's a reminder of why so many of us love to live here, even when much of it is covered with fog.

While I enjoyed the view and was looking forward to seeing Molly this evening, apprehension tugged my mind back to Raymond Zak's strange behavior. I recognized the emotion, free-floating anxiety, another nasty gift from the psycho who'd stalked me. I felt like a kid who has to check under the bed for monsters.

The next morning looked like most mornings in this part of town—gray. February or July, it's not much different in San Francisco. The fog comes in; the wind blows. Sometimes it rains. Otherwise, it's about the same.

By the Oakland side of the bridge, the fog was gone and sunshine lifted my mood. The previous night's apprehension was replaced by curiosity. And hunger.

San Pablo Avenue runs more or less parallel to the eastern shore of the bay. Its history goes back to the Spanish settlement of California, but it's fallen victim to strip development and for much of its length is lined with low-rent shops and fast-food outlets.

The Royal Café was several blocks from the Albany exit of the freeway in a pink faux-Spanish building with a little tower and a red tile roof. It had not only a parking lot but empty spaces on the street, testimony to its distance from the congested downtown area.

It was a few minutes before eight, so I wasn't surprised that Raymond wasn't there. The waitress seated me and brought coffee. My first sip reminded me that Berkeley people like their coffee strong.

As the minutes ticked by, my stomach started to feel jumpy. Could have been the coffee, but it wasn't. It was that same sense of dread that I'd felt the night before. And the longer I waited, the stronger it grew.

At eight-twenty, I ordered toast and switched to tea in an effort to calm my stomach. It didn't help. When Raymond hadn't come by nine, I headed for Cal, hoping he'd just forgotten our meeting and I'd find him there.

He wasn't there, but Paul Raskin was. "You're an early bird," he said. "I didn't expect you until ten."

"I decided to come in early so I could get back to the city after lunch," I said. "Has Raymond come in?"

Raskin shook his head. "I haven't seen him. Can I do something for you?"

Given Raymond's response to Raskin the day before, I didn't want to discuss the meeting he'd missed this morning. "No," I said, "It's nothing important. I can ask him when he comes in."

"He's usually here by nine-thirty or ten," Raskin said. "Sure it isn't something I can help with?"

I shook my head and searched for an excuse. "He's taking me to the Albany greenhouse today, and I wanted to move up the time," I said. "Do you have his home number?"

"Sure, I'll get it. You can use the phone on my desk."

I'd have preferred another phone, but it wasn't worth making Raskin suspicious, and my major concern was confirming that Raymond was all right.

I dialed the number and listened as it rang. On the fifth ring, I heard a click followed by Raymond's soft voice. "You've reached Raymond's machine. Please leave your

number and he'll call you back. Thanks, and wait for the
beep."

Damn. I put the phone down. "He must be on his
way," I said, hoping it was true.

There was enough to do to keep me busy for the next
hour, but I had a hell of a time concentrating. My mind
kept suggesting ugly scenarios. At one point, I wondered
if Raymond had fled. Perhaps he'd wanted to confess that
he had a role in the sabotage. That would explain why he
didn't want Raskin to know of our conversation. But I
couldn't see the gentle lab tech as a saboteur.

Finally, I couldn't stand to wait any longer. "I think
I'll go by his house," I told Raskin. "I'm tired of waiting
around."

He looked at me as if I were nuts. "The meeting's at
eleven," he said. "If you want to see the Albany greenhouse so much, I can take you after that."

"Raymond lives over in Albany," Julie said. "Not too
far from the Albany tract."

I filed away the fact that she knew where he lived, and
asked Raskin for the address. He grumbled a bit about
giving it to me, but in the end he did.

"I think this street runs parallel to San Pablo, a couple
of streets above it," he said. "I have to tell you that this
doesn't seem a very good use of your time."

"Not to worry," I said. "I won't bill you for it. And I'll
get back for the meeting."

He shrugged and I headed out before he could object
further.

Raymond's house was a warm gray duplex with navy-
and-cream trim. It was only about six blocks from the
Royal Café in a neighborhood of small but well-kept
houses. The house itself was fairly plain, but the yard was
from an impressionist painting. Irises of varied shapes
and sizes, riotously yellow mustard, fragile wild white
freesias and their larger, more colorful cousins, and an as-

sortment of other plants I couldn't identify created an English garden in a tiny plot.

Paving stones led to each of two doors. Raymond's was on the left. I rang the bell several times. I could hear it ringing inside the house, so I knew it worked.

The door on the right opened and a frail, high voice said, "Raymond?"

I turned toward the voice. "Hello, I'm a friend of Raymond's. Do you know if he's left for work?"

The woman in the doorway seemed about four feet tall and so thin that her faded rose housedress hung loosely on her. "I can't hear so well," she said. "Can't see much either. Would you like to come over here?"

The old woman introduced herself as Marcia Lawder, and after looking me over, she invited me in. From a distance, she'd appeared frail, but up close she was merely thin. Her skin was so white that it was almost translucent, and though she was still in a housedress, her hair was carefully combed and she was wearing a touch of lipstick.

The living room was crowded with furniture bought for a larger house. The fabric covering the generously stuffed armchairs and the sofa was a print from the fifties, faded and fraying in several places. Only the television set looked new.

But the room was far from dull. Large, brightly colored oils and pastels adorned each wall. Some were realistic, others more impressionistic; all were of flowers and each was beautiful in its own way.

"Raymond's work," Mrs. Lawder informed me.

"Do you know where he is?" I asked.

"I thought he was still at home," she said. "He usually calls before he goes to work just to make sure I'm feeling all right, and he hasn't called yet today."

"Do you know what his car looks like?" I asked.

"It's a white car, small. I don't know the make, but it's one of those foreign cars. Has a little sign with a whale on it on the bumper."

I'd parked behind a white Honda Civic with a Greenpeace sticker on it. "I'm concerned about Raymond," I said. "His car's out in front, but he doesn't answer the door."

"Oh, dear," she said. "I hope he's not ill. I haven't heard him moving around this morning."

"Do you happen to have a key to his door? I could check on him."

She hesitated and appraised me carefully. Finally, she decided to trust me. "Wait here a moment. I have one in the kitchen."

I forced myself not to rush her, or to seem in too much of a hurry myself, but it took all my patience not to bolt when she handed me the key.

There was a strange smell in Raymond Zak's house, but I was relieved that it was not the one I'd smelled at murder scenes. I called his name and got no answer. Maybe he'd just gone for a walk.

From the living room I could see through a small dining room and into the kitchen. Everything was neat, no sign of trouble. In the dining room, a door led into a hall and then to a bedroom. In the bedroom doorway, there was something on the floor.

I caught my breath. The something was a foot.

Raymond lay on his stomach just inside the door. I knew before I felt for a pulse that he was dead.

I'd parked behind a silver Honda Civic with a Greenpeace

12

RAYMOND'S SKIN WAS cold and hard to the touch. His head was turned to the side, his eyes open in an unseeing stare.

I leaned back against the wall and wrapped my arms around myself, feeling a kind of cold numbness spread through my body. I wasn't aware of the tears until I felt them drip onto my arm.

I don't know how long I stood like that before the numbness subsided so that I could think.

Raymond had been dead long enough that there wasn't much point in phoning 911, so I called the Albany police. The operator took the address and my name, and told me not to touch anything until the patrolman arrived.

I was torn between going back to break the news to Mrs. Lawder and taking advantage of what might be my only chance to look around. It wasn't much of a contest.

The police would check for forced entry. I decided to see if I could find any indication of what Raymond had planned to tell me.

The bedroom was fairly small, made even smaller by the queen-sized bed that took up most of the floor space and a heavy oak dresser with ornate brass pulls. Raymond was clearly a neat housekeeper—no clothes thrown about, no clutter on the tops of the dresser or nightstand. Too bad. Clutter often yields useful clues. Neat people throw things away; messy people often drop them into piles where they may go unnoticed for weeks.

Behind me in the hall was another door. It revealed a second small bedroom that Raymond had converted to a combination studio and office. A drafting table stood along one wall, a computer desk with a Mac faced it across the room, and in front of the window there was an easel with a partially finished oil painting. The smell I'd noticed earlier was stronger here, and I realized it must be paint.

I have friends who are artists, and I've never seen a studio that clean. I passed up the drafting table with its pencil sketch of a bold, almost predatory-looking blossom and the easel with its softer, more impressionistic rendering of bright yellow tulips, and went straight to the Mac. Computers are almost as good as filing cabinets for snooping. Their great advantage is that they force people to get their paperwork organized, so it's easier to find what you're looking for.

A stack of photos on the desk next to the Mac caught my eye. The one on top showed Scott and Julie in one of the greenhouses. I reached for the pictures, then stopped and pulled out the latex gloves I carry in my purse. If the police fingerprinted the house, I didn't want to have to explain why my prints were in this room.

There were about thirty photos, all candid snapshots of students involved in various activities in the lab and greenhouses. There were seven that included Julie, more than for any other single student—one alone, one with Paul, two with Chuck, and three with Scott. Julie had known where Raymond lived; I wondered about the nature of their relationship.

I'd just put the photos down and flipped on the power switch of the Mac when I heard a car door slam outside. Through the window, I could see the black and white. I shut down the computer, pulled off my gloves, stuck them in my purse, and backed out of the room.

*   *   *

The patrol officer was about my height, and in his early forties. A bit of a paunch pushed against the bottom buttons of his shirt. He was a redhead with pale skin and eyebrows and lashes so blond that they were almost invisible. Something about his eyes reminded me of a rabbit.

"You reported finding a body?" he asked.

"Yes," I said. "It's in the bedroom."

He followed me to the bedroom, stooped to feel Raymond's throat for a pulse, then stood up. "Been dead for a while," he said. "Are you related to the deceased?"

"No," I said. "I work for the lab where he was employed." I chose my words carefully. If Raymond hadn't died of natural causes, I didn't want the police thinking I'd misled them. At the same time, if he had, I didn't want to reveal any more than I had to of the problems at the lab. I knew I'd get to tell this story several times, and my goal was to remain as vague as possible until I was actually talking to a detective.

"And why did you come to the house?"

I described the situation in broad terms. As I talked, the patrolman took out a notebook and made some notes. "So you suspected foul play," he said. "That's why you came here."

I paused before answering. "I suspected something," I said. "But I didn't really expect to find him dead."

"I guess I better call one of the detectives," he said somewhat reluctantly. "Though it sure looks like natural causes to me."

"The woman who shares the duplex was a friend of Mr. Zak's," I said. "Do you mind if I go and break the news to her?"

If he'd believed he was dealing with homicide, he'd have refused. As it was, he looked relieved to let me deal with a task neither of us wanted to tackle.

Mrs. Lawder was at the door as soon as I knocked. "Why are the police here? Is Raymond ill?" she asked.

I waited until I was in a position to support her if she fainted. "I'm afraid Raymond is dead," I said.

Her face froze in an expression of shock and she backed away from me toward the couch and sat down. "Oh, no, not Raymond," she said.

I sat beside her. "It appears he collapsed sometime last night. Do you remember hearing anything?"

She shook her head, but I wasn't sure that she'd even understood my question. "Raymond can't be dead," she said. "He was so young." She stared into the distance, her eyes vague and unfocused. Finally, she asked, "What was it? What did he die of?"

"I don't know," I said. "They'll have to do an autopsy. Do you know if he had any health problems?"

"Nothing serious," she said. "Nothing you die from. But then maybe he wouldn't have told me. Wouldn't have wanted to worry me. Raymond was like that. Considerate.

"He always checked on me in the morning and when he got back from work. He'd call or come over. Just to chat, to make sure I was all right. He'd pick up things for me at the store. Or the pharmacy.

"He was a wonderful artist. All these paintings are his. And there are some exquisite drawings in my bedroom. So delicate. And so precise. Every detail so perfect that the flower might be alive."

Her voice was brittle with forced cheerfulness, then like a windup toy that had run down, she fell suddenly silent and sat staring across the room at a large oil painting of deep blue Dutch irises.

A second car pulled up, and I excused myself as soon as I could. Back at Raymond's, a man in navy slacks and a gray herringbone jacket stood talking to the patrolman. He was African-American, about five ten, broad shoulders and a chunky build. His black hair was shot through with bits of gray. He had his hands in his pockets, and I could hear him jingling the change.

The patrolman introduced me and identified his colleague as Detective Wilson. The detective did not look happy. He nodded a greeting to me, then said to the patrolman, "You interview that lady next door. Now."

As the patrolman hurried out the door, Wilson turned his attention to me. "Would you like to sit down," he said in a tone that made it more an order than a question. He indicated a chair at the dining room table. "You say he missed an eight o'clock appointment, didn't answer the phone, and wasn't at work by ten. Usually it takes a bit longer for co-workers to become concerned."

"I'm not a co-worker," I said. "I'm a private investigator, and I was hired because the lab has had some problems with sabotage." I told him that Raymond had wanted to talk to me away from the lab and that he'd set up the meeting surreptitiously, so no one else would know of it. "Given his desire for secrecy, I was concerned when he didn't show up."

Wilson nodded. The change jingled in his pocket. "You suggesting he was murdered to keep him from telling what he knew?"

"No," I said, "I'm not suggesting murder. But I am suggesting that you order a complete autopsy and ask the coroner's office to handle it as a potential homicide. Tell them to pay particular attention to the tox screens."

"Anything else you'd like us to do?" His tone was sarcastic.

"I'm sorry if that sounded presumptuous," I said. "My former husband was a homicide detective. I know how you guys hate civilians who're full of bright ideas."

I could sense his attitude shift. I wasn't part of the fraternity, but I wasn't a complete outsider either. In the early years after my divorce from Dan Walker of the San Francisco police, I'd carefully concealed our relationship whenever possible. Now I treated it as a valuable card to be played when dealing with suspicious cops.

I could have mentioned that my dad was a cop, too,

but Dan was in San Francisco, Dad in Denver, and I suspected that ex-wives were taken more seriously than daughters.

"I'll be honest with you," I said. "Raymond's employer hired me because she didn't want the university administration or her colleagues to be aware of the sabotage. I'd prefer to avoid a police investigation if there's no reason for it. And I expect you'd prefer not to waste your time on a bunch of interviews if there's no evidence of foul play. I was hoping you'd decide to put the investigation on a back burner until you have the autopsy results."

"I might," Wilson said, nodding. "Depends on what we find here. I'll want a complete statement from you and information on how we can reach you."

"Of course," I said, taking out my business card and handing it to him. "Would you mind if I called to find out the results of your investigations here?"

"I'll tell you what I can," he said, taking his own card from his breast pocket. "Who's your ex-husband?"

"Dan Walker, SFPD," I said. "Do you know him?"

Wilson nodded. I figured he'd be calling Dan to check on me. That, too, bothered me much less than it had a few years ago.

The coroner's investigator arrived while I was giving my statement. He conferred with Wilson outside earshot, then he began his survey of the house. From the number of photos he took and the thoroughness of his investigation, I could tell that he was treating the place as a crime scene.

13

IT WAS AFTER one by the time I got back to the lab and the meeting was long over. I found Kendra Crawford and Paul Raskin in the professor's office, she seated at the computer, he leaning over her, pointing at something on the screen. I stepped in and closed the door behind me.

They turned toward me and Crawford's brow creased in irritation. "You missed the lab meeting," she said.

Raskin read my emotions on my face. "What's wrong?" he asked.

"Raymond Zak is dead."

It took a moment to register. Both just stared at me, then Raskin shook his head once quickly as if to clear it and said, "What?"

"Raymond is dead," I said. "I went to his house to check on him and found him dead. There were no signs of struggle, and while the coroner won't know until he does the autopsy, he's guessing it was natural causes."

Raskin lowered himself into the other chair in the room and shook his head again, slowly this time. "It must have been his heart," he said. "He was so heavy. But he wasn't that old."

Kendra didn't answer. She looked stunned.

"I'd guess he died sometime last night," I said. "He was wearing the same shirt and pants he had on at the lab." I spared them the forensic evidence; no one wants

77

to know about things like rigor and lividity when they apply to someone you've known and liked.

Finally Kendra spoke. "Poor Raymond" was all she said.

"We'll have to tell the lab," Raskin said. "I think he was fairly close to Julie. I don't know that he knew the others that well."

From our conversation, I thought that Raymond knew all the students well. Whether any of them knew him was another matter. "Did you know he was a painter?" I asked.

"I think he mentioned it," Kendra said. "He did some drawings for papers, but students generally preferred photographs."

"They missed out on an opportunity," I said. "He was a botanical illustrator."

"Really?" Raskin looked surprised. "I guess that explains"—he paused only a moment, but long enough to tell me he was censoring himself—"his interest in plants."

"And?" I asked.

Raskin's features seemed to sharpen just a bit. I decided that he must tighten the muscles around his eyes when that happened, but I didn't know him well enough to know what it meant.

"You started to say something else," I said.

The muscles tightened a bit more, then relaxed. "Nothing really, just that he seemed interested in things not related to the research projects."

"What kinds of things?"

Raskin thought for a minute. "He often sketched plants that weren't of much importance. Last week I overheard him asking both Julie and Raisa questions about the strains they were studying."

I'd considered whether I should confront Raskin with Raymond's request to meet away from work. While there was every reason to assume that Scott or Dorian was the one Raymond suspected of sabotage, I didn't see why the technician would be afraid to confront a student. Far more likely, he'd prefer to conceal our meeting from his boss.

For the moment, I decided not to reveal my suspicions to Raskin.

"You want me to call another meeting?" Raskin asked Crawford.

"I guess you better. Set it for late this afternoon so we'll have time to notify people. And you'd better call Personnel about a replacement for Raymond. I want to see files. Don't let them just fob someone off on us."

If Raskin was surprised by how quickly Crawford moved on to replacing Raymond, he showed no sign of it. He unfolded his body from the chair, rose slowly, and left the office.

I closed the door behind him. "There's one thing I didn't mention while Paul was here," I told Kendra, then described the events that had led to Raymond's slipping me the note.

"What a strange thing to do," she said. "If he had something to say, why didn't he just come to me?"

A good question. A student might hesitate to speak directly to the head of the lab, but why would a lab tech? "It may not mean anything, could just be coincidence, but his secretiveness suggests that he was afraid of someone here in the lab."

Crawford frowned. "Are you saying you think his death wasn't accidental?"

Before I could answer, she went on, "Don't be ridiculous. The man was overweight, didn't exercise, probably didn't take very good care of himself. You're letting your imagination run wild." Her tone was accusatory and angry. "I hired you to keep us out of the limelight. Not to go around making wild charges."

I was startled by her vehemence. Death is hard to take, even when it's accidental. I could understand that she'd deny the possibility of foul play, but her reaction didn't feel like denial.

Word of Raymond's death was out before the meeting, and it spread quickly. The students were shocked; some seemed stunned. For many it was the first time they'd experienced the death of anyone other than an elderly relative. The intelligence and sophistication that sometimes made them seem older dropped away in the face of emotions they were ill-prepared to handle.

Some talked about Raymond's death almost compulsively, as if by talking they could make some sense of it. Others went silent. Raisa's nervous energy escalated to the manic level and she seemed to ricochet around the lab, repeating at least a dozen times, "I just don't believe it. He *can't* be dead." Scott retreated to his desk and pulled into himself, alternately staring out the window and at the floor, but never making eye contact with anyone. Dorian sat in his chair and observed the others warily, a pinched, troubled expression on his face.

I watched their reactions and thought how death had become entirely too much a part of my job recently. At least this time, the death wasn't violent, but I couldn't shake the feeling that it might not be natural. I felt sympathy for the students but I couldn't help studying them with a suspicious eye.

I was startled by laughter behind me, and heard Chuck's and Julie's voices as they came into the lab. Chuck was teasing Julie about her driving, but just inside the door he stopped in mid-sentence, sensing immediately that something was wrong.

There was a moment of silence, broken when Raisa announced, "Raymond's dead." With that statement, the energy seemed to drain from her and she sat down heavily on a nearby stool.

Julie froze, then shook her head dumbly. "Raymond?"

she said. Chuck seemed equally unable to take in the news. He blinked several times, his face blank with shock.

Raskin went to Julie and put an arm around her. "We think he had a heart attack," he said, "last night, at his home."

"He's dead?" she asked. Then, before Raskin could confirm it, she closed her eyes tight and turned her face against his chest.

As the truth sank in, Chuck looked around almost frantically. "How'd he die? What happened?" he asked. His voice was high and thin, with a panicky edge.

"He had a heart attack. At least that's what we think happened," Raskin said.

"A heart attack? It was a heart attack?" Chuck repeated. "He couldn't, I mean, oh God, oh my God . . ." The strength of his emotion drew my attention from Julie. The expression on his face startled me. I'd expected shock and sorrow but what I saw seemed closer to horror.

Suddenly aware that we were all staring at him, Chuck clamped his mouth shut. His body tensed as he struggled to force down his emotions. Finally, he took a deep breath and swallowed hard. "How awful," he said, much more quietly. Then he walked to his desk in the other room.

The meeting was short and addressed none of the emotional issues I'd observed surfacing in the lab. Watching Kendra, I decided she was even less able to deal with death than her students. She announced Raymond's demise with no more visible emotion than if he'd transferred to a different lab.

It was left to Raskin to offer the students comfort. And he approached the subject as he often did other issues; he resorted to humor. "We scientists don't *do* emotions," he said. "That's for the humanities people. But if we did, we might take it hard having a guy we work with die on us.

So Doc Raskin'll be available anytime you're feeling weird and want someone to talk to."

No one asked for help, but that would come later and probably very privately. In my short time at the lab, I'd learned that the best and the brightest do not easily admit to vulnerability.

I left right after the meeting and drove back to San Francisco. And the fog. It was like moving back a season. The thick clouds formed a low dome over the city, robbing it of color and reducing it to the dull grays of a poor-quality photograph.

The gray cityscape didn't do much for my already low spirits. Nor did the traffic. Ditto the fact that there were no parking places on the side street where I like to park my car.

I went around the block and got a parking place in front of the secondhand clothing store downhill from my office. Parking at a meter in my neighborhood is like tithing to the parking authority. Miss by five minutes and your latest bill awaits on your window. But it was late in the day and I was in no mood to hunt and hike.

I walked uphill to the white Victorian that houses our office. The neighborhood has always been transitional, rich folks up the hill, poor folks down the hill, but lately the downhill section has been moving upscale. When a law firm moved in next door several months ago, Jesse and I took it as a sure sign that the neighborhood was going to hell.

My secretary, Amy, has her office in the first room to the left. I stuck my head in and said, "Hi, Mom, I'm home." Amy's ten years younger than I am but the way she fusses and worries you'd think she was twenty years older.

"Chris called from Sacramento," she said. "She won't be back till after dinner." I'd sent Chris to the state capital to interview several produce buyers suspected of taking kickbacks. She has a gift for getting people to tell her things that make lawyers weep; that case would be wrapped up tonight.

I'd expected Jesse to be in Sunnyvale working on the missing chips case, so I was surprised and delighted to hear his voice down the hall. He was talking on the phone, and I couldn't make out what he was saying until I got to his door.

"Check your sources in Singapore, Hong Kong, and Taiwan," he said. "Those chips have got to be on the market someplace."

I pushed his door open, waved, and pointed toward my office to ask him to join me there when he finished his call, then went to see if there was any coffee left in the pot. There was half a pot, but the beer in the fridge looked a lot more inviting, and after the day I'd had, I'd earned it.

Jesse noticed the beer as soon as he came into my office. "That kind of day, huh?" he said.

"That kind of day. A guy from the lab died last night, and I found him."

"Oh, shit, Catherine, I'm sorry."

"I feel as if I'm some kind of curse," I said. "I take a case, someone dies."

Jesse did me the favor of not answering my irrational complaint with a rational argument. He sat down in the chair next to my desk and leaned forward. "I encouraged you to take this case because it looked so harmless. You just never know." He shook his head.

I took a drink of beer. "I'm spending too much time at funerals," I said. I'd meant it as a joke, but it was too true to be funny. A lump in my throat made swallowing difficult. "And the worst part is it's made me paranoid. I can't shake the feeling that this death is just too convenient."

"What makes you think that?"

"He had something to tell me related to the case, and he died before he could do it." I told Jesse about Raymond's secretly slipping me the note. "It was probably nothing of great import," I said, "and if I hadn't just handled a couple of murder cases recently, I wouldn't think anything of it."

Jesse nodded thoughtfully. "So how'd the guy die?" he asked.

"Probably a heart attack," I said. "There was no sign of a struggle."

"What makes you assume a heart attack?"

"It had to be something quick. I think the coroner's investigator would have spotted it if he'd choked. Besides, he was overweight, obese even."

"That's a risk factor, not a cause," Jesse said.

"You suggesting it might have been something other than natural causes?"

"I'm just saying that you have a damn good instinct for trouble. I wouldn't be too quick to ignore it."

A good instinct for trouble. I'd happily have traded that for the ability to stay out of trouble. But it didn't look as if I'd get the chance.

14

I'D BEEN PLANNING to go to aikido that night, and after the day I'd had, I really needed the workout.

It was dark by the time I got to the dojo. During the day, tall windows on two sides of the room bathe the mat in light, but at night the same windows glow orange with the reflected light of the streetlamps below.

The external darkness only served to make the white mats and walls seem brighter. This oblong room with its Japanese sense of order and simplicity is one of the most peaceful places I know, despite the fact that it is designed for the study of a martial art. Even when the mat is crowded with people attacking and throwing each other, the place and the art have a sense of balance and harmony.

Tonight's class was taught by Gina Lori. She's about five four, weighs maybe a hundred and ten, and can easily throw guys twice her size. One of the things that make her such a great instructor is that her students are constantly reminded that aikido is not about muscular strength. I love to watch some big guy new to the class decide he's going to resist a throw. They all have the same surprised look on their faces when they get up off the mat.

We started with stretches. The day's tension had knotted my muscles so they complained with each move. I could hear my neck crack when we did head rolls.

Gina started with *katatedori shihonagi*. She extended her right hand and her partner grabbed her wrist. As he grabbed, she slid forward on a diagonal, raised both hands to her forehead, and pivoted quickly. Her partner let the momentum turn him and stretched his body to reduce the strain on his shoulder. As she brought her hands down, he dropped at her feet.

After some practice, Gina clapped and we lined up on the mat for further instruction. Gina bowed to me and motioned for me to join her as her partner. She extended her hand and I grabbed her wrist.

"The first thing you do here, you have to get off the line," she said. "You can go in front or behind, but you cannot go into your partner." She pushed straight into me, and I pushed back. "See, here it's just a matter of who's stronger. Here," she said as she slid forward just to the side in front of me, "here, there's no resistance. Here, I take her balance." She finished the throw, and I dropped to the mat, slapping to break the fall and coming up to attack again when she signaled me.

"Aikido comes from sword work. If you face someone and you both strike, with swords you can both die." She nodded, and I brought my hand up, then struck at the top of her head. She countered with a similar strike and our arms met in midair.

"But if as your partner strikes, you step off the line . . ." This time, when she nodded, I struck, but she slid her foot forward slightly on the diagonal and turned her hips so that my strike missed and hers landed in the middle of my forearm. "You survive.

"You see, in sword work a confrontation ends in death, sometimes the death of both men. O'Sensei wanted to develop a way that didn't have to end in death.

"But in the martial arts you have to be ready to give up your life. You have to be willing to take the risk. Otherwise, you'll be afraid; you'll hold back. My teacher used to say that you should do each technique as if it were your last act on earth, with that kind of attention and power. I like to think of it as if it were your first act. No expectation, no plan, just the act itself.

"So, try again. Move off the line. Try not to anticipate."

I'd have liked to stay for a second class. A hard physical workout is the best tonic for the kind of tension I'd been feeling all day. But I was also anxious to get home to Molly so we could have dinner together, so after we bowed out from the first class, I got dressed and headed home.

Gina's words stayed with me as I drove back to my flat. Last acts I understood. I'd been in more than one situation where aikido had literally saved my life, and it's true that there's a unique clarity and power to such moments. But acting without expectation, that's even harder.

I wondered how Julie's illness and Raymond's death would look to me if I hadn't ever dealt with a murder case. Realized I'd never know. My dad told me once that he had "cops' eyes," meaning he saw the world differently because of the work he did. Maybe I was getting those eyes myself.

I'd hoped that dinner with Molly might lift my spirits. No such luck. She was in one of her silent moods. I gave up any attempt at conversation after several questions and comments were greeted with shrugs, indecipherable mumbles, or three-word answers, and wrote off her poor mood to irritation at my refusal to save her from Saturday's shopping trip with her mother.

A teenager's silence isn't just the absence of noise. It always amazes me how loud Molly's silences are. They fill the room more completely than the rock music she loves to play at top volume. As she sat hunched over her plate, pushing the broccoli around or spearing a piece of macaroni, her withdrawal was as aggressive as any confrontation.

Between Raymond's death and Molly's rejection, I was overwhelmed with longing for Peter. I hadn't realized how much I'd come to rely on him for comfort. I longed to have him wrap me in one of his warm hugs. I missed the sound of his voice. If I could have picked up the phone and called him in Guatemala, I would have, but he'd left for the countryside last week with no prediction for when he'd return.

Molly finally broke the silence as she was clearing the table. "My English teacher wants to see you," she announced.

"About?" I asked.

Molly gave a dramatic sigh. "She doesn't think I'm working hard enough. I got a D on my last assignment.

I've got a C-minus average, for Chrissake, but that's not good enough for her."

I paused and let all the things I wanted to say pass through my mind, keeping my mouth firmly shut. I did not point out that Molly might be doing better if she didn't leave her papers until ten o'clock on the night before they were due, or that she might have an easier time if she read the story *before* the class discussion. The poor kid got enough nagging from her mother.

"Do you think C minus is the best you can do?"

"It's fine," she said. "And besides, I can pull it up to a B minus by the end of the semester. I'm tired of people always bugging me about my grades. I don't get drunk, I don't do drugs, and I'm not pregnant. That's better than lots of kids."

Her face was set in challenge. I don't know what Dr. Spock recommends in situations like this, but I decided to follow Gina's admonition and get off the line. "That's true," I said, "and you don't strangle kittens, torch buildings, or date right-wing fanatics, so I guess I can't complain."

She was so startled that she just stared at me for a minute. Then the tension in her mouth eased into the hint of a grin and she said, "And I don't take money from welfare mothers and give it to fat cats."

I burst into laughter. "Well, you get an A in politics anyway," I said. "We'll worry about the rest of the stuff later."

The next morning, it took all my willpower to get out of bed. I felt an overwhelming urge to pull the covers over my head and take the day off. I changed my mind when Molly's clock radio blasted on.

The lab was nearly deserted when I got there. Clearly, I wasn't the only one tempted to retreat from the reality of Raymond's absence. Most of the students were avoiding the lab altogether. Kendra and Paul were there, and Chuck arrived a few minutes after I did. He looked tired, as if he hadn't slept well, and his usual smile was replaced with a sober, almost worried expression.

Kendra and Paul were discussing how to cope without Raymond when I came into the office.

"We should be able to get a new lab tech in a few days," Raskin said.

"Don't count on it," Kendra replied, her voice harsh. "Every day they don't fill that position is a day they don't pay a salary. The bean counters are a lot more interested in their spreadsheets than in how well this lab functions."

Paul started to protest, but Kendra silenced him with "And don't count on our esteemed VP to expedite it. He'll see this as one more weapon to force me to knuckle under. He knows we have a grant proposal due. The timing couldn't be worse."

She shifted her focus to me.

"What can we do for you today, Catherine?"

"I was going to check for other places where sabotage might occur," I said. "Any rooms or facilities you use here."

"Right," Paul said. "I'll give you a tour. Unless Kendra needs me here."

Kendra shook her head. She looked as if she needed to go home and get some sleep, but then we all looked that way.

Raskin showed me a small room with several microscopes and a boxlike PCR machine that he explained could identify a single molecule of DNA from among millions of similar DNA molecules. Down the hall, the IN USE light was on over the door of the darkroom, so we skipped it, and he took me instead to the cold room. A chilly place that lived up to its name. Noisy fans created a steady din; metal storage racks stood on one side of the room and there was a lab bench on the other. Boxes of plant material were stored under the table, and someone had left a carton of yogurt and a quart of milk in one of them.

"They're not supposed to do that," Paul grumbled when he saw the food, "but I just can't break them of using this room as their private refrigerator."

"Is it just for storage?" I asked.

"Oh, no. We use it for protein preparations and other processes where we need to keep things cold every step of the way."

I noticed as we were leaving that the door had a large paddle-shaped handle on the inside. "We make it easy to get out," Raskin said. "With the cold, you wouldn't want to get stuck in here. It's never locked."

We finished up with the tissue culture room and a long, narrow room with sinks on one side and three refrigerator-sized stainless-steel machines built into the wall on the other. Each had a large square door with a circular handle.

"Autoclaves," Paul said, pulling the largest of the heavy doors open. "They're like giant ovens, for sterilizing."

"Looks as though you could cook a small cow in there," I said, peering into it.

"Damn near," he said, then swung the door closed.

The door to the autoclave room was open, but Raskin had opened all the others, except for the cold room, with a key. "How many people have the key to those rooms?" I asked.

"That's a second-floor key," he said. "Everyone who works on this floor has one, along with all the people who worked here before and didn't get around to returning theirs. You see the magnitude of the problem. There are so many places and so many ways to screw things up. We can't watch them all."

"Not without a lot of video cameras," I said. "And that gets to be expensive."

"It's not just the expense," Raskin said. "We could

probably get away with putting them in our lab, but if we put one in any of the rooms we share with other labs and someone were to spot it, all hell'd break loose."

"So that leaves the lab and the greenhouses," I said, "assuming the greenhouses aren't shared space."

"The greenhouses are okay," Raskin said. "And their isolation makes them more vulnerable. Have you been down to the one in Albany?"

"No," I said. "I should see it."

"I'd love to take you, but I'm trapped in paperwork hell right now. I think Chuck's working over there. He can give you the tour."

Chuck Nishimura was still at his bench in the lab. He had a xeroxed article open on the desk, but his eyes were fixed on a point off to the side. I was struck again by how tense he looked, and my assessment was confirmed when Raskin called to him and he almost jumped out of his chair.

"Whoa, take it easy, Chuck," Paul said. "I just wanted to ask if you'd take Catherine to the Albany greenhouse this morning."

Chuck looked relieved and even pleased. "Sure, I've got some plants to check on there. But I don't have my car. Can I use the lab van?"

"Keys are on the nail," Raskin said. "Better check the gas. It was low last week."

I could have offered my car, but I kept quiet. You can't watch the other person when you're the driver, and Chuck's strong reaction to the news of Raymond's death made me very curious about their relationship.

15

THE VAN WAS in the underground garage. Chuck was relieved to find that it had a quarter tank of gas. He confided that it took too long to get reimbursed from petty cash since Kendra had to sign off on everything.

We drove through residential Berkeley, for much of the way following the route I'd traveled to Raymond's. Chuck was silent for the first part of the ride, but as we got to San Pablo Avenue, he said, "I hear Raymond died of a heart attack. Is that right?"

"It's likely," I said. "We won't know until the autopsy."

"When will that be?"

"A week or two."

"They wait a week or two?"

"No, they do the autopsy right away," I said, "but it takes a couple of weeks to get test results."

"Oh," he said, lapsing back into silence.

"How well did you know Raymond?" I asked.

Chuck kept his eyes on the road. "Not well."

"He had something he wanted to tell me, but he never got a chance. I keep thinking that it might be useful in figuring out the source of the sabotage."

Chuck gripped the steering wheel tighter. His knuckles turned white from the pressure. "What do you think he knew?" he asked.

"I don't know. What do you think?"

"I haven't any idea. Like I said, I didn't know him well."

Before I could say more, Chuck said, "We're almost there. That's married student housing." He pointed to the left to rows of buildings that looked like old army barracks. "It's mostly grad students, and mostly from other countries," he said. "Lots of little kids."

Beyond the apartments there was a stand of trees—pines, other evergreens, and even a couple of palms. A tiny mongrel forest in the middle of the city.

"That's the Gill Tract," Chuck said. At the corner he turned toward the bay. Beyond the trees a large field blazed yellow with wild mustard. For most of the country, the delicate beauty of forsythia and daffodils confirms that winter is truly over, but for California it's the riotous mustard, bold and profligate, that characterizes our spring.

Chuck turned into a smaller road at the end of the field. On our right the low, modern buildings with murals in bright primary colors could only have been a school. On the other side, a chain-link fence marked the boundary of the Gill Tract, and inside it another tiny forest was trying to take hold. The rows of pines and smaller fruit trees were so straight that they'd obviously been planted there.

"Those are old experiments," he said. "The guy who planted the pines is long gone, but he never took them out. Makes Kendra furious since it cuts down on the space available."

"Do you plant corn in the field?" I asked.

"They used to," he said. "But we need to use pretty strong weed killers and insecticides. City won't let us do that anymore, especially not up near campus. Albany's strict; Berkeley's the land of the environmental nazis."

We turned in through a gate, then turned right on a dirt road that paralleled the fence. The road ended at a long, low building that looked about the age of the ones in the married student housing development. The glass roofs of greenhouses rose behind it. A second building faced it and off to the right was a large, two-story barn made of corrugated tin. "This is it," Chuck announced as we parked.

He led the way to the first door and searched through a bunch of keys until he found the right one. The lock was stubborn and it took jiggling the key and pushing and pulling on the doorknob to get the door to open. Inside, the room was dark, illuminated only by a glass door and large windows on the opposite side. I realized as my eyes adjusted that the door and windows were in reality one end of the greenhouse at the back of the building.

We stepped inside and Chuck switched on an overhead bulb that didn't shed light much beyond the small area where we were standing. In the shadowy darkness of the middle of the room I could make out what looked like piles of rubber hose and a variety of round and square shapes.

"Oh, man, Scott and Rick were supposed to clean this up," Chuck said in disgust. "There's another light here someplace, but this room is mostly just storage anyway. You want to see it?"

"Is there anything here that could be sabotaged?"

"Someone could mess with equipment, I guess, but then we'd just have to replace it. No one's got plants or seed in here."

He turned and led the way to a rack on the wall with corn aprons like the ones I'd seen at the Oxford greenhouse. "We do keep our corn cards here, but since the trouble started, we've all made backups. At least we're supposed to have."

"Let's take a look at the greenhouse," I said.

"First, I have to make my preparations," Chuck said. "We're not going to be in there long, but I *never* go in without a mask."

I remembered what Raymond had said about Chuck's and Rick's allergies. "Can't we do it from the door?" I asked. "I don't want you to risk getting sick."

"I won't get sick," he said. He took a box down from the shelf above the corn aprons and pulled out a rubber mask. "You will now witness the transformation of Chuck Nishimura, mild-mannered graduate student, into Insect-man, invincible enemy of the deadly corn pollen." With a wink he pulled the mask over his face and I had to laugh because while he didn't look like an insect, he was certainly a possible extra for the cabaret scene in *Star Wars*. The lower part of his face was covered with a molded gray rubber snout with large disks of white filter material mounted on each side. Heavy black straps stretched behind his head and neck.

"Dashing, huh?" he said, his voice muffled by the mask.

"Definitely."

He slipped the mask off again. "I'd like to check on several plants while we're here. Do you mind? It won't take long."

"Not at all. I wouldn't want to put you though all this just to show me the greenhouse."

"I do it all the time," he said. "Some people, like Rick, think I'm overreacting, but they'd feel different if they'd nearly suffocated. You only need to have that happen once.

"Last summer, down in our San Jose fields, I was using a cheap little mask that wasn't very good. Suddenly, I got this weird rush starting at my feet and I couldn't get my breath. God, that's an awful feeling." His eyes had a faraway look and his shoulders tensed as he replayed the experience.

"I managed to stumble to the edge of the field and Raisa saw me. Scott had Adrenalin because he's allergic to bees. If they hadn't been there, I'd probably be dead."

"But you still work with corn," I said. "Aren't you taking an awful chance?"

Chuck shook his head and his mischievous smile was back. "You, who live in California, right on top of the San Andreas fault, ask me about risks? We all take risks.

With my mask, I'm in more danger from a quake than from my allergies." He slid the mask on again and led the way to the greenhouse.

This greenhouse was much like the one on campus with its artificial thicket of corn plants, and the air had the same damp warmth of Iowa in August. The planting beds were raised, so many of the full-grown plants were a foot taller than I was, but the majority were short and bushy like the one I'd seen in Scott's presentation at the lab meeting.

Chuck checked various plants while I studied the room for possible camera placement. It's tricky hiding a camera in a building made of glass. In an ordinary room, you can use a keyhole lens and hide the actual camera in a cabinet or behind something solid, but this room didn't offer those possibilities. The large grow lights were the wrong shape to conceal anything and the heating pipes were too thin. In the center of the ceiling, there was a large, round black metal fixture that looked like a piece of antique farm machinery. It was big enough for the camera but its location would require two cameras to cover the entire greenhouse.

Chuck's muffled voice surprised me. "What?" I asked.

"That's the heater," he said, pointing up to the fixture. "A real dinosaur. Ready to go?"

"I need a minute more," I said. "You go on out; I'll be along."

He nodded and headed for the door. I studied that end of the greenhouse as I watched him. The building and the greenhouse had been built together, and on the wall that joined them, there was just enough wood to meet my needs. If Kendra agreed, I could a drill a hole in that wall above the door and mount the camera there. The inch-square camera could be hidden behind a board, and the darkness in the room would prevent anyone from noticing it or the wire to the transmitter.

I followed Chuck out the glass door and stepped into the dark anteroom. After the bright, sunlit greenhouse, I couldn't make out a thing in the room except the light Chuck had turned on near the door. I waited to let my eyes adjust, then studied the area I was interested in. In the murky darkness, I didn't think anyone would notice the camera.

Turning, I noticed a stepladderlike stairway leading up to a loft under the roof. Looked like a good place to put the recording unit that received the signals from the transmitter. As I headed for the stairway, Chuck said, "I wouldn't go up there. The rats get pretty big, and there was a bees' nest up there last I heard."

I backed off. Rats can play havoc with wire and equipment, and while tame ones don't bother me, wild rats give me the creeps. There were lots of places to put a receiver that didn't involve rats, or bees.

Chuck had put his mask back on the shelf and was waiting for me at the door.

"That was quick," I said.

"They're not ready to pollinate yet," he said, "but they'll be ready to go in about a week, maybe less." We stepped outside and he locked the door.

As we turned to walk back to the car, a skinny guy who looked as if he'd never left the sixties charged toward us. His thinning hair was pulled back in a ponytail that reached halfway down his back, and he wore old jeans, sandals, and a tie-dyed tee shirt. His beard was frosting around the mouth and hadn't been trimmed for a while.

His feet slid on the gravel as he stopped in front of Chuck. Thin but muscular, he had that ropy all-muscle-no-fat quality that some very active guys get as they age. His face was set in a frown.

"You guys tramped through my plot again and screwed up the new plantings," he said angrily.

"I haven't been near your damn plot," Chuck replied

with equal heat. "And neither have any of the rest of us. It was probably the bio-control guys."

"Not likely. *They* understand the importance of my work."

"Yeah, right. You're all going to save the world," Chuck responded, his voice heavy with sarcasm.

"We're at least trying," the other man said. "Unlike you big shots up on campus who're too important to work on anything that might actually help people."

"Just keep pressing those sour grapes, Mather," Chuck said. He turned his back on the other man, moved around to the passenger side of the car, and opened the door for me. "If there's nothing more you'd like to see, we can go back to the lab now," he said.

The hostility between the two men was so intense that leaving seemed a good idea. I got in the car, and as Chuck got in on his side, I heard the other man say, "You tell your friends to stay out of my plot. I'm warning you."

Chuck's response was to slam his door and start the motor. His wheels slipped and threw up gravel as he backed and turned a bit too fast.

"Who was that?" I asked as we headed back down the road.

"Ethan Mather," Chuck replied, "one of the great jerks of the universe." His voice was tight with anger. "He shouldn't even be here. He doesn't have a doctorate; he's not enrolled. He's only there because one of Kendra's colleagues got interested in wild grasses and stuck his little project on a grant."

"He seemed pretty angry. Could he have anything to do with the sabotage?"

"He's certainly capable of it," Chuck said. "If it'd happened down here, I'd say yes, but he doesn't go up to the Oxford Tract or the lab much. Besides, if it'd been him, I wouldn't have any plants left."

"Why's he so angry?" I asked. I'd have liked to add, "And why are you?" but I didn't.

"Jealousy," Chuck said. "He just can't stand the fact that we're up in a nice new lab and he and his bio-control buddies are down here in the slums. He dropped out in the sixties, *says* it was because he realized the university was the tool of the establishment. Probably he couldn't make the grade."

I was surprised by the anger in Chuck's voice. My original assessment of him was that he was less affected by the tension in the lab than many of his fellow students, but his strong reactions to Raymond's death and Ethan Mather's accusations seemed a bit off-kilter.

We got back to the lab just after twelve. Raisa and two other women were there. The other lab benches were still empty. Kendra and Paul were in her office; she was talking on the phone and Paul sat across from her, listening. The door was open slightly, and I heard her say, "Yes, yes, I understand it's a real threat, and I'm taking it very seriously. I'll be there, and I'll bring the damn report."

I was about to leave when I heard her say, "Yes, definitely. I'll see you then. Bye."

I tapped on the door and Kendra motioned me in. Both she and Paul looked grave. "You've had a threat?" I asked.

Kendra looked irritated. "Oh, nothing important, just the usual administrative bullshit," she said. "So what can you tell me about our other problem?"

Life would be so much easier if clients didn't keep secrets from investigators. But they all do. "I can rig cameras at both greenhouses," I said. "I'd suggest one for each greenhouse. Two would be better but it's so hard to hide them that it's probably not practical. It'd take six to cover the labs fully, though you could probably get by with three."

"And these cameras, they tape everything that goes on, right?"

"Everything within their range," I said. "The images

are transmitted to a recorder, usually at another location. We change the tape each day, and if something happens we can review the tapes."

"You have the equipment?" she asked.

"I have a couple of cameras. We can rent whatever else we need."

"Give me a cost estimate," she said. "I want to know how much it'd be to do the greenhouses only, and how much to do the greenhouses and labs with three or six cameras. Clear?"

"Clear," I said. I was getting tired of Crawford's attitude. She was one of those women who confuse brusqueness with sexual liberation. "I'll do some checking and have an answer by late this afternoon. A couple of other things. You don't want people to know where the cameras are, because then they could sabotage them, so you'll need to have everyone out of the lab while I'm installing them. Since this is a pretty bright crew and they may be expecting cameras, I'd like to mount dummies, old junk equipment, that's visible. That way if someone is planning to take out the camera, they'll go after the dummy and we'll have a nice clear picture of them."

"Makes sense," Paul said.

"I want the figures first," Kendra said.

"I'll call you later today. Will you be in around four?"

Kendra checked her schedule and nodded, and I said good-bye and headed for the door. Paul Raskin followed me into the hall.

"I had something I wanted to ask you," I said. "Can you walk downstairs with me?"

"Sure," he said.

I waited until we were clear of the building. You never know who's just around the bend on a circular staircase. Then I said, "I met Ethan Mather down at the Gill Tract. He's a very angry man. Is he potentially dangerous?"

"Ethan?" Raskin laughed. "No, he's not dangerous. Usually he's not even angry. There're just certain people he can't get along with, and for some reason, Chuck is one of them."

"So you don't think he could be your saboteur?"

Raskin shook his head. "No."

"Chuck referred to the bio-control people. Who are they?"

"They're bug guys, started out in the entomology department. They were supposed to develop ways to control pests, but instead of concentrating on bigger and better pesticides, they got the idea of using some bugs to control other bugs. It's a real popular approach with environmentalists, doesn't go over so well with farmers or the petrochemical industry. So since the farmers call the shots, the bug guys got exiled to Gill Tract."

"Is there antagonism between them and your lab?"

"Not really," Raskin said. "They're very political, Ethan especially. Some folks up here consider them a pain in the butt. And they resent the fact that we get more money, better labs, more respect. They're working on keeping people from starving; they don't have a lot of respect for pure research, but I don't think they're hostile."

"Chuck seems pretty hostile himself," I said. "Any idea why?"

Raskin frowned. We'd reached the parking-level elevator. He pushed the button and considered my question. "Chuck's been edgy for the last couple of weeks," he said as the door opened. "He's usually a pretty mellow guy, fun to have around. Lately he's been short-tempered and quick to snap at everyone."

"Could it have anything to do with Raymond's death?" I asked.

"You're not still on that, are you?" Paul said testily. "I don't understand why you keep treating Raymond's death like some kind of nefarious plot. The guy died of a heart attack, for heaven's sakes."

I was startled by his tone. He'd narrowed his eyes, and that James Dean–dangerous look was suddenly much less attractive.

16

I HEADED BACK to the office, glad to be out of the lab. Chris had called at five to say she was staying over in Sacramento, so with Jesse in Sunnyvale I expected to have the office to myself. To my surprise, Jesse was there when I arrived.

"I need to talk to you," he said. He did not look happy.

"Can we do it over lunch?" I asked. "I'm starving, and I hate bad news on an empty stomach."

"How'd you know it was bad?" he asked.

"You're not exactly wearing your poker face," I said.

At that point my secretary, Amy, offered to go for sandwiches. I suspected she was anxious to escape Jesse's dark mood, but I wasn't going to worry about motivation when there was a pastrami sandwich at stake. I gave her my order. Jesse said he wasn't hungry.

"Boy, this is serious," I said, then to Amy, "Get two sandwiches anyway, just in case his appetite magically returns."

Jesse started to object, but I held firm. "We've been through this before, and I always end up short half a sandwich. If you don't eat yours, I'll take it home to Molly."

We settled in my office, which is bigger because I'm the senior partner, and Jesse told me about the chip case.

"Close to a million dollars' worth of specialized chips, a brand-new design. MediTech contracted for the whole lot for a new generation of imaging machines. Thursday afternoon they're packed for the president to deliver himself on Friday. He orders them put in his office to keep them safe overnight, completely overlooking the fact that he spent a bundle on security for the production facility and almost nothing on the offices. Friday morning, they're gone."

"Sounds like an inside job," I said. "It had to be someone who knew both when to snatch the chips and where to find them."

"That would include almost everyone in the company, unfortunately. These guys never heard of discretion. They had a party to celebrate the completion of the project. Just about everyone saw the boxes carried across the parking lot to the office complex." Jesse shook his head in disgust.

"My aunt Sally could have broken into that office building. Three years of R&D and a year to set up the production line, and they leave the chips in the president's office where any fool could get at them."

It was stupid but not surprising. And the chip manufacturer wasn't our first client to choose a place that felt safe over one that actually was safe.

"Any sign of where these chips ended up?" I asked.

"No," he said. "And that's what's bugging me. This should have been a piece of cake. There are fewer than a dozen places I'd expect them to turn up. I mean, after all, the damn things are only worth something to a limited number of companies. I've been on the horn to everyone I know who might have spotted them. *Nada.* No one, I mean no one, has even heard a whisper that they're available. It doesn't make sense."

"Have you checked with Kyle?" I asked. Kyle was a friend of Peter's from "the old days." He calls himself an entrepreneur, but Kyle is to other entrepreneurs as test pilots are to the boys who fly cargo planes. If it isn't risky, it doesn't interest him. I once heard him say that he doesn't deal in weapons, cocaine, or plutonium, suggesting that everything else was negotiable.

Jesse shook his head. "Last I heard, he was getting out of computers," he said. "But he still knows people. I'll give him a call."

"It's worth a try," I said. "Kyle has ways of finding out things you can't get anywhere else."

"Yeah, I always wonder how he does it."

"That's one of those things we're better off not knowing."

After Jesse left, I made some calls and put together the figures on what leasing surveillance cameras would cost Kendra Crawford. I wanted solid-state CCD cameras with wide-angle lenses. My preference was for the tiny ones that are about an inch square and can fit in fluorescent tubing containers. For each camera I'd also need a transmitter, receiver, and recorder with time-date generator.

I usually go to Jerry Green at Centaur Systems for equipment. Jerry's a genius; if he doesn't have gear to fit your needs, he can build it. But Jerry was already working on several big jobs that had cleaned him out of cameras.

Next I tried a couple of colleagues I can often hit up for an equipment loan for a job like this, but their video gear was in use. One even tried to talk me out of my two cameras. When my fallback position, a small company that does short-term rentals for a reasonable price, answered my plea with "All out," I began to suspect that half of San Francisco was watching the other half on camera.

The big guys don't like to rent short-term and they charge an arm and a leg when they do, so the figures I gave Crawford were high. She grumbled and said she'd get back to me.

It took her less than fifteen minutes to decide that she could only afford to use my two cameras for the greenhouses. I offered to install them over the weekend, and she transferred me to Raskin to make the arrangements.

"I'll need keys for the greenhouses," I told him. "And some way of making sure that the students won't be there."

"We'll post notices on the door that we're spraying, and no one is allowed inside for twenty-four hours," he suggested. "Even so, Berkeley students do pretty much what they want. I'd better help. Why don't you suggest a time, and we can meet here."

I paused. Going to the greenhouses alone with a potential killer didn't seem like a great idea. But Raskin had no reason to see me as a threat, and taking him along would give me a chance to learn more about him.

"How about Saturday afternoon?" I said. With luck I'd be out when Molly and Marion returned from their shopping trip.

"Sounds good to me," he said. "Around two?"

"I'll see you then."

I had second thoughts, of course. Like maybe my desire to know Raskin better wasn't purely professional. That perhaps I was letting my hormones run my brain. Life's never simple.

Molly went to a movie with a friend that night and I had the place to myself. I'd been looking forward to the time alone, but the empty apartment only made me more aware of Peter's absence. When he was there, a night without Molly meant a return to the kind of uninhibited lovemaking we'd enjoyed before her arrival. Now it just meant that I could watch whatever I wanted on TV.

I made popcorn, opened a beer, and started channel surfing. I ended up watching *Sea of Love*, a very bad choice for a horny woman whose lover was a thousand miles away.

Accepting Paul Raskin's offer of help in installing the surveillance cameras was also a bad idea, and for the same reason. I knew it as soon as he gave me that lazy smile.

He was wearing jeans and a heavy knit navy sweater, and I was very aware of his compact body and the easy way he moved as I followed him down the hall. When I caught myself admiring his tight rear end, I decided it was time to get a grip on myself.

My equipment was in the car, so we drove to the Oxford greenhouse even though it was less than a block away. A sign on the door warned us to stay out because of spraying, and since there was no one around, he let us into the building. While I was busy checking out the spot for the camera, he said, "I'm pretty handy with tools, and I'd be happy to help if you'd like."

"Thanks," I said. I appreciated the way he'd offered, not presuming that I needed or even wanted him to do the work. I hate it when men assume that a woman can't use a hammer or a drill, but since that wasn't an issue I was happy to let him do the work.

He stripped off the sweater. Under it he was wearing a black tee shirt with "There's No Such Thing as a Free Lunch" on the front. "One of the kids gave it to me," he said by way of explanation. In truth, I was more aware of the chest under the shirt than the words on it. He was more muscular than I'd realized, especially his arms. And I had the sense he'd earned those muscles in real work, not in a gym.

The greenhouse setup at Oxford was similar to the one in Albany, so I chose the same kind of place for the camera, behind the wall just above the door. The wall was perfect for my purpose, unfinished wood with exposed studs. All we needed to do was drill a sixteenth-of-an-inch hole for the lens, secure the camera to the wall, and tack a piece of wood across the studs on either side to hide it. Then we'd run a cable up to the top of the wall, over to the corner, and down behind the stud to a spot under a built-in table where I could mount the transmitter. We'd put the receiver in one of the empty rooms beneath the greenhouse.

I explained the procedure to Raskin, and he got a ladder and set to work.

I found a place I could attach the dummy camera to a couple of pipes that came together in one corner of the greenhouse. Getting it up there was another matter.

"I'll need a freestanding ladder to do this," I called to Paul.

"I think there's one downstairs," he said. "The light switch's on your right at the bottom of the stairs. It's pretty dark down there. You want help?"

"No, I can handle it," I said.

The ladder wasn't hard to find, but it was three-legged and so old that it looked as if it belonged in a museum instead of a greenhouse.

I got the ladder upstairs and set it up. Its legs were wobbly. "You got a gimpy ladder there," Paul said from the greenhouse door. "I'll hold; you climb."

I attached the camera with wires. It wasn't hard, but I'd probably have gotten the job done more quickly if I hadn't been painfully aware that a lurch in the wrong direction would send me smashing through a large pane of glass. Just such a lurch did occur as I was climbing down, but I was close to the bottom and it sent me into Paul instead of the window. One minute I was stepping down with my right foot, the next I was airborne.

I landed neatly in Paul's arms. So neatly I wondered if

the lurch had been an accident. But I only wondered that later. At the time I was glad to feel his arms around me and enjoyed the sensation of being held tightly against his chest. His tee shirt was a bit damp with sweat, but the musky odor was far from unpleasant.

"Nice catch," I said as I pulled away.

"My pleasure," he said, with a warm and knowing smile. "Anytime."

I'd been warned that Raskin was a flirt, but knowing that didn't lessen the attraction. I knew it was time to leave then, because I didn't want to.

Installing the camera at the Gill Tract greenhouse in Albany was even harder than at Oxford because the anteroom was so poorly lit. We discovered that the light at that end of the room had been smashed. Shards of glass still covered the floor.

The windows provided enough light, and Paul figured that he could reach the spot he needed by standing on a couple of boxes. But I needed a ladder again.

"There's one here someplace," Paul said. "I think it's over by this wall." He headed for the darkest side of the room and emerged a minute later with the ladder. It looked at least a century younger than the one we'd found at the Oxford greenhouse.

Paul helped me set it up and offered to hold it for me, but it was steady enough not to need a baby-sitter, so he went off to install the real camera while I put up the dummy.

I could hear him humming something while he worked, couldn't make out the tune, but the sound was a pleasant background. I'd decided to wire the camera to the pipe that led into the steam heater in the center of the greenhouse. The ladder wasn't quite tall enough, so I had to do the job with my arms above my head, and by the time I'd gotten the camera securely anchored so it wouldn't fall and crack someone's skull, the muscles in my neck and shoulders ached from the effort.

I climbed down and began to knead out some of the kinks. I wasn't aware that Paul had come into the room until I felt his hands on my shoulders. "Here, let me do that. Doc Raskin is an expert," he said.

And he was. He was wonderful. He seemed to know just where to rub and just how hard to press. He worked on my shoulders, then moved lower to the muscles of my upper back. I could feel the tension melt under the gentle pressure of his thumbs. If I'd been a cat, I'd have purred.

But his touch stirred a host of feelings that I'd been working hard to suppress. A sensual warmth spread through my body, and I had to work to keep it from my voice when I thanked him. As I turned to face him, his expression told me that the massage had had the same effect on him.

"We'll need someplace to put the receiver," I told him, still working to sound businesslike. "Do you have access to any of the other buildings here?"

He paused, and I could almost see him switching gears. "Yeah, sure. We don't have office space here, but I know a guy who'd let us put it in his office. Let's see if he's here."

He led the way to the building across from the greenhouses. It was a long one-story box with six doors and six windows. Paul knocked on the third door.

A short man with dusky dark skin and thick black hair opened the door. He was wearing dark pants and a tan V-neck sweater over a brown-and-gold batik shirt. He smiled when he saw Paul. "Paul, what brings you here?" he asked. His English was only slightly accented, but the speech cadence made me guess he was Indian.

"Hi, Vipul," Paul said. He introduced me, then explained the situation, and asked if he could lodge the receiver in the other man's office.

Vipul turned and looked over the room behind him,

then turned back to us. "Sure," he said. "I'm sure we can find a home for your machine. Please come in."

The room was at once crowded and orderly. The walls were covered with bookshelves, and the shelves were stuffed so tightly with books and papers that I didn't see how you'd get anything in or out of them. "We don't have much space," Vipul said apologetically, "but perhaps if I move something." He studied the room again, then said to Paul, "That box up there, that could come down and sit on the floor. Would your machine go there?"

He'd pointed to a box on top of one of the bookshelves. Paul looked at me questioningly. "That would be fine," I said.

Once we had the receiver properly situated, Vipul said to Paul, "I was so sorry to hear of Raymond's death. He was such a fine man."

"Yes," Paul said. "It was a real shock to us all. There's a memorial service on Wednesday."

"Yes, I know," Vipul said. "In Tilden Park, I believe."

"Yes," Paul said. "Here, let me write down the specifics. Please let everyone down here know."

"You will be surprised how many of us will come," Vipul said.

The sun was low in the sky as we headed back for the lab. "How about an early dinner?" Paul asked. "Have you been to the Chez Panisse Café?"

Chez Panisse is one of the world's great restaurants. The kind of place presidents and prime ministers visit on their way through the Bay Area. "I've had dinner there a couple of times," I said. "It's terrific, but they were probably booked weeks ago."

"The restaurant was booked. The café upstairs only accepts a few reservations and this early in the evening you can almost always get in."

Dinner at Chez Panisse. It was tempting, more tempting because it assured my absence from the last round of

Marion and Molly's shopping bout. Even more tempting because Paul Raskin would be across the table.

There were probably forty-seven good reasons not to get involved with Paul Raskin. Getting mixed up with a client is always a bad idea, especially a client you don't entirely trust. Especially in a murder case. Besides, even if he was a thousand miles away, I already had a lover.

There wasn't a single good reason to accept Raskin's invitation. Except for the tide of warmth his touch had sent through me. The desire to know what his lips would feel like, how his body would fit with mine.

If Molly hadn't been waiting at home, the forty-seven reasons might not have been enough.

17

MONDAY MORNING I was browsing through the *Chron* in my usual half-awake state when a headline caught my eye: GUATEMALAN OFFICIALS DENY MASSACRE. The name in the byline jolted me fully awake. Alicia Adavi. I could see her as clearly as I had two years ago when Peter and I ran into her outside a San Francisco courtroom. Tall, slender, with flawless olive skin and long dark hair, she was striking enough that I'd have noticed her even if she hadn't thrown her arms around Peter and given him a kiss that suggested more than casual acquaintance.

"A friend from the old days," was how Peter had introduced her. From the look of her, those days couldn't be very old, and from her manner, "friend" was an under-statement. They'd chatted about mutual acquaintances and exchanged phone numbers. She was a journalist now, working for a small but respected news service that specialized in investigative reporting and was covering a high-profile corruption case being tried in the courtroom next to the one where I'd just testified.

She'd called several times since Peter moved in with me. Each time she was digging into matters that powerful people preferred left unexplored, and each time she needed Peter's help. The stories always fit a lefty's definition of good causes, so he'd have helped her if she'd had three eyes and a hunchback, but it always made me uneasy to have him working closely with a beautiful woman who made no secret of her desire to get him into her bed.

After the second time, I'd confronted him about it, and he'd admitted that they'd had a brief affair many years ago. "It didn't mean anything," he said. "We weren't much more than kids. We thought free love was a revolutionary act. It didn't last long."

"Well, it's clear that Alicia'd like to give it another try," I said. "Don't pretend you haven't noticed."

Peter laughed, but it wasn't his usual easy laugh. Then he got serious. "I won't pretend I don't find her attractive," he said. "But it's just chemistry. I'm not fool enough to risk what we have for a fling."

He'd given me a big hug, and we'd made up. I never liked it when he worked with Alicia, but I had to admit that our sex life was more intense when she was in the wings.

As I stared at her byline, I wondered if Peter had known she'd be in Guatemala, and dismissed the thought almost as soon as it arrived. Peter wasn't one to sneak around. And he wouldn't have conveniently "forgotten" to mention her involvement in the project. But I was equally sure that if Alicia had known that Peter would be in Guatemala, she'd have been only too anxious to cover the story.

I thought of my reaction to Paul Raskin and how attractive I found the idea of a new romance. It didn't make me sanguine about Peter's response to Alicia's presence. While I was declining dinner at Chez Panisse, he was bunking down a few feet from a woman whose goal was to get him to crawl into her sleeping bag.

As annoying as I found the thought of Alicia Adavi trekking around Guatemala with Peter, I was even more irritated by my own jealous reactions. I knew there was nothing I could do, and therefore no point in worrying about it. Did I stop worrying? Of course not.

No matter what else I tried to concentrate on, my mind sneaked back to Peter and Alicia. But as I drove toward Berkeley later that morning, I found yet another distraction. Whenever I thought of the lab investigation, I ran smack into memories of Raskin catching me as I fell from the ladder or massaging my shoulders.

And of course, the first person I saw at the lab was Paul. The smile he gave me had a couple of extra watts of warmth behind it and had an unsettling effect on my concentration.

I made small talk while he made eye contact. Chemistry—we definitely had chemistry.

"Any response to the cameras?" I asked to get things back on track.

"They've been noticed. No one seems to object. In fact, I'd say they're relieved if anything. Lots of jokes about no more midnight trysts. Seems there's more going on in our corn patch than I realized." He laughed when he said it. An easy, knowing laugh. Almost conspiratorial.

"And no more signs of sabotage?" I asked.

The grin disappeared. "No sabotage, but Julie thinks someone's been going through her corn cards."

I felt a sudden chill and took a breath to relieve the tension pressing on my chest. "Anything missing?"

"No."

"Then how can she tell someone's been in them?"

"A bunch of them are out of order. Julie's pretty meticulous; if she says they're not the way she left them, I'm inclined to believe her."

"That makes the third time, maybe the fourth, she's been a target. There's got to be a reason." The tension tightened across my chest.

Raskin leaned back and stared thoughtfully at the ceiling, then looked back at me and shook his head. "I just can't think of one," he said. "Her genes make dwarfs normal and don't do anything to normal plants. Hers is as pure as research gets."

I found Julie at her lab bench. She was studying an X-ray film on a light box and labeling regions on it with a felt-tipped pen. "I hear someone's been fooling around with your records," I said.

She looked around quickly, checking to see who might be nearby. There was no one near enough to hear us. "Someone went through my family cards," she said. "I'm sure of it. A couple of days ago, I found the stack face up instead of face down. I always leave my cards face down because I spilled coffee in my drawer several months ago and the ink I used for field notes ran and messed up the top card.

"After I found them face up, I took several cards near the middle and I rotated them so that they're upside down. This morning I checked the stack and different cards were upside down."

"Why would someone do that?"

"I don't know. Maybe they're trying to confuse me by turning different cards. If that was a code I used, it could screw things up. Or they could be interested in what I'm doing, but they hardly need to sneak. I'd tell anyone who asked."

"Did you talk to Raymond about your cards?"

"I don't think so," she said, and sat down suddenly. "But I might have. I really miss him. He was such a sweet person."

He was, and he was dead. And that made Julie's situation far more serious than she seemed to realize.

"Julie, it's looking more and more likely that you're the real object of this sabotage," I said. "I want you to think again about who might have a grudge against you."

She bit her lower lip, and her face was very serious as she shook her head. "I've thought and thought," she said. "I really don't know. Could it be one of those things where some guy is obsessed with me and I don't even know it? You know, maybe because I'm Chinese."

I tried not to let my reactions show in my face. "I don't want to scare you," I said, "but if I were you, I'd be extra careful from now on. I wouldn't stay in the lab alone at night, and I certainly wouldn't ever go into the parking levels downstairs alone. And I'd be careful about food. Don't leave your lunch . . ."

"You don't think . . . think . . . ," she interrupted me. "When I was sick . . . Is that why you called? You thought I was poisoned?"

"I thought it was possible. What do you think?"

She looked near tears. "I don't know. I don't know what to think." She paused to get control of herself, then asked, "But when I go downstairs, how do I know who to ask to come with me? What if I ask the wrong person? And what if it isn't a guy but a woman?"

I'd hesitated to raise the issue for precisely this reason, but it wasn't my warning that had upset her. She'd recognized the danger herself. Any woman who watched the evening news had seen enough to worry about a fellow worker showing up one morning with an Uzi.

I, of all people, had no words of comfort to offer her. I'd seen it happen, and I knew it'd happen again. I just hoped that this wouldn't be the place. There was something I could do. "I'll try to arrange for campus security to escort you," I said.

"Oh, thank you," she said, looking relieved. "I feel foolish, like a real wuss, but I'm spooked enough not to fool around."

"Good," I said. "I think you should also go over your research with Kendra and see what you can do to protect it. Make duplicate copies of everything, and don't leave anything in the lab that's really important." I took one of the cards from my purse and wrote my home phone number on it. "And call me if you need help or you get any ideas about who might be behind this. I won't discuss your suspicions with anyone if you don't want me to, but I'll check them out."

"Thanks," she said, giving me her first real smile of the day. "I really appreciate your help. It makes me feel so much better."

I hoped her faith would be justified.

I called Detective Wilson at the Albany PD that afternoon to see if he had any more information on Raymond Zak's death.

"I know the test results from the autopsy won't be back yet, but I wondered if you had any preliminary findings."

There was a pause, then he said, "There's no reason not to tell you. So far there's no evidence of foul play. Mr. Zak had a problem with atrial fibrillation. That's an irregularity in the heartbeat. It's as if the electrical system that keeps the heart beating doesn't function properly. The doctor figures that his heart just stopped. So far the coroner's findings are consistent with that."

I felt a sense of relief at the news. I hadn't wanted my dark suspicions confirmed. But part of me still couldn't let go of the feeling that something was wrong. "I hate to beat a dead horse," I said, wishing I'd chosen a different cliché, "but are you checking for substances that could have precipitated the heart failure?"

"Boy, you really *don't* let go of a thing, do you?" he said in a tone that suggested that he'd talked to either Dan or someone else I'd worked with.

"Even paranoids can have real enemies," I said.

Wilson's laugh was an admission that I had guessed right about what he wasn't saying. "I know that," he said. "And I have asked the coroner to screen for any substance that might have induced the heart failure. I *am* taking this seriously, Ms. Sayler."

I had to be back to meet with Molly's English teacher by four, so I left the lab early. On my way out, I noticed that a card on the bulletin board announced, "Memorial Service for Raymond Zak will be held at 2 P.M. on Wednesday at the Quarry Area in Tilden Park." A map was posted below. I copied the information and the map. I used to hate funerals and memorial services, but as I get older I realize they help you get through the grieving process. And though I'd known Raymond Zak for only a short time, his loss had left a small hole in my life that would take a while to mend.

The meeting with Molly's English teacher was more like an ambush. The counselor sat in, and they'd invited Marion. Molly was subjected to an hour of her teacher and counselor alternately praising her intelligence and criticizing her achievement. The teacher seemed an okay sort who genuinely cared about Molly; the counselor spouted a line of psychobabble that gave me a headache.

Marion spent the hour glaring at Molly, then at me. Molly had worn a "Free Pee-wee" tee shirt and her grungiest baggy pants with numerous rips, several of which looked suspiciously new. She slouched lower in her chair and sulked, retreating into one-word answers and shoulder shrugs. I kept having flashbacks to visits to the principal's office from my own wayward youth.

When the counselor threatened to require Molly to attend lunchtime and after-school study halls, "for her own good," I lost it. "Oh, for heaven's sakes," I said, "why don't you just bring out the thumbscrews? If you think locking this kid up with her books is going to improve her attitude, you are truly deluded."

Everyone in the room looked at me as if I were a crazy woman who'd just wandered in off the street. The counselor sputtered, "I don't think . . ." as Marion snarled, "Catherine . . ." But I'd had enough frustrations that day, so I just raised my voice. "The purpose of this meeting was to discuss Molly's poor grades; you've done that, at length. But Molly's the only one who can change those grades, so let's all get off her back and give her a chance to do that. Right, Molly?"

Molly was staring at me with the same amazement as everyone else, but she nodded.

"Good," I said, standing up. "Thank you very much for your time," I said to the frowning counselor and startled English teacher. I gave Marion a smile that was probably closer to a grimace, and stepped toward the door as Molly bolted out of her seat to follow me.

"Boy, you really told them," she said as soon as we were outside. "You were awesome."

"Thanks," I said, "but you may not be so impressed when this is over." As my temper cooled, I realized that Marion had the ultimate threat to keep both of us in line; she could refuse to let Molly live with me. And I'd just provided her with two witnesses that I was not a fit guardian.

"Go sit in the car," I said.

"Why?"

"Because I'm about to do some serious groveling, and I don't want an audience." She started to argue but thought better of it.

Marion emerged from the school ten minutes later,

looking furious. She delivered a scathing appraisal of my character and manners or lack of same. "You've become hard and coarse dealing with criminals all the time. I should never have let Molly come to live with you."

I tried to look contrite and keep all traces of rancor out of my voice when I reminded her that neither of us had chosen to let Molly live with me. She'd forced us into it by running away from home. "You know Molly," I said. "If they squeeze her too hard, she'll just bolt, like she did before, only this time she won't have anyone to go to, and she'll end up on the street. You don't want that."

She didn't, of course. That didn't mean she didn't want to beat me up some more, but eventually we agreed that she'd give me a chance to get Molly back on track at school. "She's very bright, capable of getting A's, but I'll settle for a B average. For now," she said.

I don't like to deal with difficult subjects on an empty stomach, and I find Molly's much more agreeable when she's fed, so I headed for a café that has thigh-busting pastries.

Once we were settled with lattes and chocolate chip cookies the size of paving stones, I asked, "So you tell me, why are you having trouble at school?"

"I hate it," she said. "It's boring and stupid. We're reading this book that goes on and on; it puts me to sleep. I don't give a damn why Hester Prynne won't name her baby's father. And what possible good is algebra? Who cares who won the Battle of Bull Run?"

"What do you care about?"

She stared at me for a minute. "I don't know."

"I don't either. But I think it's important that you care about something."

"Like what?"

"A sport, music, drama, art, and not just watching or listening but doing. I think you need to *do* something you care about. Could be a volunteer job, working at a day-care center or a soup kitchen."

"A job," Molly said. "That's what I'd like. A job doing something interesting. I know, I could work for you."

"Oh, now, wait a minute . . ."

"It'd be great. I don't mean going out and tracking people down, but there must be stuff I could do around the office. I'm good with computers; Amy could teach me stuff."

I started to protest, but I had to admit that it might be just what she needed. School was too abstract for her. Maybe the math and writing that we did in the office would capture her interest. I'd dropped out of an accounting course in college, but when I went to work and was told I'd need to know accounting, I discovered a new aptitude for the subject.

"I have to think about that," I said, taking a bit of cookie and chewing slowly to buy time. "Jesse, Chris, and Amy'd have to agree. And if—that's a big if—we decided to try it, your schoolwork would have to come first."

Molly nodded enthusiastically.

"I promised your mother a B average."

She grimaced.

"I had to bargain hard to get it down from an A minus," I lied. "Can you manage a B average?"

"Yeah," Molly said, "if I get to work for you."

"You couldn't be involved in any case that looked dangerous. You'd always work in the office; that means no baggy pants, no rips or tears in your clothes, no X-rated tee shirts. And I would be the boss. I don't put up with arguments or weaseling at the office."

"I'll do whatever you tell me," she said.

As I looked into her face, so full of excitement and enthusiasm, I thought it was either the best or the worst idea I'd had in a long time.

18

I MANAGED TO catch Jesse before he left for Sunnyvale on Wednesday morning. Chris arrived a few minutes after him. She was wearing a deep plum suit with a mauve blouse and high spike heels in a shade between the suit and the blouse. Her eye shadow matched the blouse perfectly. I wonder how the hell she does that.

I asked Amy to join us, since, as the firm's secretary, she'd be most affected by having Molly around the office. I knew she'd be for it. She misses her five younger siblings back in Wisconsin and gets a kick out of fussing over Molly.

All three were supportive of letting Molly try her hand as office gofer. Chris, who was feeling the crunch of having Jesse and me out of the office most of the time, liked the prospect of another pair of hands. And Jesse was even more enthusiastic, which surprised me.

"Kids need jobs," he said. "My uncle let me work at his garage when I was a kid. Probably saved my life. I never had time to be hanging out on a street corner or boosting cars. More kids had jobs, less of them be doing drugs."

Jesse's dad is a civil servant and his mother's a teacher, so I'd never thought of him standing on street corners as a kid. He probably understood Molly's situation better than I did.

Amy offered to supervise Molly, and I reminded everyone that I didn't want her involved in the UC case.

"Until we're sure that Raymond Zak died of natural causes, we treat this case with special care," I said.

They all nodded soberly.

"Just be sure you follow your own advice," Jesse said.

That afternoon, as I drove into the park that caps the hills of Berkeley and spills over into the canyon behind them, I thought how appropriate it was for Raymond's memorial service to be held here. His paintings captured and reflected the beauty of the natural world; it was fitting to say good-bye to him in such surroundings.

Wildcat Canyon is a mixture of woodlands and open fields. In February those fields are carpeted in grass so green that they make the stands of trees and patches of brush seem almost gray. It's a color that reminds me of the East, where foliage is often that pure bright green. Here in the West, plants tend toward darker or bluer shades. The lower slopes and the valley itself were covered with trees from the western palette—dark green bays, dusky oaks, and gray-green eucalyptus.

At the bottom of the valley, the road to my right was closed, as it is every year at this time when the California newts undertake the trek to their breeding ponds across the tarmac.

As the road wound up the hill through the eucalyptus trees, I watched for the Quarry picnic area. I knew I'd reached it before I saw the sign. Cars lined the road and the small parking area was full.

I was glad I'd worn low-heeled shoes as I hiked up the bank and into the meadow where people were gathering. From a distance the hills were soft and silky, but up close wild grasses covered the soil with a rough stubble that made walking difficult. Brought to life by winter rains and green only so long as the rains lasted, they were hardy survivors that most gardeners would identify as weeds. I watched my footing as I stepped into them, and paid even more careful attention when I discovered the patches of slick, dark mud that covered any low area.

Most of the people in the meadow were strangers to me. I recognized six students, including Julie and Chuck, and Kendra and Paul stood with a couple of people I thought looked familiar, probably from the university. To my surprise, Ethan Mather was there. He stood with Vipul and six other men, who I assumed were from the bio-control group.

Mrs. Lawder arrived a few minutes later. She was accompanied by two men who towered over her and looked like the sons whose photos I remembered seeing in her house. I'd thought her skin unusually pale before. Now it looked as if all color had been sucked from her, making more shocking the deep blue circles that bruised the area under her eyes.

There were three picnic tables. Food had been laid out on one, and on the other two a display of some of Raymond's drawings and paintings had been set up, but a healthy breeze knocked them over as soon as they were righted. A number of people had brought flowers, the most striking arrangement was one of grasses of rust, gray, and gold accented with deep blue dried flowers. Ethan Mather worked with grasses; I wondered if it had come from him.

The service was like the food and flowers, put together from the offerings brought by numerous friends. Several read poems, others told stories or reminisced about experiences they'd shared with Raymond, a few gave brief eulogies. A large man with a full beard and a barrel chest told of how Raymond had stood his ground despite taunts and threats during a protest against the filling of an estuary. "When he believed in something, he was as tough as they come," he said, "but he was rarely angry and never violent."

We were standing in a circle and I looked across and

saw tear tracks on Julie Chun's face. A man next to her put an arm around her and handed her a handkerchief. Several people away, Ethan Mather stared at the ground.

A man with a guitar and a woman with a mandolin played "Turn, Turn, Turn," and the group sang along. It reminded me of happier times, weddings in the sixties where we gathered in sunny meadows and brides with flowers in their hair traded homemade vows with grooms in rainbow-hued shirts and jeans.

The feast after the service was also from the sixties. The table was laid with dishes from a dozen kitchens— sweet breads, cookies, veggies and dips—nothing from a caterer or a deli. Paul and Kendra and the university people stood off to the side. I'd have expected Paul to fit right in with the larger group, but he looked even more uncomfortable than the others in the university bunch. Ethan Mather and his friends were a good distance away.

Julie was the only one from the lab who seemed to know any of the other people there. She stood with a group that included the barrel-chested man. I positioned myself on the edge of the group and eavesdropped while I waited to talk with her.

"So does Darla know?" a woman in a teal parka asked.

"Yeah, the boat has a radio, but they're still two days from port," the barrel-chested man answered. "She didn't want us to wait. Said people need to get on with their grieving. I think maybe it's easier for her not to be here. She wouldn't want us to see her now."

A couple of people nodded. "She's a tough lady," another man said. "I was with her when she got the news about the death of the Partlow boy and she just went out-side and cut a whole cord of firewood. Never a tear, but you could tell she was dying inside."

Another death. I wondered if there was a connection. Decided it was time to curb my galloping paranoia.

"Well, at least she got to see him recently," said a man

in his fifties with a thin gray beard. "She was down just over a week ago, wasn't she?"

The woman nodded. "She got to spend the weekend with him. I talked with him that Monday. He said they'd had a great time together." She choked up as she said the last words and pulled out a handkerchief.

"I just don't understand it," a dark-haired woman said. "He told me last month that he'd just had a checkup, and he was doing fine."

"He was even losing weight," the man next to Julie said. "His appetite was way down and he had more energy than he'd had in years. He was feeling really great."

The group fell silent. Several had tears in their eyes. I used the break to move closer to Julie. She stepped away from them.

"I didn't realize you were so close to Raymond," I said.

"I wasn't as close as most of the people here, but he was probably my best friend at the lab."

"You seem to have a number of friends in common," I said.

She looked toward the group. "We were both members of Small World. It's a local organization of environmentalists, a think-global-act-local type of thing. Raymond did illustrations for them and some research. I met him at a meeting shortly after I began working at the lab."

"Who's Darla?" I asked.

"Raymond's sister. She lives in Oregon. I never met her, but Raymond talked about her a lot. Called her an unpaid professional environmentalist. He really admired her."

The group was beginning to break up. The woman in the parka interrupted us to say good-bye to Julie and the barrel-chested man indicated he wanted to talk to both of them before they left, so Julie excused herself and walked off with them.

I started to leave but stopped when I heard someone

behind me say, "Yeah, he was her lover before he was her right hand."

I didn't turn to see who was speaking, but I bent down and pretended to look at something on the ground.

"No shit," another voice said. "He sure does look familiar."

Across the meadow, Paul Raskin was talking to Kendra Crawford.

There really was no reason either Crawford or Raskin should have told me that they'd had an affair. No reason to assume it was relevant to the case. No reason I needed to know. Casual flirting doesn't carry a full-disclosure requirement. And it wasn't as if I hadn't been warned that Raskin was a flirt. Still, it irritated the hell out of me. I was glad I wasn't planning to go into the lab until Friday.

I put in a full day at the office on Thursday and got about halfway through the papers that had piled up on my desk. The computer searches I'd put off on Wednesday were still in the "To Do" pile. I transferred them to the Friday pile.

Molly reported for work after school and Amy introduced her to our filing system. Chris offered to let her type corrections into several reports. Jesse had left her a manual describing how to use one of our database programs and a card congratulating her on her "promotion."

Watching the scruffy teenager who slouched around my apartment transform herself into a polite and efficient employee, I suspected it was probably too good to last.

I came in early Friday to work on another case and spent two and a half hours scanning property records on the computer screen. Never did locate what I was looking for. By ten I was grateful for the excuse to shut off the computer and drive to Berkeley.

The lab was back to normal now. Most of the day

people were there, even Rick, who rarely showed up before sundown and was therefore known as Dracula. Only Kendra, Chuck, and Scott were missing.

I avoided Raskin and checked in with Julie. She was studying several photographs with the same columns of dark smudges I'd seen in Scott's presentation at the lab meeting. When she looked up, I was shocked by her appearance. She looked exhausted. The tension seemed to have sapped all vitality from her face.

"Let's go get coffee," I suggested, meaning, "Let's go where we can talk."

We walked downstairs and as soon as we were out of the building, I asked, "What's wrong?"

"I think someone messed with my solutions. My RNA is totally degraded. It could just be my own mistake. I mean, things like this can happen, and I've been distracted lately, but I haven't blown an RNA prep in six months. I have to suspect that it's someone else."

"You've taken the precautions I suggested?"

"Yes," she said. "I take my lab book home every night. I even take it with me when I go to lunch." She paused, then said with a rush of emotion, "I hate having to suspect everyone. I feel as if I'm under attack. And I don't have the slightest idea why."

She bit her lip and blinked back tears. "I just don't understand," she said. "I never did anything to anybody."

Instead of getting coffee, we walked through the campus. I don't know if it helped her. She didn't seem to notice the beauty that surrounded us—the green slopes, budding trees, wild lilies, and well-groomed border plantings. But I still walked her past every flowering tree in sight and along the creek under the sheltering redwoods.

We didn't talk much; there wasn't much to say. I could help her take precautions, but I couldn't ease the sense of vulnerability and betrayal. She'd have to find a way through that on her own.

Julie did seem in better spirits as we walked back to

the lab. She laughed at the antics of a Frisbee-chasing dog who refused to return his prize but instead dropped the disk and rolled on it.

We knew as soon as we reached the door of the lab that something was wrong. Everyone seemed to be speaking at once and there was a frenetic quality to their voices. Paul was on the phone in Kendra's office. I walked to the open door.

"Chuck Nishimura, N-i-s-h-i-m-u-r-a. The ambulance was bringing him to you," he said. "Yes, just a few minutes ago. Yes, I'll hold."

"Scott found him at the Albany greenhouse," Raisa was telling Julie. "He said he'd collapsed; his face was blue. Scott couldn't feel a heartbeat."

Julie gasped and grabbed a countertop for support. I turned back to Paul. His face was grave. He moved the mouthpiece of the phone to the side and said to me, "The medics took him to the emergency room at Alta Bates. I'm waiting for . . . Yes?" He moved the phone back to speak. "Yes, what can you tell me?" He listened and the expression on his face said it all. "You're sure? Yes, yes. I'll find out and call you back."

"Dead on arrival," he said.

19

PAUL CLOSED HIS eyes for a moment and took a deep breath. Then he collapsed into the chair behind him and sat staring at the wall for a moment.

I heard someone behind me whisper, "Shit," and the

clamor of voices fell silent as people assimilated the news. I turned and met a room full of people who seemed frozen in place. Their faces were blank with shock.

I tried to imagine how it must be for them, unfamiliar with death, encountering it twice in just over a week. Raymond had probably seemed older. His position and, I suspected, his appearance had distanced him from them. But Chuck was one of them. Too young to die.

Teri began weeping, then Julie. Joellen put her arm around Raisa and they buried their faces in each other's shoulders. This time there were none of the loud expressions of disbelief. Shock had stunned them to silence.

I realized with sadness that I was not shocked. I was surprised, but the shield of professional detachment had slipped into place almost as soon as I heard the news.

Experience has taught me to suspect coincidence. Two deaths in a little over a week could be random chance. But I didn't believe it. Not for a minute. "What happened?" I asked.

It took a moment for Paul to respond. "It must have been his allergies," he said. "He must have forgotten to put on his mask."

Just a week ago Chuck had shown me that mask and told me he *never* went into the greenhouse without it. I remembered the look in his eyes when he described almost suffocating and felt an involuntary shiver up my spine. Most of us have a secret fear. Out of the range of awful things that threaten and terrify us, our mind selects one or two that hold special horror. For Chuck, suffocation was that fear; I couldn't imagine him forgetting his mask.

I looked around at the shock-frozen faces of the students. This wasn't the time to raise the questions that bubbled up inside my head. That could wait. For now, I watched them, uncomfortably aware that in all likelihood one of them was a murderer.

*   *   *

Scott arrived from the greenhouse about ten minutes later. He had on the same 49ers tee shirt he'd worn at the lab meeting, but he looked like a different person. His skin was ashen and it appeared to take every bit of energy he had to put one foot in front of the other. As he came in the door, he was the focus of everyone's attention. He stood in the passageway and looked around the room with wide, unseeing eyes, then shook his head.

"He's dead?" he asked.

Several people nodded.

"Oh, God," he moaned. "I knew it. I hoped . . . Oh, shit." He leaned against the counter. Paul came out of the office and put an arm around Scott, led him into the office, and settled him in a chair. I followed them in. Several students followed me as far as the door but stopped just outside.

"What happened, Scott?" Paul asked gently.

Scott shook his head. "I don't know. I mean, I came into the greenhouse and there he was on the floor. He was blue. I mean it. His skin was really blue." He paused and swallowed a couple of times. "I dragged him outside. I tried to do CPR—you know, blowing in his mouth, pushing on his chest—but it didn't help. I started yelling for help, and a couple of the bio-control guys came out and I told them to call 911. I kept doing the CPR, but nothing worked."

He started to shiver and thrust his hands under his thighs as if to warm them. I took off my jacket and put it around his shoulders, but it didn't stop the shivering.

Over the next half hour as the students struggled to come to grips with their shock and grief, I watched for a false note, too strong a reaction, or too little. I didn't see it. If one of these people was a killer, he or she was not only self-possessed but quite possibly beyond feeling guilt. And such a killer is the hardest kind to catch.

* * *

After an initial period of turning to each other for support, most of the students were anxious to get away from the lab. As the numbers dwindled, my reasons for staying diminished. I was anxious to get down to Albany and pick up the tape from the hidden camera. Whatever had happened in that greenhouse, the camera was an eyewitness.

I tried to excuse myself a couple of times, but Paul was reluctant to see me leave. "I need some help with this," he told me in a near whisper. "I don't want anyone to flip out."

No one looked in danger of flipping out, but they were a somber and distressed bunch. Paul tried to locate Kendra but only succeeded in leaving messages for her at three places.

I became concerned that Vipul might leave his office, so I asked Paul for his phone number. "Why do you want that?" he asked.

"I want to get the tape from the greenhouse," I said.

"Why?"

"To see what happened to Chuck."

He looked perplexed. "But we know. Oh, wait a minute, you're not saying that this wasn't an accident?"

"I'm not saying anything except that I want to see the tape."

The office door was open and he stepped past me to close it. When he turned back to me, his mouth was a thin line and he was frowning.

"Look, it's bad enough that we've lost two people in just over a week," he said. "Bad for morale, bad for finishing the grant proposal, but if there was even a hint that something sinister was going on, that could be disastrous. Surely you can see that."

I couldn't believe he'd said that. From Kendra Crawford, it wouldn't have surprised me, but I'd expected more from him. "Surely you can see that murder is a lot more serious than an image problem," I said.

His frown deepened. "Why do you keep suggesting that it's murder? Raymond had heart trouble. Chuck had allergies. Their deaths were tragic, but they weren't murders." Raskin's voice was low but so intense that it was raspy.

"You knew Chuck," I said. "Did he ever go into the greenhouse without a mask?"

"I don't know. Obviously he did this time."

"I just want to review the tape, that's all," I said. "If there's no sign of foul play, we can all relax. But I want to see for myself."

Raskin nodded. "Okay, but give me your word not to stir up suspicions until you know something for sure."

It irritated me that he thought he needed my word, and he could probably hear it in my voice. "I'm a professional, Raskin. I don't stir up suspicions, but I also don't cover up felonies. Now, can I have that number?"

He gave it to me, but the frown was firmly fixed on his face, and the warm current of attraction we'd felt before had turned to ice.

Vipul was in his office. He assured me he'd be there for at least a couple of hours. I told him I'd be right over. As I left the office, Raskin said, "You'll let me know what you find?"

"Of course."

At the Albany greenhouse, I picked up the tape and put a new one in the machine. Vipul had been there when Scott found Chuck. In fact, he'd been the one to call 911, and he was anxious to talk about the accident. I let him do most of the talking and stuck to making sympathetic noises and asking occasional questions. I didn't want to raise his suspicions.

I needn't have worried. Vipul knew all about deadly allergies. He himself was highly allergic to bees and even a single sting could trigger a potentially fatal reaction. When he finished telling me about it, I asked, "Did you notice if Chuck had his mask with him?"

"He always wore it," Vipul said, "but this time, I don't know. I rushed inside to call when I heard the student yelling. When I came out, he was blowing in his mouth. He didn't have a mask then."

I thanked Vipul for his help and headed for my office, all the more anxious to find out what exactly was on that tape.

Traffic was light and the drive to San Francisco took less time than usual but my impatience made it seem just the opposite. I found a parking place on the street, fed the meter most of my spare change, and for once didn't worry about the Meter Maid.

Amy had a stack of messages for me, but I shook my head and walked past her to the back room, where we keep the TV and VCR.

I slid the tape into the slot and pressed PLAY. The grainy black-and-white image of the greenhouse filled the screen. Against the bright white of the windows, the plants were a uniform black. I fiddled with the controls to reduce the contrast, and the image became clearer.

I rewound the tape to noon. No sign of Chuck or anyone else. I held down the fast-forward button. The image became a snowy blur, but I could still make out enough to see that the scene hadn't changed. I was beginning to worry that something was wrong when I saw the dark smudge in the middle at the bottom of the screen. I stopped the tape, then hit PLAY again.

In the aisle just beyond the door, I could see Chuck Nishimura. And I could see that he was wearing his mask! He walked down the aisle and turned into a row of plants, so that most of his body was obscured by the leaves. Then he was out of camera range. But after several minutes he was back. Even with the corn hiding much of his body, I could tell that he was moving strangely. He seemed to be lurching.

As he emerged into the aisle, I could see that he was

clutching at the mask. He took a step forward and wrenched it down around his neck. The picture wasn't that clear, but I could see enough of Chuck's face to know that he was terrified. His mouth was wide open, whether screaming or struggling for air, I couldn't tell. He took three more steps, then collapsed.

I paused the tape and took a deep breath. My heart was pounding and my stomach felt queasy. The black-and-white images forced the reality of Chuck's death on me in a way that Scott's words had not. I stared at the snowy screen and took several more deep breaths to loosen the tightness in my chest. It didn't budge.

When my emotions settled down enough to allow my mind to function again, I considered what I'd just seen. Chuck had gone into the greenhouse with his mask on. Why would he have taken it off when he was surrounded by corn plants?

I rewound the tape and played it again. Chuck looked normal as he entered the greenhouse; no sign of a problem as he disappeared into the corn plants. But something was clearly wrong four and a half minutes later when he stumbled back out to the center aisle.

I watched as he tore off the mask and gulped for air. That was it. He'd taken the mask off because he was already suffocating. Either he wasn't getting enough air through the filters or the filters weren't protecting him from the pollen. But if the mask wasn't allowing enough air to reach him, he'd have known that when he put it on, outside the greenhouse, and he'd have dealt with the problem before going in with the corn. So it had to be that the filters weren't working; they hadn't protected him from the pollen.

I remembered the expression on Chuck's face when he described his experience in San Jose, his horror of suffocation, and shivered involuntarily. The room seemed suddenly cold.

I forced my mind back to the mask. Either it had failed or it had been sabotaged. The only way to know that would be to examine the mask itself.

I pushed "Play" again and watched the unchanging image of Chuck on the greenhouse floor as the time-date generator ticked away the last minutes of his life. A heavy sadness, followed by a sense of helplessness, settled on me as I watched the screen and waited for Scott to appear. Technology that allows us to record disaster but not to alter its course is a cruel servant.

After what seemed like hours but was less than ten minutes, Scott appeared and rushed to Chuck. He turned him over and began dragging him toward the door. I could see the mask still around Chuck's neck.

Tears blurred my vision as I stared at the screen. I tried to blink them back, gave up, closed my eyes, and felt the grief wash over me.

I couldn't bear to think about Chuck, so I turned my attention back to the case. Scott would know what had happened to the mask, but I couldn't ask him. If that mask had been sabotaged, there was a killer in the lab. I wasn't taking chances with anyone.

20

THE DRIVE BACK to the East Bay gave me plenty of time to think. Unfortunately, my mind didn't seem to be in the mood for heavy lifting.

I went first to the greenhouse. Chuck had pulled the

mask down around his neck. Scott would probably have removed it when he started CPR. I hoped Vipul could tell me who else had been there and might know what had happened to the mask.

Vipul was in his office with two other men, an Indian he introduced as Theodore and a strikingly handsome dark-skinned man named Aklilu. I asked if either of them had been there when Chuck was found. Both nodded.

"We couldn't do a thing for him," Aklilu said. "I think he must already have been gone." Theodore nodded agreement.

"Did he have a mask around his neck?" I asked.

"A mask? Yes," Aklilu said. "We had some trouble getting it off. For a moment we thought it might be strangling him, but it wasn't that tight."

"What happened to it?" I asked.

He considered a minute. His brow creased slightly and he looked up and to the side, searching for the visual memory of that moment. "I don't know," he said slowly. "I think we just dropped it there. We were all watching the boy, and after, well, did you see it, Theodore?"

"I think the other one, the one who found him, picked it up. I know he locked up the greenhouse. Maybe he put it inside."

"Ah, yes," Vipul said. "I saw him toss something in just before he closed the door. It was probably your mask."

"Do any of you have a key to the greenhouse that I could use?" I asked.

All three men shook their heads. "No one in our group has keys to their greenhouse," Vipul said.

"I think Fred in Maintenance has one," Aklilu suggested. "But he's probably gone by now."

Fred was gone; so was everyone else in Maintenance. The lock on the greenhouse was a good one, well beyond my limited abilities. I called both numbers at the lab and after listening to dead air and abrasive rings, resigned myself to the fact that there was no way into the greenhouse.

My search of the area around the greenhouse building didn't take long and yielded only two Snickers wrappers and a Snapple bottle. That left the garbage cans I found around back and the Dumpster. Dumpster searches can be vile affairs; fortunately this one turned up nothing more offensive than the remains of several lunches. No mask.

I hate to leave a job half done, and I was in a foul mood by the time I got back to San Francisco, so I went straight home. The flat was quiet, which meant that Molly wasn't there. Surprises are never welcome when you have a teenager in the house. I headed for the answering machine, hoping she'd remembered my last lecture about calling in.

The light was blinking. The first message was for someone named Connie from someone named George. He sounded depressed. The second was Molly, with crowd noise in the background. "Me and Heather and John are working on our history report at Heather's. We're going to get a pizza and work till ten. Can I spend the night?"

A boy's voice in the background yelled, "We're gonna have an orgy."

"Shut up, John," Molly said, then gave Heather's phone number.

The final message was from Jesse. "Please call me as soon as you can. It's important." I didn't recognize the phone number.

I hoped Jesse hadn't found a body today. Then I'd know for sure we were jinxed. I called him first.

"Sorry to bother you on a Friday night," he said. "But I heard from Kyle. He has the information I need but he won't give it to me. He'll only give it to you, and in person."

"Oh, great," I said. Kyle was probably in one of his

paranoid phases again. I hoped he wasn't going to put me through some elaborate ritual of phone-booth tag.

"He's flying to Atlanta tomorrow, so he'd like to take you to dinner tonight. The Alta Mira in Sausalito at seven-thirty. Can you do it?"

Maybe not paranoia, maybe just lust. I wondered if he knew Peter was out of town. "I can do it," I said without enthusiasm, "but you owe me."

"I'm yours to command," Jesse said. "I just hope he's got something worth our respective sacrifices."

I didn't tell Jesse about Chuck's death. I didn't want to discuss it. I realized as I hung up that I was grateful for the excuse not to be alone with my thoughts that night.

I called Molly to tell her she could stay at Heather's and George to tell him he hadn't reached Connie. Then I took a shower and changed my Dumpster-delving outfit for something cleaner.

The Alta Mira is a grand old hotel set high on a hillside above Sausalito. The views of San Francisco and the East Bay are spectacular. It was exactly the sort of romantic spot where I did not want to meet Kyle Jorland.

I suspected that Kyle related to women much as he did to business. He loved risk and long shots, and he was unencumbered by morality. That I was his good friend's lover only made me more attractive to him.

He waved to me from the bar and I went to meet him. The attractive blonde who'd been chatting with him was obviously disappointed by my appearance.

He was dressed in a beautifully tailored charcoal suit with a gray shirt and a tie that reminded me of Raymond's impressionistic paintings. His thick dark hair had a few flecks of gray in it and he'd grown a mustache since I last saw him. I don't usually like mustaches, but on him it looked good. He'd lost some weight and he had a tan he didn't get in northern California.

"Catherine," he said, "you only get more beautiful."

I smiled. "And you more gallant. You're looking very fit."

"You noticed," he said with a smile. "Thought I'd drop a few pounds. Never good to get fat and lazy in my business."

"And what is your business these days?" I asked as we walked to the restaurant.

"A bit of this, a bit of that," he said. "Actually, I'm into biotech right now. Fascinating stuff. Lots of money to be made or lost."

I almost told him that my current case involved biotech, but caught myself. Kyle was the last person I wanted involved in the case. He was a great source of information, but with his love of risk, he'd be a dangerous collaborator.

We made small talk while we waited to be seated and then to order. As soon as that was done and the waiter was out of earshot, I said, "So, how about we get business over before we eat. What did you find out for Jesse?"

"Always the businesswoman," Kyle said in mock complaint. "Okay, here's what I've got. Some of it's hearsay and I can't give you the sources, but I trust them. First, no one's heard any rumors about those chips, which you already know, and that's suspicious just by itself. So I took a long look at the company. They're essentially a one-product operation. Oh, they make some other stuff, but they've committed so heavily to this new chip that it's the major part of their business."

The wine arrived, and Kyle tasted it. He waited so long to give his approval that the wine steward was looking nervous. Finally, he nodded. "It's okay," he said, then gave me a sly smile behind the poor man's back.

"So I asked myself," he continued after the steward left, "what would happen if this wonder chip hit a snag?

If, say, it isn't ready to go on the date it's set to ship. Maybe there's a problem on the production line or with one of the materials they used, but anyway, the chips don't do what they're supposed to do. MediTech, the company that's waiting for these babies, would be very unhappy; investors would be unhappy. Lawsuits might happen. The bright boys who run the show might go broke.

"But if this load of chips was stolen . . ." He paused for effect.

"The company would be off the hook," I said. "They'd have time to do another production run and they'd have the insurance money to finance it."

"Very nice," Kyle said. "Like H says, a good detective has the mind of a crook. He does say that, doesn't he?"

"Sounds like him," I agreed. H was Peter's nickname from the sixties, and a few old friends like Kyle still used it.

"So if the good guy's really the bad guy, what do you do?" he asked.

"Good guy, bad guy, he's still our client. And you don't last long in this business if you rat on your clients. We write up a report saying we can't find the chips and Jesse can come home."

Kyle looked disappointed. "Would Sam Spade have done such a thing?" he asked.

"In a minute," I said, "as long as the bad good guys hadn't shot his partner."

Kyle laughed. The waiter arrived with dinner. After he'd gone, I said, "So what's your latest scheme?"

"Ventures. We call them ventures," Kyle said, and launched into a complicated story about a firm working on molecular designed drugs. I love to listen to Kyle; it's fun just to watch his devious, amoral mind at work. Not that there was anything illegal about the deal he was describing to me, but I knew from experience that slipping over the line on a couple of laws would only make it more attractive to him.

I also love to get Kyle talking about "the good ole days," since I learn all kinds of stuff about Peter that he'd never tell me. Dinner passed quickly, and as we were sitting over coffee, I asked, "Did you know Alicia?"

"Ah, the lovely Alicia. What male didn't know Alicia? God, she was a beauty."

"Still is," I said.

"And ruthless, like a man. If she wanted something, she went after it like a barracuda. That's what makes her such a good journalist. That tenacity."

"Mmmm," I said. I was ready to be done talking about Alicia.

"She and Peter had a thing, you know," Kyle said, his eyes dancing. "Well, Alicia had a thing with a lot of guys, but I think she really fell for H. He's big on monogamy, as you know, and she even bought into that for a while. Of course, Alicia is not a one-man woman, so it didn't last. What made you ask about her?"

"I saw her byline recently."

"Oh, yes. She's where?" He paused, then he gave me a wicked smile as comprehension dawned. "In Guatemala. I'll bet H has his hands full." He looked positively delighted. I could have slugged him.

He must have read my feelings in my face, since he tried to tone down his smile. "You can't really expect me to be sorry," he said. "You know I'd love to see H slip the leash. You and I could have a very good time together."

"Oh, no," I said. "You are entirely too wild for my taste, Kyle. I wouldn't take you on as a client, much less as a lover."

Kyle feigned distress, but his eyes were still smiling. "You are a cruel woman. I make a tender offer of my affections and you rebuff me. But you know, my dear, after H, anyone but me is going to be pretty dull."

Dull sounded good to me right now, and I told him so.

"Ah, you think so now," he said, "but after six or eight

months of predictable men, you'd be bored." He smiled knowingly.

21

I STARTED CALLING the lab the next morning at eight, hoping at least one student was obsessed enough to have worked through the night Friday or come in early on Saturday. There was no answer.

I called Jesse at nine to give him Kyle's information, but he was on his way out to check on a new lead, so we arranged to meet later that afternoon at the office.

Molly called at nine-thirty to say that they hadn't finished the paper and she needed to stay at Heather's to work on it.

"How was the orgy?" I asked.

"Oh, Catherine," she said. That line loses some of its effect when you can't see the rolling of the eyes that goes with it.

"Okay, how was *X-Files*?" She'd said they were working till ten, which translated to they'd be watching *X-Files* at nine.

"Really cool," she said. She'd have given me a plot summary but I stopped her and made arrangements for her to get home since I wasn't planning to stick around.

At ten-fifteen someone finally answered the phone at the lab. It was Raskin. "What'd you find on the tape?" he asked as soon as I identified myself.

"Chuck was wearing his mask when he went into the greenhouse," I said.

There was a pause. "It must have failed," Raskin said. "The damn thing must have failed."

"I'll bring you the tape," I said. "Will you be there for an hour or so?"

"Sure," he said. "But you can wait till Monday."

"I have to come over anyway," I said.

I could have asked Raskin to check for the mask, or I could have told him that I was going to do it, but I didn't. At this point it was too dangerous to trust anyone associated with the lab.

In the Genetics Building, the labs were full of people, except for the Crawford lab. No voices greeted me as I came in the door, and the only person there was Paul Raskin. He was sitting in the library. His face was drawn, making his usually sharp features even more pronounced, and he looked up at me with tired eyes.

I sat down opposite him and handed him the tape. It was a copy; the original was in the safe at my office. He looked at the black plastic case. "Such a damn shame," he said. "Such a waste."

"Can you lend me your key to the greenhouse?" I asked.

"Sure, but why?"

"Because I think the mask is there, and I'd like to take a look at it."

He reached into his pocket for the key. "Why?" he asked again.

"Because there's a chance the mask was sabotaged."

Raskin looked astonished, then sick. "Oh, shit," he said. "No one could be that dumb. I mean, surely they'd realize . . ."

"Given what's happened, it's a possibility we have to consider."

The transformation in his face was dramatic. He

looked absolutely anguished. "Oh, no," he said. "Oh, sweet Jesus, I hope you're wrong."

"The only way to be sure is to check the mask," I said as gently as I could, extending my hand for the key.

He stood up abruptly. "I'll go with you."

He was out the door before I could object.

The ride to the greenhouse was a silent one. Tension radiated from Raskin. I wondered at the cause for his urgency.

He almost jumped out of the car when we got there. "Where is it?" he asked as he headed for the door.

"I think it should be right inside. Scott probably just tossed it in there."

The feeble overhead light illuminated a small area just inside the door. We found Chuck's backpack there. Raskin looked through it. "Nothing here," he said. "Damn, I keep meaning to get that other light fixed. Can't see a thing without it."

I'd brought a heavy-duty flashlight and I searched the area around the door in ever-widening circles. Raskin became more agitated as we got farther into the room without finding the mask. "Where is the damn thing?" he repeated a couple of times.

Down the center of the room we could make out marks in the dust that traced where Scott had dragged Chuck's body to the door, but nowhere along that path was there any sign of the mask. We searched the entire room, all the way into the corners. Anyplace the mask might have landed, and a lot of places it couldn't have reached. But we didn't find it.

I checked the shelf above the corn aprons and took down the box in which Chuck had kept his things. No mask there or anywhere else on the shelf.

Next we searched the greenhouse. The bright lamps and natural light made it easy to see, but they didn't show us the mask. As we walked out, Raskin said, "The paramedics must have taken it. Or maybe Scott did."

I didn't think so, but I suggested we go back to the lab and call Scott.

"You really think someone sabotaged the mask," Raskin said as we drove back. It wasn't a question.

"I think it's very likely," I said. "And if we can't locate the mask, I'll be sure of it."

"But it could have been lost, thrown out," he said.

"Not thrown out," I said. "I checked the grounds outside the greenhouse and all the trash cans, even the Dumpster. If it's gone, it's because someone didn't want us to find it."

Raskin didn't argue the point and the tension in his face told me that he knew I was right.

Kendra was in her office by the time we got back. She was on the phone, so we went to Paul's desk to call Scott.

"Do you mind if I make the call?" I asked.

Raskin shook his head and handed me the number.

Scott answered on the fifth ring and sounded like he might have been asleep. When I asked about the mask, he paused. "I think I tossed it in the greenhouse," he said. "I know we took it off Chuck's neck so we could do CPR, and I think I picked it up after. I wasn't paying a lot of attention, you know. I was sort of in shock." His voice took on a sharp defensiveness as if he was afraid of being blamed for something.

I tried to reassure him, then asked again about the mask. "Close your eyes and try to see what happened just before you locked up," I suggested.

A long pause, then he said, "Yeah, I picked up the mask and I tossed it inside the building, then I locked the door."

Raskin had been listening on an extension. As we hung up, he looked as if he was close to tears. "What an incredibly dumb, tragic thing," he said. Then suddenly the sorrow turned to fury and he slammed his fist down on the desk so hard that the glassware jumped and a beaker fell to the floor and broke.

"Paul?" Kendra called.

The fury drained slowly from Raskin's face and he turned and led the way to Crawford's office. She could tell the minute she saw him that something was wrong. I let him tell her.

"But just because you can't find the mask," she objected, "that doesn't mean there was sabotage."

"Can you think of another reason it wouldn't be there?" I asked. I hadn't expected her to accept it easily.

"It got lost," she said. "Scott was upset; he could be confused about putting it in the greenhouse. It'll turn up."

"The only other places it could be are the hospital or the ambulance," I said. "I can check on them, but I'm not optimistic."

"I don't see why you're so sure it was taken. In all the excitement it could just have been lost," Kendra said. Her voice had an angry edge. "It could be sitting in a trash can someplace, one you didn't check."

I was at least as angry as Crawford, but I worked to keep it out of my voice. "I can't prove to you that it was stolen," I said, "but before you convince yourself that I have an overactive imagination, you should consider two things. If someone tampered with the mask as a prank or to make Chuck sick, that person is guilty of murder. He or she is likely to be fairly desperate and that translates into dangerous. Beyond that, we still don't understand the reason for the sabotage. It could be to get at you, Kendra. To ruin your lab. You could be at risk next."

Kendra took a sharp breath and her eyes narrowed. "What do you think we should do?" she asked.

"I think you should go to the police," I said. "I've got the name of the Albany detective who's investigating Raymond's death. He'd be the logical person. We can take him the tape, and . . ."

"Not the Albany police," Kendra interrupted. "We'll go to the campus police. After all, the Gill Tract is university property."

"Fine," I said. "Do you want me to come along?"

"No," she said a little too quickly. "I can handle this myself."

I had a hunch how she'd handle it. "Minor problem . . . blown out of proportion . . . overzealous investigator . . . public perception of the university." She'd make it easy for them not to take her seriously. And once they'd ruled Chuck's death an accident, they'd have an incentive to see that the case stayed closed.

And there wasn't a damn thing I could do about it with the evidence we had. The only way to ensure that the police took the case seriously was to come up with compelling proof of a crime, or to catch the criminal.

I used Raskin's phone to call the hospital. It took four transfers to get me to the person who could answer my question, and I spent so long on hold that Vivaldi was finishing up with spring and heading into summer.

The very harried secretary in the hospital morgue didn't think she could divulge information to anyone but next of kin. I put on my officious-bureaucrat voice and informed her that the mask was critical evidence in a health and safety investigation. She waffled until I demanded to speak to her supervisor. That helped her decide. She checked the paperwork and informed me that the inventory of effects did not include a mask of any kind.

It took only three more transfers to get someone in the emergency room who could give me the names and the company of the paramedics who'd brought Chuck's body to the hospital. Forty-five minutes later I had confirmation that the mask had never been in the ambulance.

Kendra was glum when I told her. She didn't act surprised. Paul had gone to pick up Chuck's mother from the airport, so we were alone in the lab.

"I know you think I'm acting foolishly," Kendra said.

"That I should push the police to make a full investigation, but there are other factors to consider." She closed her eyes for a minute and rubbed her temples, then put her elbow on the desk and rested her head on her hand. She looked exhausted. "It's not just the grant. We're under a lot of pressure from within the university. My boss's boss believes that this lab should be doing a very different kind of research."

"Leaf curl," I said, remembering our earlier conversation.

She looked surprised, then nodded. "Yes, leaf curl or some other damn thing the agribusiness community wants done. We're a university, damnit. We used to be a *great* university, but these jokers and their bought-and-paid-for legislators want us to work on leaf curl.

" 'The state can't afford pure research,' they say. It's so damn shortsighted." She stopped and shook her head. "You must think I'm pretty heartless," she said, the anger gone from her voice. "A student died yesterday and I'm getting worked up about university politics, but Chuck would have understood. He felt as strongly as I do about applied research. He didn't come to Berkeley to help farmers make money."

"I take it you're afraid that if word gets out about the sabotage the administration will use it against you."

"You better believe it. Anything that weakens the perception of this lab as an efficient research team makes it easier for the ag VP to jerk our chain. He's already threatening to withdraw funding for my lab tech and Paul, maybe even to move the lab to the Davis campus. Davis! If we lose the grant renewal, we're even more vulnerable."

"Is it possible that that's the reason for the sabotage?" I asked.

"Oh, no," she said. "Even I am not that paranoid. That's not how things work."

As I'd told Detective Wilson, even paranoids have real

enemies. I hoped Kendra Crawford would realize that before someone else died.

22

JESSE MET ME at the office Monday morning at ten-fifteen. A hot lead he'd come up with on Sunday had turned into a cold trail by ten, and he was a tad grouchy as a result.

I could tell from his reaction to Kyle's news that he'd already suspected our client. "Someone would be trying to move those chips if they had them," he said. "They're probably in a landfill somewhere."

"Well, at least they won't give you any grief for not finding the chips," I said.

"It galls me that they're using me to defraud the insurance company," Jesse said. "That's what they want the report for, I'm sure. They'll send it to their insurance company to forestall an investigation."

"A carefully crafted report can satisfy a client and still not reassure the insurance company," I said.

"If the insurance company's on the ball," Jesse said. "Well, I did my job; I just hope they do theirs. Now, tell me what's happening in corn land."

I told him about Chuck.

"Jesus, you've got a second death, and you didn't tell me. Excuse me, are we still partners?"

"Give me a break," I said. "I didn't feel like talking about it yesterday."

Jesse looked concerned. "Hey, when you're working a

murder case, and you don't feel like talking about it, we're in big trouble," he said.

"I don't need anyone to hold my hand."

"This isn't a test of your independence, you know," Jesse said hotly.

"Can we skip the psychotherapy and talk about the case?" I asked. I knew I was being bitchy. I didn't care.

Talking about the case is one of the things we do well. As we sorted through the knowns, the suspicions, and the unknowns, our anger evaporated.

"I think I understand what's going on with Kendra Crawford," I said. "I doubt that she's as unfeeling as she appears, but she was formed in a world where the work always comes first, so I'm not surprised that her first concern is protecting the lab.

"Paul Raskin is harder to peg. He reacted with much more intensity to the news that the mask was sabotaged than he did to Chuck's death, and his response seemed more personal than professional."

"You already had some questions about him," Jesse said.

"I have questions about a lot of people," I said. Too bad that was all I had.

I knew where to get one answer I wanted, and I knew that Kendra Crawford might prefer to ignore it, so I didn't ask her before I went to the Environmental Health and Safety office on Monday morning. Raskin had told me that EH and S was where Chuck had gotten his mask.

Their offices were in University Hall, a steel-and-glass box about a block from Koshland across the street from the western boundary of the campus. The huge metal beams that form X's across the outside facade of the building are not decoration. They're quake reinforcement to keep the thing together when the Big One hits.

I signed in at the desk and took the elevator to the third floor. The sign on the door of Room 350 identified it as Environmental Health and Safety. Inside was a counter and behind it a woman whose name tag read Margaret Short.

She stood up when I came in, and the irony of her name was immediately apparent. She was at least five eight, in her forties, and had probably spent most of her life listening to dumb jokes about her name. She had a long face, made longer by a high forehead and straight brown hair that hung limply to her shoulders.

"Can I help you?" she asked. Her voice was soft.

"I wanted to check on a mask that protects people with allergies," I said. "The kind that filters the pollen from the air."

"Sure, I can help you." She opened a cupboard behind the counter and took out a box. The mask she took from it looked just like the one Chuck used.

"This is the kind we recommend," she said. "It's NIOSH/MSHA-approved."

I took the mask from her and studied it, trying to see how it might have been disabled. It was a fairly simple design; most of the parts were visible. The air was drawn in through the filter disks and passed through a small valve into the plastic piece that covered the nose and mouth.

"Have you ever had one of these fail?" I asked.

"Fail?" she said. "You mean not work? I don't think so. This is an excellent mask. Here, look at these filters."

"A student died Friday from anaphylactic shock caused by his allergy to corn pollen," I said. "He was wearing a mask like this."

She gave a little gasp and stared at me. "Who?" she said in a small voice. "How?"

I told her, then asked, "Do you have any idea what might have caused it to fail?"

She shook her head slowly. "I guess if it was damaged," she said, "so that it didn't fit right, or if the filters were torn up or so old that they didn't work anymore.

But I've never had it happen. As I said, this respirator has been fully tested. It's NIOSH/MSHA-approved."

"Could it have been sabotaged?"

"Oh, dear," she said. She looked even more stricken than at the thought of the mask failing. "I don't know, but if you bring it to me, I can check it over and see what I can find."

"I'm afraid I can't. It was lost in the confusion."

"Oh, well . . ." She studied the mask in her hands, turning it over several times. "I don't know. Even if you screwed up the valves, I don't think it would disable the mask."

I looked more carefully at the valves, then lifted the soft plastic covering of one. There was a small cylindrical hole behind it. "What if someone put pollen in here?" I asked. "Wouldn't the person wearing the mask breathe it in?"

"Yes," she said, her voice even softer, so I had to strain to hear her. "Yes, but that would be crazy. Why would anyone do such a thing?"

Finally, a question for which I knew the answer.

At the lab the response to Chuck's death was similar to the reaction to Raymond's; only the students working on the grant had come to work and they didn't seem to be getting much done. I found Crawford and Raskin in the professor's office. Both looked drawn and tired, as if they weren't sleeping well. The news I had for them wasn't going to improve that situation.

As I came in, Raskin was saying, "Well, if someone did mess with his mask, they'll be so horrified by what they've done they'll never screw around again."

"I wish that were true," I said, "but I think the person knew exactly what he or she was doing." I explained why I didn't think the mask could fail accidentally. "Whoever put corn pollen inside the valves knew that when Chuck breathed in, he'd draw it right into his lungs. Given how serious his allergies were, such a heavy dose in a short time was sure to be fatal."

"Jeez," Paul said. He jumped up and went to stare out the window as he tried to take in what I'd said. Kendra just stared at me. Finally, she said, "No, I don't believe it. None of these people is a killer.

"You don't have the mask," she continued. "You can't know that's what happened."

"I can't find another logical explanation," I said.

"I met with the chief of the campus police and one of her detectives this morning," she said. "They didn't seem to think Chuck's death was particularly suspicious."

"Are they going to investigate?" I asked.

"Yes, of course," she said. "And while they're doing that, I want you to stay out of it. Your job is to prevent sabotage in the lab, nothing more. Do you understand?"

I nodded. Her tone irritated me so much that I didn't trust myself to speak.

Paul turned back from the window. "I don't know what to think," he said. "Maybe we shouldn't be so quick to ignore Catherine's concern. I've got to do something that might tell us more about Chuck." Before Kendra could object, he went on, "Someone needs to help his mother go through his apartment and pack stuff up."

"That's not our job," Kendra said sharply. "I don't mean to be unkind, but we have a lab to run, and we've already fallen behind. I need you here, Paul, and I can't afford to pay Catherine to hold Chuck's mother's hand."

"There're files and papers there that are related to his work here," Paul reminded her. "Mrs. Nishimura's already said we could take them. I'll send Margot. She's taking over his research while we adjust."

Kendra pursed her lips and tapped her pencil on the desk. Finally, she said, "We're too shorthanded here to spare Margot or anyone else. All right, Catherine, you can get Mrs. Nishimura started. Set aside anything that's related to the lab, and Margot can go through it later. And while you're doing that, you can take a look around. But if you find anything, you don't mention it to her. You bring it to me."

I picked up Mrs. Nishimura at the Marina Marriott. She was waiting for me in the lobby, and it seemed to take all her effort to rise from the floral armchair in which she sat. She was a small woman with a trim, athletic body. Her hair showed no sign of gray, and her face was relatively unlined. But sorrow sat on her shoulders like a lead weight and aged her face.

Chuck's apartment was in El Cerrito, about twenty minutes north of the campus. In East Bay neighborhoods, as in much of the world, income rises with elevation. Chuck's place was in the flatlands. Four identical two-story buildings lined up with their ends toward the street. They were typical California low-rise construction—cheap materials thrown together in a manner you'd never get away with in a harsher climate.

Mrs. Nishimura stared at the building from the car and made no move to get out when I turned off the engine. Her eyes were moist when she turned to me. "It's so hard to go in," she said. Before I could respond, she gave a sigh and opened the door. "Enough of this," she said more to herself than to me, and got out of the car.

Paul had given me some cardboard boxes for packing, and I pulled several of them from the back of the car and followed her to Chuck's apartment. It was on the ground floor in the middle. A card with his name printed in faded ink was tacked above the bell.

Inside, the air was stale. There was a hint of something rotten, probably from the kitchen. The living room was furnished sparsely with a comfortable-looking old gray tweed couch, a couple of end tables that didn't match, an easy chair in a faded pink floral print, and two bookshelves made of bricks and boards. A portable television sat on the floor in the corner. The walls were bare.

"He didn't have much money," Mrs. Nishimura said. I guessed she was trying to explain the sparse furnishings.

"It looks very comfortable," I said. "Just right for a student."

"We couldn't help much with money," she said. "Not with his sister still in college." She paused and looked around again. "He was proud he could live on his fellowship."

Then she sighed as she had in the car, gathered her strength, and announced, "I'll start in the bedroom."

I followed her down a short hall that opened onto two bedrooms and a bath. Chuck had used the smaller bedroom for sleeping. An unmade queen-size bed and a dresser were the only furniture in the room.

The other bedroom was his study. He'd made a desk from a door supported by a file cabinet on one end and a three-drawer chest the size of a nightstand on the other. His computer sat on one end of the desk; the rest was covered with papers. A half-eaten Mars bar lay next to the keyboard.

A long, narrow table ran down the opposite wall. It was empty except for a few books. Cardboard file boxes were stored under it, and books were piled in stacks on the floor. The walls were covered with articles and pictures that he'd taped or tacked up.

I don't know what I expected to find, or how I'd know if I found it, but the best place to look seemed to be this room. I started with the desk. The papers were mostly handwritten notes and a couple of xeroxed research articles. They might as well have been written in Chinese for all I could understand of them. I stacked them in one of the boxes.

That left the computer and the three-and-a-half-inch disks piled up next to it. I carry a portable hard drive in my car, and I'd brought it in to copy Chuck's hard disk. I switched on the computer and took a look at the word processor files. The root directory showed eleven subdirectories. One was labeled "Letters."

I browsed through the files in that directory, not reading but just checking the ones directed to people in the lab. The ones I spotted were all business-related. Nothing sinister. About halfway through, I got tired of browsing and started on the job of copying the hard drive.

While the computer was doing its thing at high speed, I sorted through the boxes of files at a much slower speed. They all looked like research and I piled them in the living room to be taken to the lab. There were remarkably few personal papers in the study: a pile of letters from home, a file of bills, a file of instructions and warranties. Nothing very revealing.

With all the file boxes out, I could see a few scraps of paper that had fallen behind the table. I pulled them out. There was a grocery list, a dental appointment reminder, and a newspaper article. The article was a profile of five East Bay biotechnology firms and included photos of their founders. A thin pen line drew my attention to one name, Galen Wells, and his company, Biosolutions.

Wells was identified as a former professor of biochemistry at the University of California at Berkeley who had resigned two years earlier to start his own company. As a researcher he had made promising discoveries in the area of mammalian sugar metabolism, and his company was developing a drug that promised improved treatment for diabetes and hypoglycemia. Testing on the new product was scheduled to be completed in late March.

I put the article in the box of personal papers, then pulled it out again. The name Galen Wells was vaguely familiar. It took me a few seconds to figure out where I'd seen it. The copying procedure was complete, so I went back to the letter directory. A third of the way down the list of documents was "GALEN-WE.LLS."

The letter was short and totally ambiguous. It read

simply, "I'm enclosing the info you asked for. I hope you can make more sense of it than I can."

IN MY BUSINESS you pay attention when someone who works for a client is too friendly with a competitor. I didn't know if Chuck's relationship with Galen Wells was unusual in the academic community, but I'd certainly ask Kendra Crawford. I printed out a copy of Chuck's letter and stuck it and the article in my pocket.

We got Chuck's possessions packed that afternoon and wrapped them to mail home. Mrs. Nishimura took surprisingly little, only a few boxes. The rest she set aside for the lab or packed up for charity. She was businesslike and efficient as we sorted and packed, but when the job was done, she seemed to sink under the weight of emotional exhaustion. Her shoulders slumped and she seemed barely able to lift her feet as she walked.

It was clear she needed to go back to the hotel, and I didn't want to make her wait while I loaded the boxes for the lab, so I decided to pick them up later. She didn't say a word on the ride back, and when she thanked me, it was with the thin, strained voice of an old woman.

I drove back to the apartment to pick up the boxes of files and disks. As I was walking down the path to Chuck's apartment, a door opened behind me and a tall guy in a white tee shirt poked his head out and called to me. "Say, you the lady's picking up Chuck's things?"

"Yes."

"Just a minute there," he said, stepping back into the apartment. He emerged carrying something in his hand and hurried toward me. His skin was the color of white paste, and his long brown hair was pulled back in a ponytail. There was something wrong with his left leg, so he walked with a lopsided, swinging gait.

"You a family member?" he asked.

"No, I'm a colleague. I'm helping his mother. She was here earlier."

"Well, could you give her this?" he said, thrusting a pile of mail into my hand. "And could you ask her to notify the post office so the mail goes to her?"

"Sure," I said. "Thanks for keeping the mail."

"No trouble. Too bad about Chuck. He was a nice guy. She won't be wanting the rats, will she?"

"The rats?" I asked.

"Pinto, Poco, Chub, and Twitch. Chuck's four rats. He gave them to me about a week before he died."

"No," I said. "I don't think his mother will want the rats. I'll ask her, but I expect she'll want you to have them."

He smiled, revealing a missing upper incisor. "They're doing really well. Poco and Pinto have put on a lot of weight, just like he said they would. They're almost as big as Chub and Twitch now."

"That's nice," I said, thinking how grateful I was that Chuck had bestowed his rats on his apartment manager before he'd died. I'm very fond of Molly's gray mouse, but I don't much like rats. And I was just as glad not to have to handle a multiple adoption.

"Well, gotta go," he said. "I left dinner on the stove." With that he spun around and made his way back to the front unit.

I sorted through the mail in my hands. A couple of advertising circulars, three charity solicitations, a credit card offer, and two bank statements. I wondered as I entered Chuck's apartment what the law says about opening a dead person's mail. I didn't wonder long, just until I found a knife.

The first statement was for a checking account. Beginning balance was $527. Ending balance was $584. The summary showed one direct deposit of $1,150, which was probably his fellowship, and a slew of checks. The only revelation from the canceled checks was that Chuck was very fond of pizza and bought his groceries at Safeway.

The second statement was the surprise. It was for a savings account that contained a nice round twenty thousand dollars.

It was after five when I got back to the lab. Raskin was gone, but Kendra and several students were there. She delegated Dorian and Rick to bring the boxes up from my car. "And no whining," she ordered Dorian before he could open his mouth.

As soon as they were gone, I closed the office door and handed Kendra the article and the copy of the letter I'd found at Chuck's. "Any idea why Chuck would be interested in Galen Wells's work? Or why Wells would be interested in Chuck's?" I asked. She read the article and letter, frowned, then read them again. When she picked up her pencil and began tapping the eraser on the desktop, I knew she was taking them seriously.

Finally, she looked up at me and shrugged. "I have no idea what it's about," she said. "I know Galen, of course. He used to teach here in Nutrition. But there's no overlap in our research. He's never been interested in plants."

"There's something else," I said, handing her the bank statement. "It may be connected or may not. Did you hear anything about Chuck coming into a sum of money recently?"

"No," she said. "You're sure it's recent?"

"Check the beginning date for the statement. It doesn't cover a full month. That probably means the account was established less than thirty days ago."

"Have you asked Mrs. Nishimura?"

"No, but I will tomorrow, when I explain that this statement got mixed in with some other papers."

Crawford started tapping the pencil again. "He shouldn't have that kind of money," she said.

"If he didn't come by it honestly, I'd bet on theft or blackmail," I said. "I think you'd better check on any expensive equipment that's portable."

Molly was still enthusiastic about working in the office, even when Amy put her on cleanup and plant maintenance duty. The kid who scoured the coffee room at the office was not the same one who spent the evening inventing excuses for why she couldn't get to the dishes.

After dinner and before our nightly battle about the dishes, I asked about school.

"I got a B on my history quiz," she announced.

"Great."

"It's no big deal," she said. "And I'm still bored. I've got another dumb English paper to write."

"What's it on?"

She rolled her eyes. "I'm supposed to describe some dumb person I know. Boring."

"Why don't you write it as if you were briefing a lawyer about a witness he'd never met. They want a description that lets them recognize the person when they walk in the room and prepares them for the kind of responses they'll get during questioning."

"You do that? I mean, you write stuff like that?"

"Occasionally. Peter does it all the time."

"Okay," she said. "I could do that. I think I'll describe Chris."

*   *   *

Kyle called that night to ask how Jesse's investigation was going. I had the feeling that I had become his new project. "What do you know about Biosolutions?" I asked.

"What?" he said. "Is that a laundromat chain?"

"Come on, Kyle, it's a biotech firm. Don't tell me you haven't heard of them."

"Actually, I have. They're working on ... wait a minute, I'll get it, they're working on ... cholesterol reduction. No, no, that's somebody else. Biosolutions is ... insulin. Am I right?"

"You got it. Founder's a former Cal professor named Galen Wells. Do you know him?"

There was a pause, then Kyle admitted he didn't. "But I could if it was worth something to you."

"How much?"

"Dinner, dancing, whatever."

"Dinner and dancing," I said. "No whatever."

"We'll see," he said. "I'll get back to you."

I knew Kyle would get back to me. I knew he'd find out things I couldn't. But I still wanted to meet Galen Wells and see what he had to say about Chuck Nishimura.

The next morning I called Kendra Crawford. She assured me that she could get the information I wanted over the phone.

"Do you tell your doctor how to treat you when you're sick?" I asked.

"No. What's this got to do with my doctor?"

"It has to do with hiring someone and trusting them to know their business," I said. I say that a lot. People pay more attention to the advice of halfwit cousins than they do to an investigator.

It sounded as if the line had gone dead. Finally Crawford said, "All right."

Next I called Biosolutions and asked for an appointment with Galen Wells. The two lures most people find irresistible are the opportunity to make money and the chance to talk about themselves. I offered Wells the latter. I told his secretary I was writing a profile of former professors who'd started their own companies. Fifteen minutes and a detailed vita was all I'd need, I promised.

She checked with her boss and gave me an eleven forty-five appointment. "He has to leave exactly at noon," she warned me.

I took extra time with my makeup and chose a teal dress that was softer and more feminine than the suits I wear when I'm trying to remind people that they're under scrutiny. I accented it with a scarf in shades of blue and green and wore my fancy suede heels that feel like stilts compared to the comfortable low-heeled pumps my feet prefer.

I arranged to see Mrs. Nishimura before my appointment with Wells. She sounded pleased to hear from me and I decided to leave San Francisco early so that I could spend extra time with her if she was in the mood to talk.

She looked a little better than she had the day before. Getting the packing done must have been a relief.

She thanked me for my help and invited me to have a cup of coffee with her. The hotel is located at the Berkeley Marina and sits right at the edge of the bay. Its restaurant has a terrific view of the water and San Francisco beyond.

We got a seat by a window. The sky was overcast. We looked out on a world of grays—smooth pearl above, choppy slate below, with the Oz-like silhouette of San Francisco, the delicate span of the Golden Gate, and the dark mountains of Marin strung between them.

We chatted for a few minutes, and when there was a pause, I handed Mrs. Nishimura the mail and the bank statements. "The apartment manager was holding these for you," I said. "He wanted to know if he could keep Chuck's rats."

"His what?"

"Chuck had four rats that he gave the manager a week before he died," I said.

She looked surprised and a bit perturbed. "Of course he can keep them," she said. "I had no idea Chuck had rats. He never liked rodents as a child. He was always afraid of the one at preschool."

Four rats were a lot for someone who didn't like rodents. Unless they weren't pets. Before I could ask more, Mrs. Nishimura said, "Oh, good, there's a bank statement. I'm glad to have this. I was wondering about his bankbook. I didn't find it. Did you?"

"No," I said, wondering if we might not have been the only people to visit Chuck's apartment. "The statements got mixed in with lab notes, but I didn't find a bankbook. You're sure it wasn't with the things you sorted?" It was a dumb question to ask a woman so bereaved that she'd barely been able to address boxes to her own home.

She shook her head. "I didn't think of it then, but I'm sure I didn't see it. I thought it must be among his papers."

"I'll check for you," I said, but I was thinking, "Damn, I wonder what else disappeared from that apartment before we got there." Chuck's backpack with his keys in it had been at the greenhouse for over twenty-four hours.

I was anxious to see Mrs. Nishimura's reaction to the bank statements, but she left them lying on the table. I realized she wouldn't open them while I was there, so I excused myself and went to the ladies' room.

When I got back, she had the savings statement laid out in front of her. She looked perplexed.

"He had twenty thousand dollars," she said as soon as I sat down. "Wherever did he get that kind of money?"

My question exactly. Inheritance, I suggested, a gift, payment for a previous job? Her answer was no to all three.

As I looked at the exhausted, grieving woman across

from me, I longed for an answer that would leave her memory of her son intact. I shook my head involuntarily.

24

BIOSOLUTIONS WAS ONLY about five minutes from the Marriott, just across the freeway and about eight blocks north in the industrial section of Berkeley. The area reflects the changes American industry is undergoing. Some of the old factories still function, but a lot have been replaced by service-oriented businesses whose architects specialize in turning warehouse grunge into nineties chic. I think of the area as meat and potatoes meets quiche and sushi.

Biosolutions' building had not benefited, or suffered, from the attentions of an architect. It was an honest, square, stucco-covered box, unlovely, but utilitarian. Inside, a receptionist who didn't look old enough to be out of high school directed me down a hall to Galen Wells's secretary.

It was a smallish operation, judging from the number of offices. The majority of the building was probably lab space, but that was sealed off from view.

Wells's secretary could have been the receptionist's mother. She was an attractive brown-haired woman who studied me from behind thick glasses. She began by reminding me that "Dr. Wells" had to leave "right at noon," then handed me a packet with information on the company, Wells's vita, and a black-and-white photo that was the same one I'd seen in the newspaper article.

Wells was younger than I'd expected, probably in his mid-thirties. He was just under six feet, medium build, with a softness to his body that suggested inactivity. His face had a boyish quality, accented by the shock of sandy-blond hair that slipped down over his forehead. A pleasant face, though the nose and ears were a half size too big for the rest of it.

He greeted me warmly and I thanked him for his time.

"I'll do this quickly, I promise," I said. "Let me start by asking if you always wanted to start your own company."

"Oh, no," he said with a smile. "I was going to be a professor, settle into the halls of academe, do my research in the ivory tower." He pushed the shock of hair off his forehead. It slipped back down.

"What changed your mind?"

"I discovered that the university is like any other bureaucracy. More interested in rules and procedures than in getting things done. They'd rather talk about the way you list your supplies than the results of your research. And I found I didn't really enjoy teaching. I wanted to explore new areas, not serve undergraduates' career needs."

"So you decided to go out on your own."

"Well, it wasn't quite that easy," he said, taking another swipe at the errant shock of hair. "I was working on complex carbohydrate breakdown in bacteria, and I began to wonder what would happen if I could use a dietary supplement that would break down to glucose at a constant rate. I thought if you could better control sugar levels, you'd have a drug that could change the lives of millions of diabetics and hypoglycemics. I had other similar ideas for dietary supplements to improve nutrition. But I knew if I tried to work through the university it could take decades to do the research. I needed to have my own lab, to be able to focus on my work, and to fund it properly of course."

He began to describe that work in more detail, and as

he did, his voice became deeper, more resonant. His blue eyes radiated energy. He leaned toward me, drawing me in so that I felt his excitement as my own. Experiencing his charisma, I understood how he'd gotten investors to buy into his dream.

"So once I had those results," he continued, "I applied for a patent and went looking for people who could see the potential of my work and scientists who wanted to join me in doing real science."

"Sounds like a gamble," I said.

"Sure. That's part of the fun of it," he said. His eyes lit up as he talked about the risk, the difficulties of getting backing, the excitement of discovery. "You know, being at the university's like being a farmer. Once you've got tenure, you know the dirt is all yours, but there's no support and the university makes sure that no for-profit company can invest in your lab. If you don't want to do the sort of research currently funded by government agencies, then you have no crop. In the private sector, I raise money and take risks. It's a hell of a lot more fun."

"So the risk doesn't bother you?" I asked.

"Adds a bit of spice," he said with the same big smile.

"But your product isn't on the market yet," I said. "If your trials aren't successful, you could lose everything."

"Won't happen," he said confidently. "Oh, sometimes things take a little longer than expected, but we're very sure we have a solid product." He checked his watch to remind me that time was short.

He didn't need to remind me. I had my own clock running. I asked a couple of quick, easy questions, then with three minutes left I said, "That's about it for my questions. I know you're very busy, but I wondered if one of your employees could give me a quick tour of the lab, just so I can describe it in my article."

"Oh, sure," he said. He pushed his chair back from the desk, but before he could rise, I said, "By the way, I think we have a friend in common. Chuck Nishimura. He's a graduate student at Cal."

His features froze for a split second, then he shook his head, "No, I don't think I recognize the name. But, of course, I had a lot of students."

"Then he never worked with you here?"

"Oh, no," he said. "Well, not with me, I suppose it's possible that he might have been a summer hire." He rose from his desk and he was still smiling his easy, confident smile but his voice was slightly higher and there was tension in his jaw as he ushered me out.

Wells's secretary called a supervisor to give me a tour of the lab. A man with a bushy mustache and thinning hair combed across the top of his head appeared. He introduced himself as Henry Porrill and led me toward a plain, unmarked door.

The temperature in the warehouse was at least seventy-five degrees and the air conditioners were working overtime. Stainless-steel barrels and vats lined the walls, and the warehouse floor was filled with rows of boxes the size of small rooms. As we walked close to one, I realized they hummed. My guide informed me that they were flow hoods used to ensure sterility.

Except for the sound of the machinery, the room was silent. The only signs of human presence were the white rumps of seated, lab-coated technicians that stuck out into the corridors between the boxes. The space was immaculate.

But what interested me most was what wasn't there. There was no sign of corn, either plants or kernels.

"Is your other facility just like this one?" I asked as we were walking back to the main door.

"What other facility?" he asked.

"I thought you had another building," I said.

"No, this is it."

As I left, I stopped at Wells's secretary's office and thanked her for the tour. Then as I left, I dropped one of my business cards in front of her desk where she couldn't miss it. It would be interesting to see what Galen Wells would do when he realized I was an investigator.

I was only a matter of blocks from the Albany greenhouse, so I decided to stop in there before going back to campus. I needed to know more about Chuck Nishimura. Since a man's enemies often tell you things his friends won't, it was time to talk to Ethan Mather.

An old white Chevette was parked in front of the greenhouse, and I found Teri Shaw inside the building in the middle of a row of mature plants. She was holding a waxed-paper envelope with what I assumed must be pollen in it and was shaking the contents onto the silks of an immature ear.

"Hello," I said.

She was so intent on her work that she jumped when I spoke. When she looked up at me, I was struck by the size of her eyes and the depth of their blue color. She was a very attractive young woman.

"Oh, hello," she said. "You're the detective, aren't you?"

"Yes."

"I was just taking care of Chuck's plants," she said, looking down at the ear she was holding. I remembered that she'd been Chuck's girlfriend and realized that his death must have hit her especially hard.

She sniffed and said, "I can't believe he's gone. I mean, Thursday he was kidding around and Friday he was gone." She looked up at me with tears in her eyes. "It just doesn't seem possible."

I nodded.

"I can't believe he was so careless. I get so angry when I think about it. I guess that's pretty stupid, to be angry at someone you cared about for dying." She looked away as if she was embarrassed by the unseemly emotion.

"It's pretty normal, actually," I said.

"It is?" She looked relieved.

"You knew Chuck pretty well. Do you know if he ever worked for a biotech firm?" I asked.

She thought for a minute, then shook her head. "Not that I know of. He might have, but he never mentioned it to me. Of course, we only met last September." She slipped a paper bag over the ear she'd been holding.

"I suppose most people at the lab knew about Chuck's allergies," I said. "Did they all know about his mask?"

"Yeah, I think everyone knew. I mean, they all worked together, and Chuck was always on Rick's case about taking precautions."

"Who else knew?" I asked. "The other people down here?"

"You mean the bio-control guys? Sure, they probably did. Everyone understands about allergies."

"How about Ethan Mather?"

"He's the grass guy, isn't he? I know he knew because he and Chuck used to fight a lot, and once he said something about Chuck's allergies being nature's way of telling him he was in the wrong business. I thought it was pretty insensitive. Why do you ask?"

"Just curious," I said.

"Oh," she said. She sniffed again and put the waxed envelope back in her corn apron and took another one out. "I guess I better get back to the corn."

I felt sorry for her. She was so young, and working so hard at being grown up. Looking at her, I understood Kendra Crawford better. You bottle your emotions up that tight, in time you're bound to have a short fuse.

I left her in the greenhouse and went looking for Mather. I found him on his hands and knees pulling green shoots from a patch of ground that was covered with neatly planted patches of grassy foliage. He wore a blue baseball cap and his long ponytail hung down behind it. His jeans and white tee shirt were clean but faded and frayed.

"Hi," I said.

He turned and squinted up at me, then got to his feet. "Hello," he said. "I know I know you, but I'm sorry, I've forgotten your name."

"We were never actually introduced," I said. "My name's Catherine Sayler, and I've been helping with some problems at the Crawford lab. I was at Raymond's memorial service."

He nodded. "Yeah, sure. And I think I saw you here once, too."

"That's right, with Chuck Nishimura."

His features tightened just a fraction, I couldn't read the expression. "Pretty awful thing," he said. I wasn't sure whether he was talking about Chuck's death or Raymond's, or both.

I agreed. He stared down at the ground, then looked up and asked, "What can I do for you?"

"Someone at the lab sabotaged several people's work. Chuck was one of the victims. I was hoping you could tell me how people felt about him."

He looked away, staring into the distance. "I don't know about the others. I didn't like him much, but then I don't like many of the wunderkinder."

His voice had a hard edge of derision, and a hefty undercurrent of superiority. I could see why he was considered a pain in the ass. "Why not?"

The left side of his mouth contracted in a slight grimace. "They're young and arrogant and they think they own the world," he said. "And Crawford's bunch is the worst. They're so sure that biotechnology will solve all the planet's problems, they've forgotten to tune in to the real world. They *say* they're interested in basic research, but it's mostly just an ego trip."

"Julie Chun was another victim," I said.

"Now, Julie's different from the others," he said, turning to face me. "She's a really fine person. She has a real sense of values."

I liked him better for that. "She told me that she and

Raymond were both members of Small World. Are you a member, too?" I asked.

"Sure am. I'm one of the founders. The rest of Crawford's people don't give a damn about anything but their careers. They don't have a clue." He jammed his hands in the pockets of his jeans. "They play around in their labs and ignore what's happening in the world, but it's all connected. When people are starving, they do desperate things. And when you poison soil or water in one part of the globe, you're poisoning your own backyard."

He spoke with real passion. And anger.

"Did Raymond tell you much about what was going on at the lab?" I asked.

"Only general stuff."

"He had something he was going to tell me the day he died," I said. "Did you see him around that time? Do you have any idea what it might have been?"

He made the slight grimace again. "I saw him Tuesday. I could tell something was bothering him. I even asked, but he wouldn't tell me."

I got a quick lunch at a place that advertised itself as the Nothing Fancy Café and served amazingly good Mexican food with free salsa verde, then headed back to the campus, the "ivory tower" Galen Wells had been so anxious to escape. Having met the man myself, I was curious to have Kendra Crawford's take on him.

I'd expected the lab to be almost empty, but most of the students were there. There was no chatting or laughter; everyone was intent on their work. As I walked in, I heard Kendra say to Raskin, "Call Scott and Tony again. I want them in here. We're falling way behind. I need their write-ups for the proposal by Friday at the latest." Her voice was sharp with irritation.

As soon as she caught sight of me, she motioned me into her office. "Catherine, in here," she ordered in the tone she used with her students.

I stopped in the doorway. "Excuse me," I said, the edge on my voice matching the one on hers.

"Close the door," she said.

I stepped in and closed it, but before she could say anything, I said, "I know you're used to ordering people around, but I don't work that way."

"You don't work for me at all," she said angrily. "I got a call from my department chair about twenty minutes ago, chewing me out for having a private eye snooping around."

"Twenty minutes," I said. "Even faster than I'd expected."

"What?"

"Did your chair tell you how he'd found out you'd hired me?"

"A colleague, someone who's highly respected in the field, called to ask what the hell was going on."

I couldn't help smiling, which annoyed her even more. "You don't seem to understand the seriousness of this," she said.

"Oh, I understand all right. It means we've got a hit. Galen Wells is not only involved in your problem, he's mighty nervous about being found out."

"You think it was Wells?"

"I'd put money on it. I saw him just before noon and managed to drop into the conversation that we had a mutual friend, Chuck Nishimura. He denied it, but it rattled him enough that he's putting on pressure to force you to back off."

Crawford considered my point. She picked up her pencil and began her annoying habit of tapping it on the desk. "But what the hell has Wells got to do with Chuck?"

25

"**H**OW WELL DO you know Galen Wells?" I asked Crawford.

"Pretty well. We were colleagues for several years."

"Tell me about him."

"He's brilliant and ambitious, quite charismatic actually. He never really fit in here. I don't think anyone was surprised when he left just before the tenure decision."

"What do you mean by didn't 'fit in'?"

"He was impatient with the system, hated teaching, hated the bureaucracy, couldn't or wouldn't hide his feelings about it all. I mean, we all hate the bureaucracy, the red tape can drive you nuts, but you learn to play the game. And Galen just wasn't interested in doing that.

"Early in his career a British pharmaceutical firm wanted to give his lab a million pounds. Their lawyers flew in. After twenty minutes with the university's patent folks, the lawyers walked out, right past Wells, without saying a word, and just took off into the friendly skies. He never got over it."

"Was there ever any indication he was unethical?"

"Not that I know of. He's a good scientist, a brilliant scientist. It's just that the university isn't for everybody."

"I know it's probably hard for you to accept," I said, "but your old colleague is your new worst enemy. You can pull me off the job, but that won't get him off your back."

"How can you be so sure he's involved?"

"The timing of your call from the department chair. Think about it."

She did, tapping the pencil all the while. Finally, she said, "What do you advise?"

"First, I'd suggest you get the campus police to find out who wrote that twenty-thousand-dollar check to Chuck." I gave her a photocopy of Chuck's bank statement. I didn't mention that I'd kept a copy for myself. It's damn hard to get that kind of information, but not entirely impossible.

"Then, if you want me to continue, I'll do some checking on Wells, try to figure out if there's any reason he'd want to disrupt your lab."

More tapping, then she nodded. "All right," she said.

"One last question," I said. "Was there ever anything between you and Wells that would give him personal reasons for wanting to hurt you professionally?"

She waited long enough before answering that I knew there was. Finally, she said, "We had a 'thing' a number of years ago, while he was still at Cal. I broke it off after about six months, and he took it rather badly. Not that he cared for me that much. But it hurt his pride. I don't think he ever forgave me."

I stared at her in amazement, wondering how long she'd have waited before she decided to share that bit of information with me. Wondering, too, what else she might be keeping to herself.

Jesse was finishing up his report for the larcenous chip maker when I got back to the office.

"Read this for me and see if it works," he said.

"You mean check to see that you left enough room between the lines?"

"That and that my suspicions aren't as obvious to the client as I hope they are to the insurance company," he said with a wicked smile.

The report was a masterpiece of the unsaid. The client

would probably read it as a straightforward if overly detailed statement of Jesse's investigation. A sharp insurance investigator would see red flags flying.

"You sure it's okay to do this?" he said. "I mean, these guys *are* our clients. Is it ethical to screw them like this?"

"The ethics might be a bit questionable," I said. "But it has a lovely twisted morality to it, don't you think?"

Jesse looked worried. "I'm supposed to be the wild child here," he said. "You are supposed to be the voice of reason."

"Screw that," I said.

With the chip case finished, Jesse tried to sucker me into taking half of the pile of papers stacked dangerously high on his desk. I left him complaining about poor team spirit.

I started a background check on Wells and Biosolutions that afternoon, but I knew that Kyle was much more likely to turn up something useful than I was. I called to see how he was coming along.

"Wow, talk about psychic connection," he said. "I think of you and you call. With that kind of long-distance energy, can you imagine what sex would be like?"

I couldn't. I wouldn't. Sex was on its way to becoming a distant memory. "Biosolutions," I said. "Speak to me about Biosolutions."

"Sex is a biosolution."

"Death is also a biosolution, Kyle," I said. "What about Galen Wells?"

"I don't talk about other men over the phone," he said. "But I do have something for you. I'll pick you up at five. We're taking the ferry to dinner in Tiburon, so dress warmly. Underwear is optional."

"In your dreams," I said. "I'm missing my aikido class for this. It had better be good."

"Oh, it is. I promise you won't be disappointed."

"And I promise you will be," I said.

I finished up quickly at the office, so Molly and I could

have a little time at home together before Kyle picked me up at five. Of course, she wanted to work late. I only got her out early because Amy sided with me.

"You're going out to dinner with that guy again?" Molly said.

"It's purely business," I said.

She gave me a look that was an exact duplicate of the one I use on her when she's shining me on, and for a moment I felt like a guilty fifteen-year-old. "He's a friend of Peter's," I said.

"Sure. Poor Peter's tramping through some Guatemalan jungle, and you're having dinner with some other guy."

I didn't tell her that in all likelihood "poor Peter" was tramping through that jungle with Alicia Adavi. "How's your English class?" I asked in retaliation.

"Still boring, but I turned in my paper on time," she said. "And I got a B on the algebra test. Satisfied?"

"That's terrific. I knew you could do it. Aren't you pleased?"

She sighed, a heavy fifteen-year-old sigh. "It's not such a big deal," she said.

Molly shot to the front door when the bell sounded. "Hello," she said to a startled Kyle, "I'm Molly. Please come in."

"This is my daughter," I said, giving Molly an evil smile, "the product of a youthful indiscretion."

"I consider it my job to make sure she doesn't repeat past mistakes," Molly said, returning my smile.

Kyle just stood and stared at us.

"Actually, Molly is my niece," I said. "It seems she's also appointed herself my moral guardian. She wants to make sure that your intentions are honorable."

"My intentions are never honorable, Molly," he said. "Your aunt will be late tonight."

* * *

It was just getting dark as we parked near the Ferry Building and walked to the dock behind it. The building is a reminder of older, slower times when visitors to San Francisco arrived after a sail across the bay. The bay's smaller now, thanks to numerous fill projects, and the Ferry Building, once one of the city's proudest buildings, is dwarfed by modern high-rises.

We joined the line of tired men and women in business suits making their nightly commute home. As we boarded the sleek ferry with its bar and comfortable seats, I thought that if you had to commute, this was the way to do it.

Then something struck me and I stopped just inside the door. "This is a commuter ferry, Kyle," I said. "Does it come back to San Francisco?"

"First thing in the morning."

"Good night, Kyle." I turned back toward the gangplank, but he stopped me with a hand on my arm.

"Hey, it was a joke. I had my assistant leave the Jag over there," he said, giving me his best disarming smile. He didn't fool me for a minute, but I smiled back, thinking that at least I could count on him to be consistent.

"Can I get you wine or something harder?" he asked as the ferry pulled away from the dock.

"White wine would be nice," I said. "I'll be out on deck."

It was a mild evening, but the wind was still brisk and cold. I was glad I had on a warm jacket. Still, the view was worth the discomfort. San Francisco was a city of lights, the buildings just dark shapes against the darker sky, their lit windows like cutout peepholes into a hidden shining world.

Near the dock they loomed over us, close enough that you could actually make out some of the features of the lighted rooms. As we pulled out into the bay, they shrank and became a spectacular backdrop.

Kyle joined me at the rail and handed me a glass of

wine. "Nice way to see the city, isn't it?" he said. "In a few months when it warms up, I'll take you night sailing on my boat. It's even more beautiful that way."

"Peter and I'd love that," I said.

Kyle groaned.

"So tell me what you found out about Galen Wells."

"You are such an impatient woman," he said. "I'll bet you always peeked at your Christmas packages."

When I didn't respond, he gave in. "Okay, I'll tell you now. Two tidbits, each interesting. Together, *very* interesting." He paused for effect. "Biosolutions was supposed to go for a public stock offering this spring; but they've postponed it. Rumor has it that the new drug isn't progressing the way they expected, and they may be at least a year behind schedule.

"Now, that's just a whisper, not even a real rumor yet. But it's interesting. Second tidbit is even better. A guy I know was approached by Wells several weeks ago about a new start-up company. The principal researcher is a newcomer, a former student. Wells was very cagey, claimed he couldn't talk about the product yet. All he'd say was that it would be bigger than NutraSweet."

"Bigger than NutraSweet? What's that supposed to mean?"

"I don't know. My friend tried to get something more specific because he was curious as hell, but Wells wouldn't talk."

"Is that common?" I asked. "Is that how you guys operate? I've got a secret, give me money and I'll tell you?"

"No, of course not. But it's an interesting strategy for testing the waters. Sort of like fishing. You toss some bait out and watch to see who acts most interested."

"What do you think he's got?"

"Damned if I know. But NutraSweet's a food product, so I wouldn't be surprised if it has something to do with food."

"Corn syrup's a major sweetener," I said. "Could that be the connection?"

"You tell me. You're the one who's working with the corn people."

I shrugged. We were far enough out into the bay so that the wind was stronger and I shivered inside my jacket. But looking back at the sparkling city and the strings of lights that outlined the Bay and Golden Gate bridges, I wasn't about to go inside.

NutraSweet was not just a sweetener; it was a diet aid. Sweetness without calories. Something tugged at my memory. Two of Chuck's rats had been putting on weight since he gave them away. Thin rats. Skinny mice. That was the connection I'd been struggling for since I heard of the rats. The skinny mice in the greenhouse.

And that wasn't all. There was Raymond Zak's unexpected weight loss. He'd mentioned it in the coffee shop and his friends had commented on it at the funeral.

Kyle's voice interrupted my thoughts. "You look as if you've got bells going off all over the place," he said. "Talk to me."

Normally, Kyle was the last person I'd have told about the case. But with Peter gone and Jesse away so much, I missed having someone to discuss work with. Besides, I told myself, the case fit right into his expertise. Maybe he'd see things I missed. So I told him about Kendra Crawford's lab, Raymond's and Chuck's deaths. The whole thing.

There's a feeling of elation when the pieces of a case begin to come together. Random facts take on significance; things that made no sense fit a pattern. It can be infectious, and it had that effect on Kyle. He gave up his flirtatious games and plunged into it with me.

"So you figure that Wells's product has to do with weight loss," he said.

"It fits," I said. "And it'd be worth a lot of money, wouldn't it?"

"Oh, hell, yes. In this country the diet industry is a multimillion-dollar business. And it's growing. Any product that can actually cause weight loss would be worth a fortune, several fortunes."

We were past Alcatraz now, and the water seemed choppier. A gust of wind peppered my face with drops of briny sea spray.

"We don't know what it is, but we do know it came from Crawford's lab," Kyle continued. "Who found it— Zak or Nishimura?"

"Nishimura, I think. Zak seemed genuinely surprised that he was losing weight, and I doubt that he'd have mentioned it to me if he'd been involved in the plot. He'd have wanted to hide it."

"So Nishimura found it, which explains the rats in his apartment and the twenty thou in his bank account."

"Whatever it is, it must be in Julie's corn," I said.

"Why Julie's?"

"Because of the skinny mice," I said.

Kyle looked at me as if I were a bit screwy. "The skinny mice?" he asked. "I think I missed that one."

I told him about the skinny mice in the greenhouse. "That's where Julie's corn was drying. And it was the only corn there. Chuck must have noticed the mice and realized that something in the corn was affecting them."

"So Nishimura sees the skinny mice and decides to feed the corn to rats to see how it affects them. They get skinny, too, and he figures he's going to be a millionaire. He feeds it to the fattest guy he can find. The fat guy dies. But if the corn killed the fat guy . . ."

"Raymond," I interrupted. "His name was Raymond." It annoyed me to hear the gentle lab tech reduced to "the fat guy."

"Okay, but if it killed Raymond, then it's not going to be any good as a commercial product. I mean, people want to get thin, not dead."

"We're not sure what killed Raymond. He had some medical problems, so he might have been a special case. It's also possible that Raymond found out, that he was going to tell me about the corn, and Chuck or someone else killed him to keep him quiet."

"But who killed Chuck?"

"That," I said, "is the big question."

"Wells?"

"Why would he kill the person who was going to help him develop the product?"

Kyle straightened up, turned, and leaned his back against the rail. "Doesn't make sense," he said. After a couple of minutes of silent thought, he added, "I need more fuel. You want another glass of wine?"

We had a wonderful dinner of mesquite-grilled shrimp at Guaymas in Tiburon. The restaurant sits on the water, near the dock, and we had a table next to the window so that we looked out across the dark bay at the lights of San Francisco in the distance.

Anyone watching us would have seen a couple so intensely involved in conversation that they seemed unaware of food, wine, and even the shimmering beauty of the view. They would probably have assumed that a great love was flowering. They'd have been wrong. What animated our passion that night was not romance but murder.

26

I WOKE THE next morning with a slight headache from too much wine and a sullen, reproachful niece. A small price to pay for the information Kyle had brought.

I got to the lab at nine-thirty, only to find that Julie hadn't come in yet. I went downstairs and got a cup of coffee, then sat on the patio, hoping to spot her when she arrived.

About twenty minutes later she emerged from the parking lot elevator and headed across to the Genetics Building. The backpack she was carrying didn't look particularly heavy, but she moved slowly and there was no spring in her step.

I called to her and motioned her to join me.

"Hi," she said. "I'm afraid I can't stop. Kendra's on a tear because we've fallen behind on the research. Even though my project isn't part of either proposal, she's laid down the law that everyone has to be there. She had me working on some of Chuck's stuff yesterday." There was exhaustion and more than a little resentment in her voice.

"Sit down for a minute," I said. "This is important. I'll cover for you with Kendra."

She nodded and sank into the chair. I checked around us and decided that there wasn't anyone near enough to overhear our conversation.

"I need your help. There's something going on that I don't understand, but your research is at the center of it. First, I think that the person who stole your corn used it in an experiment involving rats. I don't know exactly what he did with it, but I'm guessing he used it as a feed, and the result was that the rats lost weight."

"But why would . . . ? Oh, wait a minute, that was around the time of the skinny mice. In the greenhouse." She started to explain, "You see . . ."

"I know about the skinny mice," I said. "They must have been eating your corn. The question is what was there about that corn that caused the mice to lose weight?"

"Maybe they just didn't like it, so they didn't eat it."

"It must have been something more than that," I said, "because after the experiment with the rats, someone paid a lot of money for the corn."

She looked confused. "Who? Who has my corn?"

"Don't worry about that," I said. "I'll explain all that later. But first I need to know what's going on with the corn. Could it have caused animals to lose weight?"

She gave me a puzzled look. "I don't see how. The mutation I'm studying affects plant growth. It shouldn't have any effect at all on the nutritional quality of the corn."

"Don't answer too quickly," I said. "I'm sure there's something there if you can just put the pieces together."

She stared at me for a moment, then leaned back and gazed up at the building as she thought it through. Her eyes took on a blank, unseeing look.

Suddenly she sat up straight, jumped to her feet, and ran for the building. "I've got to tell Kendra," she called as she ran.

I followed Julie upstairs. By the time I got there, she was already in Kendra's office with the door closed. I could see the two of them huddled over a sheet of paper, Julie drawing and talking excitedly.

They didn't even notice when I came into the room. I couldn't understand much of what Julie was saying, but I didn't need words to tell me what was going on. Energy radiated from the two women, and it built as Kendra questioned and commented on what Julie had told her. At several points they were talking at the same time, seemingly undisturbed by the overlap.

Suddenly, Kendra shouted, "Yes. Yes," and jumped up from her chair. She and Julie hugged. When they parted, they just stared at each other for a moment. Kendra murmured, "Oh my God." Her face was flushed with excitement.

Julie's face mirrored Kendra's excitement. She was radiant. She opened her mouth a couple of times, but words didn't come.

I felt out of place, to say the least. The quality of the emotion was orgasmic, too personal for an outside observer.

My presence hadn't even registered with the women. But when they became aware of me, they enveloped me in their excitement.

"You must think we're crazy," Kendra said. "And we are. A discovery like this is so rare. You're blessed if it happens once in a lifetime.

"Finding what you expect, proving what you think is true, that's no big deal. It's important, but ..." She shrugged, dismissing it. "When the pieces come together and the picture is something you didn't even dream of, well"—she smiled and nodded happily—"it's ... it's great."

She turned to Julie. "This is going to be terrific for you. You have arrived, my dear. We'll put this together, publish it in *Nature*, and departments'll be begging you to come. You can write your own ticket."

Julie beamed, and I watched in wonder as the cold, driving woman I'd known heaped praise on the postdoc. It wasn't just her manner that seemed transformed. Her voice was deeper and warmer, and her face glowed with excitement and joy.

"We've got to tell the lab," she said. She flung open the door and called Paul. "Tell everyone to come to the conference room. I want them all to share in this." Given the situation around the discovery, I'd have preferred to keep it quiet, but that clearly wasn't going to be an option.

The tone of Kendra's voice was enough to get everyone's curiosity piqued. The professor grabbed Julie by the arm and they hurried down the hall talking excitedly. The students who followed them traded startled looks.

In the conference room, Kendra beamed at the students. "This is a day you'll remember for the rest of your careers," she said. "Julie, tell them."

Julie took her place at the head of the table and began describing her work. Most of what she said was way over my head, but I understood enough to learn that Kendra and Julie believed something in the mutant corn suppressed appetite.

As Julie talked, you could feel the excitement build in the room. Students leaned forward; some of them nodded. I watched a smile bloom like a sunrise on Scott's face. The questions started as soon as Julie paused for breath, but this time there was no hostility, just curiosity and exhilaration.

There were several undergraduates in the room, and they seemed more confused than inspired, but all the graduate and postdoc students were completely caught up in the thrill of the discovery. They were a different group of people than I'd watched at the earlier lab meeting. When this meeting was over, old animosities seemed to have disappeared and they chattered excitedly to each other as they returned to the lab.

As the mass of excited scientists surged out the door, Paul Raskin appeared beside me. "You understand what's going on?" he asked.

I shook my head. "Only that everyone's very excited."

"Like an explanation?"

"Yes," I said. "I'm curious as hell."

We sat back down at the table and he began. "Interrupt me if this gets confusing," he said. He took a pen from his pocket and looked around for a piece of paper. He found an announcement for a seminar and turned it over to write on.

"Remember how I told you we found *Bonsai 4*—looking for mutants, then crossing them with a special strain to produce lots of jumping genes, then looking for the offspring that weren't dwarfs." He drew six tall, stick-figure corn plants, then an X and six short, stick plants. Beneath them he drew four short plants and two big ones and drew a circle around the tall plants.

"The offspring that looked normal were the ones where the jumping gene had landed in the *Bonsai 4* gene and messed it up, so those were the ones we were interested in. But, of course, in science any single effect can have any number of causes.

"We crossed a bunch of Bonsai 4s with normal corn. The offspring should all have been dwarfs, but some weren't. So you'd think that the *Bonsai 4* gene must have been screwed up, but it wasn't. It was normal. Those are the plants Julie's working with."

"How does that lead to an appetite suppressant?"

"*Bonsai 4* disrupts the receptors for GA3, gibberellic acid, that's the growth hormone. The plants stay small because they can't recognize the hormone. It's like a lock-and-key situation. *Bonsai 4* changes the lock so the GA3 can't fit into it and signal the plant to grow. Julie figured out that in her plants there'd been a further mutation that changed the GA3 itself. The altered GA3 sneaks through the Bonsai 4 receptor and restores the plant to normal size."

He paused and asked, "You with me?"

"I'm not sure. I see why the new mutation makes the plant bigger. I don't see why it affects appetite."

"That's the exciting part," he said. "GA3 is a plant steroid. The mutation must have changed it so that it acted like an animal steroid. One of the things steroids can do in animals is affect appetite. If the altered GA3 mimicked an animal steroid, it could affect the appetite of animals, or humans, who ate it. That's what we think must be going on.

"And that's what's so exciting to all of us. It isn't the effect on appetite; it's the idea of a plant steroid acting like an animal steroid. It's completely unexpected. It opens up hundreds of questions, whole new lines of research. It might explain some herbal medicines. . . ." His voice took on the same almost ecstatic excitement I'd heard in the others. His laid-back, just-doing-my-job pose disappeared and I could see the scientist beneath it.

Back in Kendra's office, some of the adrenaline was wearing off, but both Kendra and Julie still had goofy grins on their faces. Paul leaned against the door and watched them with bemused pleasure. I hated to burst their bubble, but it seemed like time to remind them that their breakthrough had a darker side.

"I hate to bring this up," I said, "but you're not the only ones pursuing this discovery. I'm fairly sure that it's the reason for the theft of Julie's corn and the other sabotage. It's also the most likely reason for the twenty thousand dollars in Chuck's savings account."

I told them about Galen Wells's claim that he had something "bigger than NutraSweet." As I talked, the joy drained out of their faces, replaced by grim concern.

"So you think Chuck figured out about the altered GA3 and stole the corn to give to Wells?" Kendra asked.

"He probably stole it to test it himself, though he could have done the test earlier with a small amount of corn. By the time Wells gave him the twenty thousand dollars he must have given him the corn. I'm guessing on that. But it fits."

Kendra was quiet for a few minutes. She picked up a pen from her desk and absentmindedly tapped it against her thigh. "The bastard," she said.

I didn't know if she meant Wells or Chuck. The epithet fit both. "There's still one piece missing," I said. "And it's the big one. Who killed Chuck?"

Julie almost jumped when I asked the question and her jaw dropped.

Kendra responded with irritation. "What do you mean, 'Who killed Chuck?' Chuck died in a stupid accident. That's all," she said impatiently, moving on immediately. "Galen's involvement complicates things. He'll probably try to beat us to a patent. I'm not going to let him get away with that."

The pen tapped faster against her thigh. "I'll have to talk to Al Perkins in Technology Transfer, but I don't want to leave it to them. We'll need a lawyer with experience in human hormone and growth substances."

She turned to Julie. "Get together your lab notes, corn cards, everything, so we can get the documentation started. That patent belongs to this lab, and you should be on it. It won't mean money, since the university gets that, but you deserve the recognition and I won't let Wells take that away."

Julie looked shell-shocked. No wonder. In less than an hour she'd discovered that her research could lead to a major scientific and commercial breakthrough, that a man she thought was her friend had stolen her research, and that his death, which she'd assumed was an accident, might be murder.

When she answered, her voice was shaky. "It'll take me a day or so to put everything together," she said. "Because of the sabotage, I've been keeping some of my stuff at home. And my notebook isn't completely up to date; there's data that I haven't entered yet."

"No problem," Kendra said. She turned to Paul. "Get someone to take over what Julie was doing. And give her whatever help she needs."

Paul gave a mock salute and escorted Julie out. Kendra turned back to me. "This patent business could be complicated. Galen will claim he got that corn someplace else. He may already have filed. If Julie doesn't have enough mutant seed to do the rodent tests now, we're three months behind him. Can you prove he stole the seed?"

I shook my head. "It's all circumstantial. Even if the police can trace Chuck's check back to him, he can just argue that it was in payment for some other kind of work. I think you'll need good legal advice on this one."

"I wish I trusted the university lawyers. They just don't have the expertise for a case like this." She stopped tapping the pen against her thigh and slapped it down on the desk. "I hate all this administrative crap," she said with feeling. "This is a great discovery. I can't wait to start unraveling what's going on, and I'll probably spend the next year fighting Galen Wells for the damn patent.

"But I can't let him steal it. It's too important to the lab. It'll get us out from under the thumb of the ag VP and his Sacramento cronies. If they handle it right, this patent could generate more money for the university than the entire ag budget.

"And it proves what I've been trying to tell these ag guys; the really big breakthroughs come from pure research. You'd never have gone looking for an appetite suppressant by studying the alteration of gibberellic acid."

"I hate to bring up an unpleasant subject," I said, "but there's still a murderer loose out there, and he or she is probably in your lab."

Kendra glowered at me. "I told you that the police consider Chuck's death an accident. As far as I'm concerned that issue is closed. In fact, since he was obviously the saboteur and he's dead, the problem I hired you for is solved. If you'll put together a report and a bill, I'll write you a check."

"You really don't seem to realize that both you and Julie could be in danger," I said. "Imagine, just for a minute, that I'm right and Chuck was murdered. We don't know why, but there's a good chance it's related to the discovery of the appetite suppressant. If it is, and the killer didn't get what he or she wanted, Julie is a possible target, and so are you. The murderer isn't going to want to let you develop this research."

She didn't even slow down to consider my point. Instead, she said, "It comes down to this. I don't believe anyone killed Chuck. I believe that Galen Wells wanted to steal my research, that he'll still try if he thinks he can get away with it, but with the full weight of the university behind me, I don't think he's going to be a problem. So I appreciate your time, your work, and the fact that you've opened up an exciting new line of research for this lab, but I no longer require your services."

I was stunned. With two people dead and a murderer on the loose, such denial was worse than irresponsible. It might well be deadly.

27

IT'S NOT THAT unusual for a client to decide he or she doesn't really want to know what I might find out and close the case. I've gotten used to being left with questions that won't get answered. But those questions have never involved murder, and I wasn't ready to just walk away from this one.

Julie was still surrounded by excited students. This was her big day and I didn't want to spoil it, but the stakes were too high to wait. I worked my way into the group and told her I needed her. Her colleagues were reluctant to let her go, but I led her down to the outside courtyard, where I could be sure no one was listening.

"What did you mean when you said someone killed Chuck?" she asked before I could say anything.

"It's true," I said. "Kendra doesn't want to believe it, but someone tampered with Chuck's mask. His death was no accident."

"Oh, no," Julie said, collapsing into a chair. "Why? Why would anyone do that?"

"I don't know," I said, "but that's why I wanted to talk to you. To warn you that you have to be very careful."

"You think someone might come after me?" she asked. She looked concerned but not frightened. Either she was still too high on the excitement of the discovery to recognize danger or her self-confidence had gotten such a boost that she no longer felt vulnerable. Usually a good development, but not now. Not for her.

"I think it's possible. You may be safer now that the secret of the discovery is more widely known, but there's no way to be certain. I think you should be extra careful about the things we discussed—make sure that there're always several other people around when you're at the lab, never go into the parking garage alone, and watch what you eat and drink."

"Having people around shouldn't be too hard," she said. "I'm really popular right now. Everyone wants to know what I'm doing and how they can be part of it."

"That brings me to another question," I said. "Did anyone show particular interest in your research during the last couple of months?"

"Chuck, of course." She shook her head. "I can't believe he was stealing my research. I feel pretty foolish thinking he was interested in me. Not that I was in love or anything. I told you I'm a real drudge. But he seemed like a good friend; I enjoyed talking about work with him." She wore a small amethyst ring on her right hand.

She took her ring finger in her other hand and began to turn the ring absentmindedly. Her nails had been bitten so far back that it hurt to look at them.

"Anyone else show an interest, in the work?"

"Scott. But with him I was pretty sure it was a way of trying to get something going. Still, he's a really bright person, and he did have some good insights. He taught me some valuable things."

"But you also told him about your research."

"Of course. There was nothing secret about what I was doing. I talked about it with anyone who asked."

"Who else asked?"

She shrugged and continued to turn the ring. "I don't know. Raisa, I guess. We talked several times when we were alone here at night. And Margot, she and Chuck were working together, so she was sometimes part of our discussions. And there were a couple of undergraduates—Bill Estes and Susan Eggers."

"Teri Shaw?"

"No, I don't think so."

"Did she resent it when Chuck started hanging out with you?"

"Not that I knew of. She was still friendly. In fact, with his death, she seems to feel as if we have some kind of a bond. I think it hit her much harder than it did me. She's really just a kid."

"She was in love, but she didn't resent the breakup?"

"I don't know," she said. "I'm not real good with emotional stuff."

Behind me, a voice called, "Hey, Julie, way to go." I turned to see a guy in jeans and a bomber jacket waving at us from the walkway. Julie called thanks and waved back. Word was spreading quickly.

"Okay, let's get back to the research," I said. "Who else was interested or worked with you on it?"

"No one. Except Paul, of course. He helped me out

several times. He knew what I was doing, but then, he knows what everyone is doing."

"So, Chuck, Scott, Raisa, Margot, Paul. And Bill and Susan. That's it?"

"That's it. You're really sure about Chuck? That he was killed?"

"As sure as I can be," I said.

Julie nodded, still trying to absorb the news. Then her face contracted into a stricken look. "Raymond," she said. "Raymond lost his appetite a week or two before he died. I remember him saying he just didn't feel like eating. And he was losing weight. You don't think . . ."

"I don't know," I said. "What do you think?"

"I—I don't know what to think." She leaned across the table toward me. "Could he have figured out about the appetite suppressant and decided to try it?"

"Possibly. Or possibly someone gave it to him, probably baked or mixed into some other kind of food, to see how it would affect him."

"Oh, no. No one would do that," she protested. "Not with a substance we knew so little about. One of the first things you learn is that you can't do human subject experiments. Not without approval."

"I don't know what happened," I said, "but I'm fairly sure that someone in the lab is very dangerous. I want you to be careful."

I left Julie looking very somber. Next life, I want to come back as someone who gets to deliver the good news.

There was no way I could poke around Kendra Crawford's lab without her approval, but I couldn't just let the case go. The only thing left to do was act the good citizen and make sure the UC police knew everything I could tell them.

At Cal, the campus police force is larger than some small-town departments. There was a time when their work involved mainly drying out drunken frat boys, but times being what they are, they now handle rape and murder as well.

Their office is in the basement of Sproul Hall, the administration building made famous by the Free Speech Movement and other sixties protests. These days in the plaza where thousands of demonstrators chanted defiance, tables are more likely to be manned by the Young Republicans than by the Young Socialists.

It took a while to locate the detective handling Chuck's death. He was a pleasant young man with red hair and freckles and a well-scrubbed quality that seemed out of place on the Berkeley campus. The plaque on his desk read DETECTIVE DREYER.

I told him about the results of my investigation. He nodded and made a few notes. He didn't ask questions. "Going through the motions" pretty much summed up the situation.

I gave him Detective Wilson's name and suggested they confer. He assured me the situation would be carefully investigated. Unkind words came to mind. I kept them to myself.

Next, I called Detective Wilson.

"I'm glad you called," he said. "We've got the autopsy results on Raymond Zak. There's no sign of foul play."

I told him what I'd learned about the appetite suppressant and Raymond's sudden loss of interest in eating. "Seems like a hell of a coincidence that he'd lose his appetite at just the time we think Chuck was testing the stolen corn to see if it had that effect."

"You think corn suppresses appetite?" Wilson asked sarcastically.

"It's the steroid in the corn, Detective. Crawford's lab is working on identifying the chemical."

"I might just leave that case open for a while," Wilson said. "No need to rush on it."

"Did the UC police contact you about the death at the greenhouse at the Gill Tract?" I asked.

"We knew about it, of course. But the investigation's their jurisdiction."

I told him about the videotape and the disappearing mask. "Another case of a too convenient coincidence," I said.

"What's UC say?"

"They're not inclined to share their thoughts with a civilian, but I get a strong impression that they're not taking what I told them very seriously."

"Lots of coincidence there," he said. "I don't much like coincidences."

"Neither do I."

The nightmares were back full force that night, and the dark-haired woman I associated with Julie played a major role. In one, I struggled to reach her from the other side of a river and watched helplessly as she was cut down by a dark faceless figure that turned into a bird and came after me. In another, I pulled her into the river with me, only to realize that the water had turned to blood and we were drowning in it.

I must have woken at least four times, each time with my heart pounding and my body drenched in sweat. At least I didn't cry out, or if I did, Molly slept through it.

I was a wreck the next morning. I've had heavy hangovers that left me feeling better than the nightmares. Over breakfast, I decided to call Crawford and suggest that she consider moving Julie's research to another site. She'd refused to believe in the possibility of murder, but if I could convince her that sabotage was still a danger, I might get her attention.

When I got to the office, there was already a message to call her. I dialed the numbers with a mounting sense of dread.

"Is something wrong?" I asked as soon as she answered.

"You're damn right something's wrong. Last night someone broke into the corn room and stole all the seed from Julie's research. Every ear is missing—about sixty boxes of corn, including the parents of the plants that made the seed Chuck stole."

"Is Julie all right?"

"Of course she's all right. But the seed is gone. I'm sure Wells stole it."

"Have you called the police?"

"They called me. A student found the broken window when he came in early this morning."

"What did they tell you?"

"Nothing. They're investigating, but frankly, they weren't very encouraging. I can't seem to get them to understand the seriousness of the situation."

I didn't mention that I'd had that problem myself. "What do you want from me?" I asked.

"I want to hire you again. I think I can get the Technology Transfer Office to help with your fee, but if not, I'll pay it myself. This is very serious. Without that corn, we have no way to counter a patent application by Wells. He can claim he developed that strain of corn, and we'll have no proof that he stole it from us."

"What about Julie's lab notes?"

"By the time it got to court, he'd have his own set of notes. We have to find the corn. And we have to prove that he stole it."

By the time I got back over to Cal, I had the beginnings of a plan. I outlined it to Crawford.

"If Wells is setting up his own corn lab, he'll need grow lights and equipment. You put together a list of what he'll need, and I'll start checking suppliers. I'll also put surveillance on him and hope he leads us to it. And I think I can get someone undercover as a potential investor." I'd debated long and hard on that last point. Kyle would love to do it, but he was such a wild card I hated to use him. If it hadn't been a matter of life or death, I wouldn't have considered it.

"Finally, to protect the research, you should send Julie to another site to work on it. She's too vulnerable here and so is her work."

Crawford had been nodding until I got to sending Julie away, then she soured up. "No," she said. "I want that research done here, under my direct supervision. The other ideas sound fine, though. I'll have Paul put together an equipment list."

"If you're going to keep Julie here, I think I'd better spend some time coming up with ways to protect her research," I said. "It's possible Chuck had a confederate in the lab or that Wells might recruit a replacement."

"All right," she said. "But my priority is getting the corn back or at least proving Wells stole it."

"Understood," I said. "Now I need two things from you. First, I won't take the case unless you agree to let me investigate Chuck's death."

She started to protest, but I held up my hand and she let me finish. "I know you think it was an accident. I know you don't want a scandal. But if there's a killer here, people are still at risk. So, if you want me on the case, you have to let me do things my way."

She frowned, but she nodded. "And the second thing?"

"If I'm sending someone undercover, I don't want anyone knowing about it except you, not even Paul. Let's keep the surveillance quiet, too."

"You're not worried about Paul?" she said.

"Under the circumstances, I don't know who to trust," I said, "so the safest thing is not to trust anyone."

28

THE PLAN I'D outlined to Crawford was only half a plan, but since she'd only grudgingly agreed to let me investigate Chuck's death, there wasn't any point in telling her the other half. It was possible Wells was involved in the murder, but the killer had to be someone who knew about Chuck's allergies and the precautions he took, someone with access to the mask. I doubted that Wells had either the knowledge or the access. The people in the lab had both.

With no evidence and no promising leads, I had only one alternative. Poke at the suspects and hope I'd rattle one enough so that he or she would make a mistake. It's not my favorite tactic. It can have nasty consequences, but the alternative was to do nothing and risk leaving Julie in jeopardy.

The mistake I hoped for was that the killer would run or start inventing elaborate lies to deflect attention. Of course, there was always the chance that he or she would come after me. Not a desirable outcome. Especially not with this killer.

If I have to face an attacker, I like to see him coming. But a killer who used weapons as subtle as corn pollen would be more devious. The attack could come in any form. At any time. It could happen in front of a dozen people while you sipped your tea. It made my heart speed up just to think about it.

I started the second part of my plan by hanging around

the lab for about an hour and watching the reactions. My presence didn't have much effect on the students. They were still exhilarated by Julie's discovery. Though Kendra was keeping the pressure on the ones working on the grant proposal, they seemed calmer and gentler with each other.

I wanted to talk with Scott. He was at his bench, gluing something to a small, flat aluminum cylinder. A small plastic box with similar cylinders sat open next to him.

"Can I talk with you for a few minutes?" I asked.

He looked down at the cylinder, then back at me. "A few minutes," he said. "I need to get this finished. I promised Kendra it'd be ready for the scanning electron microscope today."

I led the way to the interview room. "Remember I asked about what happened to Chuck's mask after they took him to the hospital?" I said as he sat down on the other side of the table.

"Sure," he said. "I put it in the greenhouse before I locked up."

"Did anyone else ask about the mask?"

"No. Why would they?" He seemed tense, a bit defensive.

"Because we never found it," I said. "So either it wasn't put in the greenhouse or someone stole it before I was able to search for it."

He sat up straighter. "Stole it? Why would anyone steal the mask?"

"To get rid of evidence. Because instead of protecting Chuck from pollen, the mask was sabotaged so that it fed him a heavy dose of it."

Scott was staring at me. His mouth dropped open. "You're sure of that, that someone . . . ? But if the mask is gone, how do you know? And if that's true, how come the police aren't doing anything?"

I didn't reply, just kept my eyes on his face.

"Oh, man, this is too weird. What the hell's going on?

Are you trying to suggest that I had something to do with Chuck's death? Just 'cause I found him? Look, he was blue when I got there. I pulled him out as fast as I could.

"The bio-control guys were there; they saw me. Look, I don't understand. Why're you asking me this? If it's really true about the mask, why aren't the police doing something?"

"They are investigating," I said. "The case is open, but without the mask, the major evidence is gone."

"Well, I didn't take it," he said with feeling.

"I understand that you were dating Julie before she started going with Chuck."

"Julie?" he said, his voice rising. "I asked her out a couple of times. It wasn't a big deal." The pitch of his voice contradicted his words.

Again, I stayed quiet and let the silence work for me.

"What're you saying? That I was jealous of Chuck? 'Cause I wasn't. I mean, I only took her out a couple of times. It's not as if I was in love with her or anything."

"So maybe your interest was more in her research," I suggested.

He shifted in his chair, raised his hand to his mouth, and bit down on the thumbnail. He watched me closely, as if he were trying to read the right answer on my face.

"I don't know what this is about," he said. "I didn't do anything wrong. I need to get back to work." With that, he almost fled from the room.

Next I went after Dorian Barker. The anger I'd witnessed in his argument with Chuck didn't seem like enough motive for murder, but with someone stretched as tight as Dorian, you didn't want to bet on the length of his fuse.

Dorian was arguing furiously with Margot about the quality of a table for their paper to be submitted with the grant proposal. "But the columns aren't properly aligned," he fussed. "You really have to go back and reset the tabs and margins."

"Look, Barker," Margot announced in the tone of a woman who'd had too many discussions like this. "An eighth of an inch doesn't matter. It just doesn't fuckin' matter. You want it perfect, you stay to do it over. Me, I've got more important things to do."

"Yeah, I'll bet you do. With Lloyd, no doubt."

I dragged him away before she could twist his skinny little neck. Nearby students looked disappointed.

"You and Chuck worked near each other in the lab," I said when we got to the interview room. "I was wondering if you saw or heard anything suspicious before he died."

Dorian turned his head slightly to the right and looked at me out of his left eye. It was a strange mannerism, almost birdlike. "What do you mean, suspicious?" he asked.

"I don't know. Anything that suggested he was involved in sabotage, or might be working with or for someone outside the lab."

His head bobbed slightly as he stuck his chin out a bit and drew it back. The man really did look like a large blond bird. "No, I don't think so. We never talked much. He was annoying."

"Annoying how?"

"He was a slob," Dorian said, "and he made stupid jokes."

"Julie seemed to like him," I said.

The head bobbed again, and Dorian's eyes were almost fierce. "She just put up with him because he hung around and acted interested in her work. Julie doesn't like guys much."

"You like Julie, don't you?" I said.

"She's a nice person, too nice for Chuck. So's Teri. I'll never understand how smart women can be so stupid about men. Why're you asking me this?"

"Because there's strong evidence that Chuck's death wasn't an accident."

He almost leaped forward in his seat, startling me and causing me to pull back from the table. "What do you mean? You mean someone killed him?" he asked, his voice an octave higher.

I nodded.

"But how? I mean, I thought he died of allergies. He was allergic, you know." He asked four questions in a row, never pausing for an answer, then abruptly stopped. "Oh, wait a minute. You're not saying you think I have something to do with this? Just 'cause I didn't like the guy. Lots of people didn't like the guy, but they're too mealymouthed to say so now that he's dead."

He reeled off a list of people he claimed had disliked Chuck. I jotted them down. When he started on the ones who might have wanted to frame him for Chuck's death, he convinced me that we should add "paranoid" to his list of personality disorders.

Before Dorian could reconvene his argument with Margot, I asked her to join me in the interview room. Curiosity shone in her face as she agreed.

I asked who'd been interested in Julie's research and got the same answer Julie'd given me, with one important addition. Dorian Barker. "Dorian is always interested in *everything* about Julie," she said. "Dorian gets these crushes; it's really sort of cute, but sad. Half the time, all he does is talk about the girl and never even asks her out. I think he's getting braver. He did ask Julie out. Probably because of Teri."

"Teri?"

"Because before Julie, he was hot for Teri, but while he was mooning over her and trying to get up the nerve to ask her out, Chuck snapped her up."

So Chuck had taken both the women Dorian liked. It'd be ironic if his death had nothing to do with the breakthrough he was pursuing. But then, I suspect at least as many people are killed for thwarted love as straight-out greed.

I asked more about Chuck and the other students but didn't get anything new. However, I did achieve my second goal, which was to spread word of my suspicions about Chuck's death. When I told her about the sabotage of the mask, she reversed our roles and began shooting questions at me.

Within minutes of leaving me, she was deep in conversation with four other students. By five that evening everyone in the lab would know what I'd told her. Margot was better than a PA system.

My next stop was the campus police department. I didn't expect that Detective Dreyer had developed a burning interest in the case overnight, but I hoped the stolen corn might have awakened his curiosity about Chuck's death. It hadn't.

However, urgent calls from the Technology Transfer Office had definitely gotten his attention, and he was considerably more cordial on this visit. He asked me to tell him everything I knew about the corn and Galen Wells, and this time he took notes as he asked questions.

When I finished my part of show-and-tell, I asked, "Did you question Wells about the break-in?"

Dreyer nodded. "He denied having anything to do with it, of course. He did seem genuinely surprised. He mentioned that you'd been down to see him, representing yourself as a journalist. He suggested that Dr. Crawford's allegations are the result of an unfortunate affair in the past."

"There's a lot of money at stake," I said, just to keep his attention focused.

"So Mr. Perkins in Technology Transfer tells me. He wanted us to get a search warrant, but we simply don't have enough evidence to go to a judge for one."

"Are you tracing the check that Chuck Nishimura received before he died?"

"Absolutely. But I have to tell you that even if it is from Galen Wells, if he gives us a satisfactory reason for paying Nishimura we still won't have any proof of wrongdoing."

Wells was smart enough to come up with an excuse. And he'd have a story for why he didn't recognize Chuck's name, or he'd deny I asked about the dead student. The police were going to have a hard time getting anything against him.

"Let me ask you one thing," I said as I rose to leave. "Do you believe Dr. Crawford's allegations that Wells sabotaged research and stole material from her lab?"

"What I believe or don't believe isn't important. I'm only concerned with what I can prove," he said officiously.

I knew then that the UC cops weren't likely to be of much use to us.

I'd promised Crawford lots of scut work. That's what checking on suppliers and watching Wells would be. Important but incredibly boring.

Scut work is where being the boss pays off. I called in Chris as soon as I got back to the office. "I've got a load of background checks for you," I said.

I gave her a list that included Wells and everyone in the lab, even Crawford. Chris gets more than her share of scut work, but she accepts it good-naturedly because she's killing time till her husband finishes graduate school and gets a job so she can start business school.

She grimaced as she looked over the list. "I take it we're shelving the four cases you have me working on," she said.

"Can we get away with that?"

"For a week or so, not much longer."

"A week should be enough," I said. "I also need to know if anyone has ordered equipment to set up an indoor greenhouse in the past month. I'll have a list of supplies and likely suppliers by this afternoon."

"We should talk to someone at DEA. I think they pay attention to such things," Chris said.

"Go for it," I said. "You really should consider a career in security. You're awfully good at it."

"I have a career in security, and at the rate Don is finishing his dissertation, it may be the only career I'll ever have."

"Don't expect me to lament that," I said. "Jesse and I are delighted by Don's modest pace."

She uttered an expression completely out of character with her elegant appearance and tapped the papers I'd given her on the desk to straighten them. "Anything more for your humble servant?"

"Please, don't let Molly get involved in any of this," I said. "Even if she asks about it."

"Especially if she asks," Chris said, and headed for her office.

The next job was surveillance on Wells. I've always hated surveillance; Jesse does, too. Fortunately, he decided the solution was to hire someone else to do it for us and found the Mascotti brothers, retired police officers who'll take any job that doesn't conflict with a 49ers home game or their Wednesday night poker party.

I called Joe; Frank's usually out during the day.

"A job? Sure, we'd love to," he said, almost shouting into the phone. I suspect he's a bit hard of hearing, but he won't admit it. "We can start anytime you want. Yeah, it'll be fine with Frank. He spends too much time playing golf and bowling. This'll be good for him. Tell you the truth, retirement is a bit dull, you know what I mean?"

I arranged for them to stop by later so I could brief them on the case and give them the photo Wells had so conveniently provided.

The last part of the plan was the most difficult, getting someone to approach Wells as a potential investor. I'd put off calling Kyle because I still didn't like the idea of involving him in the case. He had the perfect background for the job, but he was such a wild card. I'd feel much more comfortable using Chris or Jesse. Before I could resolve the issue, Amy buzzed to say Kyle was on the line.

"Guess who I had dinner with last night?" he said gleefully.

I knew the answer before I said it. "Not Galen Wells, I hope."

"Now don't get upset. I don't want you to think I'm horning in on your case, but this was just too good to pass up. I got a call from one of the guys I asked about Wells. He said our man is still looking for investors and would I like to meet him. So, of course, I said sure, I'd love to hear more about his venture."

I should have been delighted. It was just what I needed, a man on the inside. And just what I didn't, a loose cannon.

"So did you learn anything?" I asked.

"I did indeed. The hot product is an appetite suppressant," he said, sounding very pleased with himself. "What'd you find out at the lab? Could the corn be the thing?"

"Very likely," I said. "But there've been some new developments. Can you come to the office?"

"Be there in twenty minutes," he said. His flirtatious manner was gone, a sure sign that he found his involvement in the case more exciting than trying to seduce me. I should have realized then what a bad idea it was to get him mixed up in this case.

29

IT WAS EXACTLY twenty minutes later when Kyle arrived, with flowers for Chris and Amy, a take-out latte for me, and a box of diskettes for Jesse. "He'll know what it is when he boots up," he said with a smile. If he couldn't seduce me, Kyle was going after my staff.

"So what do you know?" I asked as we settled into my office. It was a very good latte.

"Wells is good," he said. "Very good. He's not only smart, he could sell shoes to snakes. Or fleece suckers with the shell game. I'm good at spotting hucksters . . ." He gave me a sly smile, an unspoken recognition that it took one to know one. "But I'm still not sure whether he's blowing smoke or on the edge of making a million."

"What did he say about the appetite suppressant?"

"He was cagey about that. He says he's in the process of putting together a patent application and can't talk till that's set. You know how that works?"

"No."

"Well, if your grad student actually tested the corn on rats and if he gave Wells the notes on that test, then Wells has both the theoretical explanation of how the suppressant functions and preliminary experimental evidence that it works the way he predicted. That's all he needs to apply for a patent. It'll take about a year to get approval, and during that time, he can do more experiments and amass more data to buttress his case."

"But he hasn't applied yet?"

"Says he's in the process. That could mean almost anything. The only sure thing is that his application hasn't been officially accepted. Once you've got a number and a place in the queue, you use the term 'patent pending' and proceed as if it's a done deal.

"Wells isn't there yet. He made a big point of the fact that he was prepared to offer me better terms because it's so early in the process. That makes sense. Once he's at the patent-pending stage, it'll be much easier to attract investors. Biotech start-ups do that all the time; some are marketing the product before they can pry the patent out of the feds."

"But what if Cal protests the patent?"

"Now you're in over my head. Obviously, Wells did not mention that there might be a nasty fight over the paternity of this particular discovery. He was too busy describing how rich he was going to make me."

"How did he explain the fact that a lab dealing in insulin had come up with a discovery involving corn?" I asked.

Kyle took a drink from the latte he'd brought for himself and leaned back on the sofa. "He says it's the brainchild of a buddy in genetics. A former student. Claims they were telling stories over a couple of beers and one of them hit on the idea of a plant steroid mutating to mimic an animal steroid. A few months ago the guy called him out of the blue and said he thought he'd pulled it off and wanted help in setting up his own company to develop the thing into a product."

"I don't suppose he identified this friend. Or where he works."

"Couldn't do that. This fellow wants to remain anonymous until he's sure he can pull off setting up his own lab. He's not ready to give up his university job till he's sure."

"So Wells is looking for someone to front for him," I said.

"That'd be my guess."

"You think you can get him to show you his facility?"

"I'll try. I didn't want to act too interested. I think the best approach is to play hard to get. Wells needs money. Now that he sees me as a potential source, I don't have to do much but hang loose and let him woo me."

"And watch your back," I said. "Don't forget that this is a murder case. And Wells is right in the middle of it. If he senses you're not what you appear to be, you could be in real danger."

When Kyle smiled, I realized that I had said exactly the wrong thing. He loved the danger, was having the time of his life. I just hoped it wasn't the last time of his life.

Molly arrived at the office around four. I'd told her about Julie's breakthrough the night before when it looked as if we were off the case. It had been such a high to experience the excitement of discovery that I'd wanted to share it with her.

I'd picked up enough around the lab to give her a general picture of how plants were bred and mutants identified, and she was as fascinated by it all as I was. I'd have loved to take her to the lab and let Julie explain it to her in more detail. But that was out of the question now.

She proved that she had an aptitude for investigative work when it took her only twenty minutes to discover that Chris was trying to keep certain files from her. She accepted Chris's admonition that the case was off-limits, but once we were home she started in on me.

"I don't see why you can't even tell me about it," she said.

"Because at least one person has been killed in this case," I said, "and I don't want you anywhere near it."

"But I won't be doing anything. I just want to know."

"No. You're not going to be working on anything connected to this case, so you don't need to know about it. I told you when I agreed to let you work for me that I'm the boss."

"But it doesn't make sense."

"It doesn't have to. Ask Jesse or Chris—as a boss I can be irrational and arbitrary. Also, very mean if I'm crossed."

"So don't tell me as a boss. Tell me as a sweet, supportive substitute parent figure, so we can have one of those neat bonding experiences," she wheedled.

I repeated Chris's unladylike expression and threatened to make her cook if she didn't get out of my kitchen.

The next morning Jesse got a call from the insurance company on his chip case. He was wearing the smile of the truly smug when he informed me that they wanted to hire him to do some further investigating.

"I will now call our former clients, the chip company, and ask their permission to release the records of my investigation to the insurance company and to continue on their behalf."

"And they will either refuse, in which case the insurance company can deny their claim, or they will agree, and you can nail them," I said.

"Just so," he replied with a grin.

Friday was the grant deadline. With all that had happened in the lab, I couldn't see how Crawford would make it, and I wasn't looking forward to dealing with her if she didn't. She and Paul were in the office with piles of paper stacked on every surface, but they didn't seem to be in panic mode.

"The damn Radioactivity Use Authorization Form is missing," Crawford complained as I walked in.

"I've got one in the files," Paul replied.

"Looks as if you're going to make it," I said.

"Not by five o'clock today," Crawford said. "But today's just the university deadline. They make a big fuss about needing two weeks to process it, but they can turn it around faster than that. We'll be done by Monday or Tuesday, and I can walk it over to the Sponsored Projects Office with a bottle of wine and a mea culpa, and we'll be fine."

She turned back to the piles of paper, and I walked into the lab to see who was there. I was glad to find Teri at her bench. As an undergraduate she spent much less time in the lab than the others and might miss out on the gossip I'd so carefully planted. The other undergraduates were only peripherally involved in lab politics, but Teri's relationship with Chuck made her someone I wanted to know better.

She was discussing something with Raisa, so I waited until they finished, then asked if she'd join me in the interview room. As I reached the door and saw blue sky and sunlight through the window, I changed my plans. "Why don't we go downstairs and sit outside?" I suggested.

"That'd be great," Teri said. "We don't get many days like this."

We got coffee and sat out on the patio. It wasn't as warm as it had looked from the window, but then it never is in Berkeley. The cool air pouring through the Golden Gate keeps the city constantly air-conditioned. I was glad I'd worn a heavy sweater.

"How are you getting along?" I asked. "I know Chuck's death must have been hard on you."

She nodded, all trace of her earlier smile faded from her face. "Yeah," she said. "I really miss him. I can't quite believe that he's not there. I mean, I'm always looking toward his bench and being surprised not to see him."

"You were pretty close. It must have hurt when he broke off the relationship."

"It did, but not like you probably think. I mean, I was sort of sad that Chuck didn't hang with me anymore, because I enjoyed his company, but it wasn't a great passion. What was special to me was that he took me seriously. He treated me like a real scientist, not just a dumb undergrad."

Teri leaned forward across the table, and her voice was earnest. "That probably doesn't sound like much, but it was really important to me. See, when you're little and blond, guys think you're some kind of Barbie doll. They're impressed you can tie your shoes."

She must have caught the smile that flickered across my face, because her voice and manner became more insistent. "It's true. If you're blond and people think you're cute, they automatically subtract fifty points from your IQ. Even women do that." Her voice was bitter now.

I was reminded of how young she was. Like Molly, she couldn't imagine that anyone my age could possibly understand what it was like to be her age. Wouldn't have believed that I had also experienced the unconscious mathematics of IQ subtraction.

"Did he break it off, or did you?"

"He did," she said. "I told people it was mutual since I felt a bit, I don't know, embarrassed, but one day he just said he was too busy for a serious relationship. He stopped inviting me to his place, didn't call. He was still nice at the lab, and sometimes we talked like we had before, but he seemed preoccupied. We just didn't connect anymore."

"Did he ever mention someone named Galen Wells?"

"I don't think so. It's an unusual enough name, I think I'd have remembered it. Who is he?"

"He owns a biotech company."

The wind came up and scattered a stack of papers a girl was working on at a nearby table. She jumped up and chased them down as they fluttered across the paving stones like wounded birds.

"Did Chuck always keep his mask at the greenhouse?" I asked.

"Whenever he had plants there he did," she said. "Why?"

"Because the mask obviously failed him, and now it's disappeared."

Teri stared at me. "What're you saying?" she asked.

"That there's a good chance Chuck was murdered."

Her eyes widened in shock, then she shut them tight and put both hands to her face. I expected her to burst into tears, but she simply breathed hard several times, then lowered her hands to beneath her eyes and looked at me over her fingers. "I heard a rumor. I didn't want to believe it. Are you really sure?"

I nodded.

"Oh, God," she said, and lowered her face into her hands.

It took a while for Teri to calm down. She never cried, but she looked devastated. She asked some questions, then just sat and stared at her coffee cup.

When she looked back up at me, she asked in a small voice, "Why? Why would anyone do that?"

Another answer I didn't have.

When we got back upstairs, Kendra was looking for me. Her features were compressed in an angry frown.

Once in her office she exploded. "I just got a call from Galen Wells. You know what the bastard had to say for himself? He said he just wanted me to know that he hadn't stolen this corn. Just like that. Didn't bother to deny that he'd stolen the first batch of corn. Or that he was trying to steal my patent. But he wants me to know that he didn't steal this corn. What a nerve!" She slammed her palm down on the desk and everything on it jumped.

"I wonder why he did that?" I said, as much to myself as to Crawford.

"To twit me, of course. Just to thumb his nose. He's

like an obnoxious eight-year-old boy yelling, 'Yanny, yanny, yah, yah.' "

"Maybe," I said. "Or maybe he didn't steal it. Maybe he's worried that there's a third agent out there and he wants to clue you to go looking."

"Oh, don't be ridiculous," she said. "He's just trying to hassle me."

"Just for argument's sake, if you knew it wasn't Wells, who would you suspect?"

She started to protest, then thought a minute. "Julie," she said. "She's the only one who knows enough to make use of the corn. If she screwed up the research here, so we couldn't get results, she'd be in a position to redo it when she got a job at some other university."

Kendra reached for the pencil, and I knew she was going to start tapping the damn thing again. It was all I could do not to grab it out of her hand.

"It happened when I was in grad school," she continued. "A guy named Oscar Brickman discovered that the professor had given him a lousy reference, so he killed his research project. Then when he got a job at some state school, he did the research there and published it under his own name.

"But I really don't see Julie doing that. This research is big enough that it'll spawn plenty more projects, and if we're successful, it'll get her a job anywhere she wants. No . . ." She tossed the pencil down on the desk. "Wells is just messing with my mind."

30

IT WAS ELEVEN-THIRTY. I wanted to get Paul Raskin away from the lab to talk, and lunch seemed a convenient excuse. I found him digging through a file cabinet. "Is your offer of a meal at the Chez Panisse Café still good?" I asked.

He looked up, checked his watch, and considered for a minute. "Sure," he said. "Now that we've got till next week on the grant, I can spare an hour to eat. If we hurry, we'll get there before the wait's too long."

The brown-shingle, two-story building that houses Chez Panisse is only about seven blocks from the lab. It looks as if it should be on a quiet residential street instead of sandwiched between low-rise commercial buildings. A wooden arch separates the small bricked courtyard from the sidewalk traffic, and the elegant restaurant inside preserves some of the feeling of a home.

We climbed the stairs to the café and waited by the bar to see if they had a table. A young woman dressed in black led us past the open kitchen to the dining room in the back. On the high counter that separated the kitchen from the walkway and dining room, a large round platter held artichokes, oranges, and leeks in an edible still life.

The dining room was rather small. The French posters on the walls were from the forties, and the room's wooden ceiling and craftsman geometric designs reminded me of Frank Lloyd Wright, but the menu was strictly nineties.

I ordered avocado and grapefruit salad with smoked trout and Paul chose the pizzetta. I agreed to his suggestion of wine, hoping it would loosen his tongue without destroying my concentration.

As we waited for our food, I said, "Wednesday's meeting was pretty exciting."

"Yeah. We're just incredibly lucky to have stumbled on this thing. It opens up such fascinating possibilities for research. Everyone's sort of walking on air."

"Yes, I noticed," I said. "Even the corn room break-in doesn't seem to have brought them down."

He frowned and shook his head. "It's a real bummer, that's for sure. Makes everything much harder, but with luck we'll still be able to salvage enough seed to get back on track fairly quickly."

"There's more seed?"

"We're hoping there'll be a few kernels in the planting envelopes. See, when you plant, you keep your records on an envelope, and you usually try to keep a few extra kernels, just in case. Later, you transfer the information to the corn cards, and then into the computer files. You stick the envelopes away someplace as a sort of ultimate backup."

"And Julie has envelopes?"

"She thinks she does," Paul said. "But she's not sure where she put them. They're either at the greenhouse or at her house. I'm hoping for the greenhouse, since I've seen her place. She lives with several other people and it's a jumble. She's not even sure there'll be kernels in all the envelopes, so we won't know till she finds them."

"What if she doesn't find them?" I asked. The waiter delivered dessert to the table next to us. Paul and I were momentarily distracted by the pear and blueberry tart.

We realized at the same moment that we were making the recipient of the tart uncomfortable and looked away, then smiled guiltily at each other. Paul picked up where he'd left off. "If she doesn't find the seed, we could have a hard time of it. We'll have to start over and hope that we get some of the mutants we got before, but without the seed, there's no guarantee. Mutations are like rolling dice with the gods. A lot of random chance. And at this stage there's no way we know enough to make that mutation happen."

"I'd think everyone would be depressed and disappointed," I said.

"Well, no one's happy about the break-in, but even without the corn, we have the concept. It's like we know something about this little piece of the universe that we didn't know yesterday. And no one can steal that."

With the companies I work for, money's always the bottom line, and when there's a crime, the motivation is usually greed. The desire for money or power, sometimes both. But what I'd seen the day before was about something else entirely.

"Is that what drives Kendra?" I asked. "That desire to know, to be the one who discovers something new?"

"That's a lot of it. There's the desire for success and recognition, just like in other professions, but beneath that there's this very special kind of curiosity. It's like a fire inside, that kind of passion. You saw it yesterday in Kendra and Julie. Not everyone has it, but the best ones all have it."

"How about Ethan Mather?" I asked. "He seems to have plenty of passion, but he's disdainful of people like Kendra."

"Ethan's fire is a different kind," Raskin said. "Ethan wants to save the world. Or at least to feed it. Science is just a tool for him, a tool he enjoys, and one he's very good with, but always as a means, never an end. He just doesn't understand a person like Kendra. To him, her passion is self-indulgence."

"And you, which kind of fire is yours?"

He smiled, but it was a rueful smile. "That fire's too

hot for me," he said. "I got too close to it once. I've learned to keep my distance."

"Really?" I said. "I could have sworn I saw it flicker yesterday in the lab."

"Just a flicker," he said. "You know what I'm talking about. You've gotten too close to some fire yourself." His gaze was so intense that I felt almost trapped in its implied intimacy. I didn't know what he was talking about, but I felt his words cut through to someplace inside me that I didn't want to look at.

"What makes you say that?" I said, trying to keep my tone light.

"The way that you're always watching. That you never let yourself trust, even for a little while. You keep this barrier between yourself and the world."

"It has to do with my job," I said. "An investigator can't afford to trust any more than a scientist can afford to disregard data."

"Must be pretty lonely."

"It's one reason I don't mix business with pleasure," I said. "Especially in a murder case."

He nodded soberly. "Maybe you're right," he said. "It can be dangerous to trust anyone too much."

It didn't sound exactly like a warning but it was certainly more than a casual observation. On an impulse, I said, "Raymond didn't trust you. Why?"

He looked surprised. "He didn't?" he said. "I don't know. I thought we got along well."

Unfortunately, the waitress arrived just then with our food, and Raskin switched his attention to his plate. My salad looked beautiful and tasted even better. It took me a few minutes to remember that I wasn't there just to enjoy the food.

"Galen Wells called to tell Kendra he didn't steal the corn from the corn room," I said.

"Kendra told me. She's furious."

"If we assumed that Wells didn't steal the corn, who would you suspect?"

"One of the students, I guess. Almost have to be a postdoc, since they'll be going on to their own jobs soon and could conceivably use it there."

"Julie?"

"She'd be able to do it most easily, but really, she's the least likely one."

"Why?"

Raskin put down his fork and took a minute to answer. "Because of who she is." He grimaced slightly. "It's always tricky when you get into stuff based on culture, too easy to get into racial stereotyping, but Julie's first generation. Her parents both came from southern China, though I don't think they met till they got here. She's had a very traditional upbringing. Family is terrifically important to her. And her parents wanted her to become a doctor. For them, medicine is a guarantee of security. You can see why that'd be important to immigrants. So in going into science, getting a Ph.D. instead of an M.D., she defied their wishes."

I remembered my first interview with Julie and her anguish at the thought that the sabotage might destroy her chances for a job at a university and a lab of her own. She'd sacrificed a lot for that dream; no wonder she was so upset by the threat to it.

"But if success is doubly important to her, wouldn't she be more inclined to break the rules to get it?" I said.

"If she were an ordinary American," Raskin replied. "But since she opposed her family once, she's all the more anxious not to disappoint them in any other way. Tell the truth, I think that's why she's so cool to the guys in the lab. Marrying within the culture is even more important than following a particular profession. She told me once that her parents would forgive her almost anything as long as she married someone Chinese."

He took a drink of wine and picked up his fork, then

put it down again. "There's one other possibility. Could be the thief's a spoiler. Not out to steal the research, just to make sure that Kendra and Julie don't benefit from it. Someone who's jealous or has a grudge."

"Which means it could be anyone in the lab," I said. "And probably even a number of outsiders."

" 'Fraid so," Raskin said as he picked up his fork again and went back to eating. For the rest of the meal we stayed away from the difficulties at the lab. By dessert, we'd both relaxed a bit, and Raskin was making lightly flirtatious banter and serious eye contact. A few days before, it would probably have set my hormones racing. Not today.

"Why didn't you tell me you'd had an affair with Kendra?" I asked.

He looked startled, then shrugged. "I didn't think it was relevant. It happened before I came to work for her, never affected anything in the lab."

"Really?" I said. "You must be awfully good at keeping your emotions separate from your work."

"There wasn't a lot of emotion involved. Strong chemistry, but not a lot of emotion. We both realized that fairly early. We'd talked about her problems at the lab. At some point, she offered me the job. I was tired of bouncing around; this was a great opportunity. Maybe I'm getting old, but I decided I needed a job more than I needed a lover."

I didn't quite believe that it was that easy to switch roles, especially not when his new role was subservient. For all his easygoing manner and apparent warmth with the students, Paul Raskin didn't strike me as the kind of man to take orders easily. I realized that was something that had troubled me from the beginning. "It doesn't bother you to be ordered around by your former lover?" I asked.

He laughed and his sexy grin seemed genuine. "Sometimes. But when Kendra gets too far out of line, I just tell her she's full of shit. Does it bother you that she was my lover?"

"No," I said, though that wasn't quite true. "What bothers me is that you and she withheld information."

"I just didn't see how it was relevant to the investigation," he said. "It isn't even relevant to anything that might happen between you and me. It was just chemistry. It didn't mean anything."

That was what Peter had said about his affair with Alicia Adavi. I resisted the temptation to comment on the male concept of chemistry. "My work's a lot like yours," I said coolly. "You never know what's going to be relevant, so you want all the information you can get."

When I got back to the office that afternoon, the relaxing effect of the wine had worn off, leaving me slightly tired and more than a little irritated by my conversation with Paul Raskin. I still didn't trust him. I had no idea what he meant by his comment about being burned by getting too close to the fire. It was probably just a clever way of putting me on the defensive for keeping him at a distance, but it had struck home.

I hadn't been able to trust my reactions since I took this case. Mooning over a client was bad enough, especially a client I didn't trust. And trying to keep a rein on my skittish psyche long enough to figure out where the real threats lay wasn't making my job any easier.

Chris popped out of her office as soon as she heard my voice. "I've got something," she said, looking pleased with herself.

"Already? That's fast work. Let me get some coffee before we talk," I said.

I poured myself the last of the suspiciously dark brew that was left in the pot, and we settled in my office. "I think Paul Raskin has a fake identity," she announced as I sat down. "Everything for the last fifteen years checks out; before that, the info is bogus."

The shock hit me like a blow to the solar plexus. "You're sure?"

"I'm sure that what we've got is bogus. Something happened fifteen years ago that caused him either to change his name or to change the information about his past."

The sense of shock passed, replaced by excitement. "Well," I said, "things are starting to get interesting."

31

KENDRA WAS GONE when I called the lab, and Paul informed me that he didn't expect her back until Monday. "Her mother was hospitalized with an irregular heartbeat, and she flew home to see her. The doctors think they can treat it with drugs, but Kendra wanted to be sure she was all right," he said.

I didn't ask who he'd been fifteen years ago. I wanted to do that in person.

Molly was a good deal more enthusiastic about working on Saturday than I was. As soon as I got home from aikido, she suggested we go to the office. I suggested she tackle her homework. She sulked.

"Don't forget our deal," I said. "Schoolwork comes first."

"I'll get B's," Molly said. "But that's it. I'm not doing that straight-A crap."

"You have some objection to A's?" I asked.

She hunkered down in her chair. I could see a major sulk coming on.

"What'd I say?" I asked.

"I'm not busting my butt just so my mom can brag to her friends. That's why she cares so much about me getting A's. She's in this bragging contest with all her Junior League buddies."

"Are you going to become a bag lady just to thwart her?"

Molly hunched lower. I was afraid she was seriously considering it.

"You could achieve the same thing by becoming a liberal Democrat," I said. "Or opening a soup kitchen in her neighborhood. Or writing a best-selling autobiography."

A grin twitched the edges of her mouth. "Or becoming a talk-show host. Or a public-interest lawyer; maybe I could sue her."

"Director of the IRS, so you could audit her."

"A private eye, just like you."

I groaned as she hooted with laughter.

Monday was cold and overcast in San Francisco. And cold and overcast in Berkeley. It looked as if it might even rain, which would have been a source of rejoicing a couple of years ago when there was a drought, but would only bring grumbles in this year of floods.

Kendra wasn't in the lab when I got there. Raskin was.

"She's with the university lawyers," he said. "Expect her to be in an ugly mood when she gets back."

My news would only make it uglier.

I didn't feel like making conversation with Raskin, so I went to see if Julie had found her seed. She had a box of dirty envelopes in front of her, and she was checking through them and noting their contents on a pad.

"Do you have enough to make up for the corn room loss?" I asked.

She frowned. "I don't know yet. I already know I'm missing some. I just don't know how important they are. In most cases, I only have three or four kernels. But that's better than nothing."

"Be sure to keep those envelopes with you at all times," I said. "Don't leave them here in the lab, even for a few minutes."

"Don't worry," Julie said. "They go where I go."

Teri came into the room looking excited. She was wearing a navy down jacket and a wool cap. She looked around, then hurried over to us. "I don't mean to interrupt, but I need some help with the protein purification machinery, and I can't find Raisa. Could you give me a hand—that is, if you're not too busy?"

Julie smiled. "Sure," she said.

"Would you like to come, too, Catherine?" Teri asked. "You might find it interesting. Raisa and I are trying to isolate the *Bonsai 4* receptor. We're studying the actual structure and sequence of the protein. We're in the cold room, so it's pretty chilly, but you don't need to be in there long."

Julie picked up her box of envelopes, and I followed the two women down the hall. Teri gave Julie the background on her work. They might as well have been speaking Urdu for all I understood of their conversation.

At the cold room Teri pulled the heavy door open and we stepped inside. The frigid air cut through my sweater and raised goose bumps on my arms. On the bench sat a Rube Goldbergesque machine with three tall, skinny columns of gelatinous fluid dripping their contents into a seemingly endless line of small test tubes that snaked along on a conveyor belt. The mechanism at the bottom of the columns clicked as it finished with each tube, and the line moved on.

"That's a fraction collector," Teri said. She practically had to shout to make herself heard above the fans that forced cold air into the room. "They count exactly ten drops into each tube."

"What I don't understand is this," she said to Julie, and began describing her problem. It was way too complicated for me. My mind wandered and I was sure I smelled the sweet, slightly cloying scent of overripe strawberries. When I glanced beneath the bench, I saw a basket of them sitting on top of a tub of yogurt. Raskin's ultimatum about storing food obviously hadn't had much effect.

Teri stopped talking and put her hand to her head. "The cold must be getting to me," she said. "I . . . I don't feel so good. I think I'll go get an aspirin. Can you keep an eye on this for me?"

"Sure," Julie said as Teri hurried out. She started to explain the protein purification process to me, but I found I couldn't concentrate on what she was saying. A succession of weird thoughts danced through my head—a windy night at the beach, cross-country skiing, but not through any landscape I remembered. Then suddenly I was back in a sunlit office staring at the grotesquely positioned corpse of a woman I'd known. The body rose and floated toward me; I tried to scream but couldn't.

Then I was on the floor, feeling the cold rubber mat pressing against my cheek. A pale blue shape jutted up in front of my face, filling most of my field of vision. I realized slowly that it must be the back of Julie's tee shirt. Above her I could see the underside of the lab bench. I knew I had to get to the door.

The body on the desk was back. It was reaching out to me. I tried to stand, couldn't even get to my knees. I dragged myself forward though it felt as if my body weighed five hundred pounds.

The floor dipped, making it easier to crawl. I was no longer on the mat. The cement was icy. The cold against my face cleared my head a bit, but my body still felt like lead.

My head hit something. I prayed it was the door and tried to reach up for the handle. I couldn't raise my arm. The smell of strawberries was so strong that the air was thick with it. I felt I was suffocating in strawberry jam.

The corpse was back. It rubbed itself against my body. I hadn't the strength to pull away. I tried again to raise

my arm for the handle, and felt icy fingers on my elbow.
I tried to pull away, then realized they were pushing my
arm upward.

My fingers hit something hard and metallic. I pushed
against it and it gave. It had to be the paddle that opened
the door, but the door hadn't moved. It took all my
energy to keep the pressure on the paddle, but it wasn't
enough to budge the heavy door.

A voice, a woman's voice, ordered me to push. I tried,
but my arm had no strength. The only thing left was to
use my head. I tried to push myself forward with my feet.
The first time they simply slipped over the mat, but the
second my toe caught and I had just enough traction to
press my body forward.

The door was hard against my head, then it moved.
Warm air flowed over my face and I gave one last heave
of my body that pushed it open even farther. I gulped in
the air and the strawberry jam thinned. I still couldn't get
to my knees but I dragged myself out into the hall.

Julie was right behind me. We lay on the floor together, unable to do more than breathe. My head felt as
if someone had hit me with a hammer and nausea sent
my stomach to my throat. The icy air continued to pour
over us.

I don't know how long we lay there. After a few minutes we were able to get out of the doorway so that the
door could close and our bodies began to warm up. Eventually, I heard footsteps that stopped, then hurried closer
until a large pair of dirty white running shoes were only a
few inches from my nose. A baritone voice asked anxiously what had happened. Neither Julie nor I was able to
answer.

Things got chaotic after that. Lots more shoes and voices.
Soft, warm jackets were piled on top of us and a hand
raised my head from the floor and stuffed something
under it as a pillow. Some of the voices were familiar,

but my head hurt too much for me to understand what they were saying.

The herd of running shoes and sandals was replaced by heavy white oxfords beneath white pants, and large hands lifted me onto something flat that was softer than the floor but not by much. A plastic mask was pressed over my nose and mouth. I'd have knocked it away, but my arms weren't working right.

With the oxygen, my head began to clear. By the time they had us in the ambulance I knew where I was, and I could begin to talk. Julie seemed to be coming around, too. I could hear her talking to the paramedic who knelt next to her.

The headache wasn't any better, and being bounced around on the stretcher had only made my nausea worse. I suffer from migraines, and I've always assumed they're about as bad as a headache gets. I'd been wrong.

A young woman in a jumpsuit sat on the seat next to my head and began asking questions. It was hard to hear her above the siren and the crackling radio. The driver seemed to be talking to someone on the other end who was issuing instructions. I'd have liked to suggest that he slow down. The rocking of the ambulance made everything worse.

At the ER they rushed us inside and hooked us up to machines, poked us with needles, then abandoned us in a room full of equipment where the lights were much too bright. Either I'd died and was in hell or they'd decided I was going to live.

32

BY THE TIME the doctor got there, my mind was clear and my body was functioning again. The nausea had eased, but the headache was fierce. It squeezed the top of my head like an inquisitor's vise.

Dr. Kopecko was probably about Julie's age. Her blond hair was cut very close at the hairline and sprang into a crown of curls on top. She questioned us about the chemicals we'd been using and Julie answered, assuring her that there was nothing in Teri's experiment that could have poisoned us.

"Did you smell anything unusual?" she asked.

"Strawberries," I said. "There were some in a box on the floor and I remember smelling them and thinking they were a bit off."

"I remember that," Julie said. "They shouldn't have been there. Paul's been on everyone's case not to leave food in there."

"They might have masked another odor," the doctor said. "I'm afraid we won't know what it was until the environmental safety people check the room, but your vital signs are good and you appear to be recovering well. I think you're going to be fine."

"I have a crushing headache," I said. "Can you give me something for it?"

"I'd rather not right now," the doctor said. "Since we don't know what the chemical was, I don't want to risk any interaction. The safest thing right now is just to rest and let the stuff get out of your system. We're going to transfer you to a regular room where you can rest for a couple of hours. If you're feeling all right by then, you can contact someone to take you home. But you shouldn't be alone tonight, just in case it has effects we don't expect."

"Can we have visitors?" I asked.

"Sure."

"Would you contact either Kendra Crawford or Paul Raskin from the lab, please. I need to talk to one of them."

"Mr. Raskin is outside right now," she said. "I'll send him to you once we've got you settled in the room. I'll stop by to see you again before we release you."

With that, she was gone, and a couple of nurses hurried in to move us to another room. I wanted to walk; they took me in a wheelchair anyway. Julie wanted to go home and rest there. They didn't listen to her either.

They let Raskin in once we were settled. He was pale, and worry furrowed his brow. "How are you feeling?" he asked us both as he walked in.

We assured him that the doctor seemed to think we'd be all right. "Any idea what did this to us?" I asked.

He shook his head. "We have a lot of dangerous chemicals around the lab, but everyone knows how to handle them. I did a quick check; nothing obvious is missing."

"How's Teri?"

"She seems fine, though she's got a bad headache. She must have been more sensitive to it than you were."

"She was working in there earlier," I said. "If the air is recirculated, whatever it was would have built up over time."

"That's right," Raskin said. "I've got EHS checking the room. Sorry—EHS is Environmental Health and Safety. They're decked out in moon suits going over the cold room. The director, the supervisor, and the grunt workers all delivered stern lectures on the evils of negligence. These guys are the new puritans."

From my hospital bed, I was considerably more sympathetic to those puritans than he was. "Are you going to tell me this was another accident?" I asked.

He shook his head grimly. "No. No more playing ostrich. The police are going over the lab right now."

"I'm surprised Kendra called them. She's been working hard at not facing reality."

"I called them," he said.

"Without her approval?"

He nodded. "She's pissed, to say the least. Told me she'd fire me if she wasn't so short on manpower."

"I'm sorry," I said, though I wasn't sorry he'd called the cops, only that he'd gotten in trouble.

"Don't worry. By tomorrow she'll have thought it through and realized it had to be this way. It's just taking her a bit longer to see what she doesn't want to see than it took me."

"So you finally believe Chuck was murdered," I said.

He nodded. "I really wanted to believe it was an accident, or at worst a prank gone wrong. I just couldn't accept that one of us was a killer." He looked miserable as he said it.

I heard Julie catch her breath and turned to look at her.

"So it really is one of us," she said. "And that person was trying to kill us today." Her voice was thin and strained. I sensed she was on the edge of tears.

"We probably weren't the intended victims," I said. "It was Teri's experiment. The killer couldn't know she'd ask us in to look at it."

"Why Teri?" Julie asked.

Why, indeed? I'd have given a good deal to have the answer to that one. I didn't really want to discuss it with Julie. Or with a man who had no past.

Raskin could tell we weren't in the best shape to talk, so he excused himself after a few minutes to go check on the lab. As he was turning to leave, Julie stopped him. "My envelopes, they're in the cold room. Would you get them for me?"

He promised to keep them someplace safe and left us, but he was back two hours later when Dr. Kopecko decided that we could go home. He'd arranged for one of Julie's housemates to take her, and he offered to drive me to San Francisco.

I told him Chris was on her way to pick me up.

"Can we talk for a minute before you go?" he asked.

I didn't feel much like talking. My stomach had settled down some, but my head still felt like someone had bored a hole straight through it. I started to put him off, but one look at his face changed my mind. "Sure," I said.

"I think it's time for me to be straight with you. But I need your word that you won't repeat what I tell you."

"I can't give you that before I know what it is," I said. "I try to protect what people tell me, but I won't go to jail for you, and I won't withhold evidence related to a murder."

He stared at me for a minute, then looked down at the floor, trying to make up his mind. Finally he said, "I don't think it's related. I hope to hell it's not, but after what happened today, I don't want to take any chances." He paused and cleared his throat.

"Fifteen years ago, I was a grad student up in Oregon. I was also something of a radical, involved with a group of environmentalists. We were pretty militant, at least we talked that way. We were fighting for a better world." He sighed heavily, and his tone was bitter when he added, "As if fighting ever brings a better world." He poured himself a cup of water from the pitcher next to my bed.

"There was a young kid, Jimmy Partlow. God, I think he was only a freshman. We should never have let him get involved with us. He was too angry." Raskin took a drink of water. His eyes had a faraway look, and his pain was so real that it seemed to shroud him.

His voice was hoarse when he spoke again. "For some reason Partlow attached himself to me. That spring we were fighting a chemical company that was dumping poison in the river—picketing, distributing leaflets, shooting off our mouths about how they were killing us. Our language got pretty extreme.

"We all felt very strongly. Maybe that's why I didn't realize that Partlow was going off the deep end when he kept railing about the killers. I should have paid more attention, but he was just a kid. I didn't take him seriously." Raskin swallowed hard. I wasn't sure he'd be able to go on.

"One fine afternoon, Jimmy marched up to the chemical plant with a backpack slung over his shoulder. The note we found later said he was going to blow up the capitalist bastards who profited from poisoning our water. But he slipped climbing over a wall, fell backward on the pack, and blew himself into a million pieces. If there hadn't been a note, they wouldn't even have known who he was."

Raskin leaned forward and put his head in his hands. We sat in silence for a few minutes. I wanted to comfort him, but he was locked in his own private place.

"The police assumed it was a conspiracy, of course, and started rounding up members of the group," he said, looking up at me. "I was closest to him, and I felt so damn guilty, I figured they'd be sure I was involved. So I threw my stuff in the car and disappeared. There was a warrant for a while. I don't even know if I'm still a fugitive or not."

Something in what he'd said stirred a memory. I tried to follow it but couldn't. I felt as if my brain had turned to steel wool.

"Does Kendra know?" I asked.

"No."

"Anyone else in the lab?"

"No. I'd appreciate it very much if you could keep it confidential. Will you do that?"

Keeping my eyes open took all the energy I could manage. Making decisions was way beyond me. I told him that.

33

THE MONSTER HEADACHE was down to human size by the next morning, and I felt a lot better than I'd expected to. I must have looked better, too, since Molly was sufficiently reassured to give me a bad time about the bare state of our luncheon larder.

"I suppose I could take cold leftover rice," she said in martyred tones.

I handed over money for lunch and made a note to add shopping for food to her list of duties at the office.

I didn't look good enough to keep Amy from fussing over me like a mother hen. She urged me to go home. Chris, who was looking for help with the papers piling up on her desk, argued that I shouldn't drive to Berkeley. I didn't have to deal with Jesse since the chip manufacturers had foolishly agreed to the insurance company's request to hire him directly.

Trying to work just made the headache worse. It only took me forty-five minutes to admit that I'd be better off at home. But before I left, I called Raskin.

"How's Julie?" I asked, after assuring him that I was no longer at death's door.

"She called in a while ago to say she's fine but she's still got a headache and is spending the day in bed. Teri hasn't been in, but she seemed all right last night."

"Any news from the police or EHS?"

"Lots," he said. "The police think they know what poisoned you and who did it. They've taken Dorian into custody."

"Dorian?"

"Yeah. They found a vial of EMS hidden behind the books on his lab bench. EMS is ethylmethane sulfonate. It's a Class 1 mutagen. A nasty chemical. We use it a lot to cause mutation, but we're real careful with it.

"EHS found a paper towel saturated with EMS in the cold room, behind the basket with the strawberries. There's no way it could have been an accident."

"Has Dorian confessed?"

"We don't know yet. He was protesting his innocence when they took him away."

"The vial could have been planted," I said.

"That's what Dorian claimed. But they also found a printout about the danger of EMS hidden in one of his books."

"That could have been planted, too. They'll need a confession to make the case," I said. "Are you surprised that it's Dorian?"

There was a pause. "Yes and no. He's high-strung and blows up easily. And he certainly never liked Chuck, but I still have trouble seeing him as a killer. I guess I'd have that reaction with any of the students, though. He really is the most likely one."

At home, I didn't have the energy to do much more than listen to music. I tried watching television. I got one of those talk shows where people reveal their most disgusting and embarrassing secrets in front of a national audience. This one was about a family that was suing their former baby-sitter for child abuse because she'd had sex with their son. The baby-sitter, just a kid herself, had gotten pregnant and was now suing the boy for child support. The program that followed it had a nineteen-year-old boy whose claim to fame was that he was a virgin and several teenage girls behind a screen who described, in detail, what they'd do to make his first time special.

I don't know what appalled me more—the fact that they put this stuff on television or that I'd just spent two hours watching it. It felt like the video equivalent of gawking at the wreck on the side of the road.

I had the disquieting realization that my own life wasn't any saner than the ones being probed on the tube. Maybe I could go on with Peter, Paul, and Kyle in "Women Who Are Attracted to Wild Men" or with Molly and Marion in "Women Who Subvert Their Nieces." Of course, I could just go solo on "Women Who Keep Finding Bodies."

I had lots of time that day to think about Dorian Barker's arrest. I should have been pleased that the killer had been caught; instead I was uneasy. It wasn't that I couldn't imagine Dorian killing someone. We're all capable of killing; it just depends on the circumstances. But Dorian was such an in-your-face guy, more a shooter than a poisoner.

Our killer was a planner, stealthy, indirect. That description fit almost anyone in the lab better than it did Dorian. And Dorian, with his tweaked personality and interest in guns, was exactly the kind of person that a brilliant, stealthy killer would pick for a fall guy.

The day wasn't a complete waste. As I was watching my tea steep, I made a connection I'd been struggling with since Paul had told me why he'd changed his identity. Something in his story had tugged at my memory. I realized it was the name of the ill-fated bomber. Partlow. At Raymond's memorial service, a friend had referred to his sister's reaction to "the news about the death of the Partlow boy."

It wasn't a common name. If it was the same Partlow,

Raskin and Raymond's sister had probably known each other at the time of the abortive bombing. She'd visited Raymond the weekend before his death. If she'd recognized Raskin, she might have told Raymond about his past. That would explain Raymond's reaction when I asked about Raskin and Crawford on the way back from the Oxford Tract. It could also explain why he acted as he had the afternoon before his death. If he'd decided to reveal Raskin's past to me, he'd have been unnerved by Paul's appearance just then.

I called Raskin to check it out.

"Did you know a Darla Zak in Oregon?" I asked.

"I knew a Darla, but her name wasn't Zak," he said. "Are you saying she was related to Raymond?"

"Could be. He had a sister in Oregon who knew the Partlow boy."

"Has to be Darla Criner. She rented out rooms. Jimmy lived at her place. But I don't remember her being married. No, wait a minute, I do remember her complaining about an ex-husband, so maybe she'd changed her name when she married."

"I wonder how she'd have recognized you. You didn't see her when she visited him, did you?"

"No, but I called that weekend. Could she have recognized my voice?"

"That's rather a long shot."

"The lab photo," he said. "Raymond took a bunch of photos just after the first of the year. He thought it'd help build a sense of community. I know he had a set of prints, because he was planning to bring them in."

"That's right. I remember now that I saw them. Darla must have recognized you."

"But what does that have to do with Raymond's and Chuck's deaths?"

"Probably nothing," I said. "But it explains why Raymond was so anxious to meet me away from the lab the morning he was killed."

So the incident that had made me suspect foul play in Raymond's death probably had nothing to do with it. Of course, it was possible he did know something about Chuck's sabotage of Julie's research. That was something we'd never know for sure.

The headache was gone the next morning. A good thing, since I don't think I could have managed a second day of talk television. On the drive to Berkeley I realized something else that had eluded me earlier. While Teri was the most likely target of the cold room murder attempt, Raisa was also a possibility. She was supervising Teri and had probably set the equipment up. The killer might easily have expected her to be the one in the cold room that morning.

I was surprised to find both Julie and Teri at the lab when I got there. Julie admitted that she still had a dull headache, but was too anxious to finish work on the corn envelopes to stay home.

I'd forgotten all about the envelopes. In the confusion after we collapsed, they'd been left unattended in the cold room for hours.

"Can you tell if anything is missing or has been tampered with?" I asked.

She frowned, then shook her head. "Not really. There're still kernels in some envelopes, so everything wasn't stolen, but someone could have switched them."

"And there's no way to know if that happened?"

She shook her head again. "No."

Kendra was at the police station or with the lawyers, Paul wasn't sure which. "About what I told you at the hospital," he said, as soon as we were alone in the office.

"I don't see any reason to tell anyone at this point," I said.

He looked relieved. He walked over to the window and leaned against the sill, looking out as he spoke. "I probably should have told Kendra, but I didn't see the point. I wanted to put it behind me."

He turned back toward me, but the glare from the window made it difficult to see his face. "I guess that's just not possible," he said with a sigh. "From the beginning I've been looking at things in terms of what happened fifteen years ago. I felt sorry for the saboteur, even sorrier when I thought he'd killed Chuck accidentally. I was so busy seeing myself in him that I was blind to what was really going on."

"It happens to all of us," I said. "We always see the present framed in terms of the past." I was struck by the irony of the situation; both Raskin and I had been struggling with our personal histories. His past had made him resist the suspicions that mine had stirred in me. We had to get beyond that now. There was too much at stake to let the past intrude.

"Tell me more about what the police found," I said.

"Well, I told you about the EMS . . ."

"Tell me more," I interrupted. "Tell me what effects it's likely to have on me."

"I wish I could answer that," Raskin said. He came back to the desk and sat down opposite me. "We don't know. We know it's a powerful mutagen, which means it's also a carcinogen, but we have no idea how much it takes to do damage."

"Oh, great, so we won't know for twenty years, at which point I'll either get cancer or I won't."

"And if you got it, you wouldn't know it was from EMS," Raskin pointed out. "From everything I can find, I think you're probably all right. You got an intense exposure but only for a short time. I'd like to be able to give you a definite answer, but that's the best I can do."

"What else did the police find?" I asked.

"A printout of information downloaded from the Internet. Seems there's a newsgroup on toxins, *alt.plants.poisons*, or something like that. It's mostly people working in labs but also some from industry, and they discuss various chemicals, their dangers, and so forth. Dorian had downloaded a notice reminding people to always use a panel in front of their faces when working with EMS in a hood. The notice describes how even a little bit can cause dizziness and loss of coordination, leading to loss of consciousness and ultimately death. It even mentions the sweet smell, a bit like overripe strawberries."

"Sounds familiar," I said. "And he got it off the Net."

"That's the thing that seems so strange," Paul said. "Dorian was the last person I'd have expected to go searching for this in cyberspace. Lots of us subscribe to the *bionet.plants* newsgroup. You can ask a question and an hour later have answers from researchers around the world. But one of Dorian's little idiosyncrasies was his distrust of that kind of communication. I don't ever remember him using the Net."

"Did anyone check to make sure it was he who logged on and downloaded that information?"

"I tried," Raskin said. "But it was done from the machine in our library, so it could have been anyone in the lab."

Julie, Teri, and Raisa were talking together when I came out of the office. It was almost lunchtime, and I suggested we walk up to the Northside to get lunch. When I added, "My treat," they were ready to go.

The high fog had thinned and was beginning to break up, leaving patches of blue sky and promising a sunny afternoon. Most of the fruit trees were leafed out, but we passed one splendid apple covered with pink-white blossoms.

Northside is the back door to Cal, or maybe the side door. Located across the campus from the Sather Gate entrance at Telegraph Avenue, it's much quieter—and before the university recently erected two concrete pillars to simulate a gate, it looked like a driveway.

Restaurant selection is more limited on the Northside,

but we found a narrow courtyard surrounded by small restaurants that allowed us to choose from five different cuisines. Julie ordered a feta and spinach crepe, Teri chose a Japanese bento box, and Raisa and I got *bimidbab*—beef, vegetables, and egg over rice—from the Korean restaurant.

We found a table in the sun and waited for our food.

"I feel as if I've been on a roller coaster," Julie said. "Sometimes I'm all excited about the discovery, then I'm sad about Chuck and Raymond, and now I'm scared. One good thing, though: when I told my parents, it was maybe the first time they haven't suggested I made a mistake by not going to med school. Of course, I didn't tell them about the bad stuff."

"Your parents wanted you to go to med school?" Teri asked.

"Yeah, they *really* wanted me to be a doctor. They were worried I wouldn't make nearly as much money being a scientist."

"Well, at least they wanted you to be successful," Teri said. "My parents wrote me off. My older brother's at Harvard and my younger brother's a freshman at Stanford. I outscored them both on the SATs and I got better grades, but I'm at Cal because my parents wouldn't pay for a private university."

"But Cal's a really good school," Julie protested.

"Not good enough for my brothers," Teri said, "just for me."

" 'Cause you're the girl, right?" Raisa said. "My dad was like that. 'Your brothers'll have to support a family,' he'd say, like I was going to go through life on a full scholarship. Course, my brothers didn't get any more than I did since in my family there was nothing to get. You're lucky your family has money. At least they can help you out if you get caught short."

"I suppose," Teri said.

"Believe it," Raisa said. "I've been just scraping by

since I started college. Thank God for fellowships. But I figure that if I get a good job, in five years I'll be making more than either of my brothers. That'll be sweet."

Teri nodded knowingly. "My brothers keep bragging about how much money they're going to make, and my dad just eggs them on. Boy, would I like to show them."

Raisa and Teri had clearly found a subject of shared passion. I could see why they'd been attracted to Kendra. Not only did she provide a role model, they needed someone to take them seriously.

Once we had our food, I asked what they thought of Dorian's arrest. They all seemed relieved and none voiced the misgivings that Raskin and I had.

"I don't understand why he did it, though," Julie said.

"Because he was nuts," Raisa said. "Why else would anyone do a thing like that?"

34

IT WAS FOUR by the time I got back to the office, and Molly was there. She and Chris appeared at my office door before I'd gotten my jacket off. Molly had an expression I couldn't read; she seemed both excited and apprehensive.

"We may have something for you," Chris announced. "I think we know who stole the seed."

"Great," I said, then stopped myself. "I thought I told you not to involve Molly in this."

"You did, and I didn't," Chris said. "Molly involved herself."

I turned sternly to Molly. She was shifting from one foot to the other and looking increasingly guilty. "I, uh, well, I sneaked a look at the file on your desk," she said. "I know you said not to but I thought that reading it couldn't do any harm. I was just curious."

I resisted cat clichés.

"Anyway, Chris asked me to put some papers on your desk, and the one on top was her report on orders for grow lights. I noticed something I thought you should know."

"Which was?"

"Neither Galen Wells nor any of the people from the lab ordered lights, but Ethan Mather did," Chris said.

"Ethan Mather?" I said in surprise.

Chris and Molly nodded in unison. "He wasn't on my list, so I missed him. Molly remembered his name from the case file."

"The case file you were forbidden to read," I said.

Molly tried to look abashed. It's a new expression for her. She didn't quite have it down yet.

"You're grounded," I said. "For a week."

"But not fired?" she asked in a hopeful voice.

"No, not fired," I said. "This time." I thought to myself that if I could ever get her to follow instructions, she'd make a damn good assistant. "Now, get back to work while Chris and I figure out what this means."

Molly hustled out. I thought she looked a bit disappointed.

"Don't be too tough on the kid," Chris said. "You know it's exactly what you'd have done in her place."

"Which is a good reason to be tough on her," I said. "I don't want to see her get into some of the fixes I've been in."

"So does that mean you'll call the police and let them handle Ethan Mather?"

"I probably would if it were the Albany police; Wilson seems like a sharp cop. I'm less impressed by Dreyer at

UC, and he's the one I'd have to go to. According to Teri Shaw, Mather knew enough about Chuck's allergies to sabotage the mask, and he could have had a key to the greenhouse. But he couldn't have set up the poisoning in the cold room. And he's about the last person I'd have figured would steal the corn. I really want to question him myself."

"Just like Molly," Chris said. "Too damn curious to follow the rules. I don't suppose you'd consider having someone back you up for this interview."

"Don't fuss," I said. "Of course I'll take backup. Where's Jesse?"

"Jesse's in Santa Cruz. He may or may not be headed for Monterey tonight, depending on what he finds."

"I guess I can wait," I said. "Unless, of course, you want to ride shotgun."

"Not me," Chris said. "I might chip a nail."

And I would have waited, if Kyle hadn't called a half hour later.

"Wells claims he doesn't have a facility he can show me," he reported. "I've pressed pretty hard. I don't think it's going to happen."

"It looks as if he doesn't have the corn room seed after all," I said. "Though I'd still bet on him having the seed Chuck stole from the greenhouse."

"I feel like a failure as an undercover operative," Kyle complained.

"Nah, finding out who doesn't have something can be as valuable as knowing who does. I may need someone to watch my back during an interview tomorrow. Want to volunteer?"

"Sure," Kyle said with a little too much enthusiasm, reminding me why I'd hesitated to involve him in the first place.

"I'll give you a call if I need you."

"Why don't you just tell me where to be and when and I'll be there."

"I'll call between nine and ten," I said.

Jesse did go to Monterey, and against my better judgment I called Kyle. He agreed to meet me at the Albany greenhouse at ten-thirty.

Ethan Mather wasn't at his grass patch, but he was inside one of the greenhouses. This one was full of pots of what looked like healthy weeds, late summer vacant-lot mix.

"You stay by the door," I told Kyle. "This is a seen-and-not-heard job."

"Yez, boz," he said. "You sure he's not armed?"

I looked in at Mather. He was wearing Levi's and a sweatshirt that had shrunk. There wasn't anyplace on his skinny frame to hide a gun. "I think we're safe," I said.

Mather looked up and smiled in recognition when I came into the greenhouse. "You're the detective," he said. "I'm sorry, I still don't remember your name."

"No problem," I said. "It's Catherine Sayler." By now I was standing only a few feet away. The bright light of the greenhouse made it easy to see his face. "I've come about Julie's seed from the corn room."

He should never have tried being a thief. His face gave him away immediately. First his eyebrows shot up in shock, then he drew his head back a bit, and his eyes bounced around as if he were looking for a place to hide. "I . . . I . . . I didn't," he said, looking as guilty as anyone I'd ever confronted.

"Come on, Ethan," I said, in my kindly mother-confessor voice, "I have the evidence."

"No," he said. "You can't prove anything. I don't have to talk to you."

"No, you don't. Would you rather talk to the police?"

Guilty gave way to scared. "I'm not talking to anyone.

I don't have to," he said. The defiance in his words was contradicted by the tremor in his voice.

"Look, Ethan, if I go to the police with this, you'll end up with a police record. That's bad. But much worse is that you become a suspect in a murder investigation."

"Murder?" His voice cracked as he said it.

"Chuck Nishimura's death was no accident. His mask was sabotaged," I said.

"You don't think I . . . I mean, just because we argued, you don't think . . ."

He stammered, then reached up under his sweatshirt.

I moved in fast, slapped his hand down, and caught it between mine.

Mather didn't struggle. He stared at me in shock. "Please," he said. "I need my inhaler." He sounded as if he had a head cold.

"Show me," I said.

"It's in my shirt pocket."

I kept my grip with one hand and raised his sweatshirt with the other. As he'd said, there was an inhaler in his pocket. I gave it to him.

"I'm sorry," I said, "I thought you might be reaching for a weapon. Do you need to go outside?"

He took a couple of deep breaths from the inhaler, then shook his head. "This time of year, outside's no better than inside. Damn allergies."

"I guess you and Chuck had something in common after all," I said.

"Thank God mine aren't as bad as his. I wouldn't have wished that kind of death on my worst enemy. And he wasn't my worst enemy; I just didn't like him much."

"I believe you, but there's no telling what the police will think."

He looked at me long and hard, then took another hit from the inhaler. On the right side of the greenhouse, the pots sat on a wooden platform that was raised about three feet above the floor. Mather sat down on the edge of it.

"Okay," he said. "I give you the seeds, you forget where you got them. Is that the deal?"

"As long as I don't find any evidence that you were involved in any of the sabotage or attacks on students."

He sighed heavily. "Okay. I don't have the seeds here. I'll pick them up tonight, give them to you tomorrow. That acceptable?"

"Why not today?"

"Because I promised Vipul I'd do a bunch of work on his plants. The seeds'll wait; the plants won't."

"Why did you steal them?" I asked. "You seemed like the last person who'd want to hurt Julie or to profit from her discovery."

"I didn't want to hurt her," he protested. "I wouldn't have. Her career depends on the discovery, not the patent. And I wasn't trying to get rich, not for myself. Sit down, for Chrissake, you make me nervous."

I sat down on the bench. Kyle stayed in the doorway. Mather seemed unaware of him.

"Julie and I had arranged to have dinner Wednesday night, not a date, just friends getting together. She told me all about the great discovery. I was happy for her. We had a couple of drinks, got to talking about how ironic it was that she'd wanted to work on ways to feed poor people and she'd ended up helping rich people lose weight.

"After she left, I got to thinking about all the money this thing would generate, and how it'd either go into some capitalist's pocket or back to the university to fritter away. And I thought how sweet it would be if money from this appetite suppressant could be used to fund research to feed hungry people.

"You know there's a lot we could do, a lot we need to know, but we can't do the research because there's no profit in it. Private enterprise only wants to figure out how to use more fertilizer and pesticides. People like

Crawford think they're too good to deal with such mundane problems; everybody else works for agribusiness.

"We could have used that money to set up an independent lab, one where we'd work on real problems, ways to increase yields without using chemicals. Aklilu was in India last month; he saw farmers who'd stirred the chemicals with their arms because no one had warned them not to. You have any idea what that did to them?"

His voice was stronger now and I could hear anger in it. He was probably right. His cause was certainly just, but I raised my hand to stop him.

"I'm not going to look the other way, Ethan. Not and let you keep those seeds. They belong to Julie and the lab, and I want them back."

He nodded. "Tomorrow. One o'clock. Here. I'll have them for you."

As we left, Kyle could barely contain his excitement. "That was great," he said, as soon as we were in the car. "What a scheme! The guy's a real Robin Hood, using profits from an appetite suppressant to feed the hungry. I love it. This has been terrific. I think I could really get into this detecting shit."

"Down, Kyle," I said. "I really appreciate your help, but believe me, there's not nearly enough excitement or profit in detecting to interest you."

He thought a moment. "You're probably right. I have a high-maintenance lifestyle."

I said a silent prayer of gratitude. It was bad enough having Molly involved in my work. Kyle would be a disaster.

35

SHOWERS ARE THE mothers of invention. Warm water streaming over the body frees the mind to make the kinds of leaps it refuses to perform when pushed in the workaday world.

It was in the shower that I figured out who had killed Chuck Nishimura. The pieces had been there, I realized, but so cleverly hidden that I'd missed them entirely. Knowing who the killer was didn't mean I could prove it.

This was the kind of case where only a confession would be strong enough to stand up in court. There was no witness, no concrete evidence, not even the proof that a crime had been committed.

That left me with only one option, to design a trap that would net a confession. It took longer than a shower to figure it out, but I solved that one as I was fixing dinner. Unfortunately, I burned the spaghetti sauce, so we ate canned soup and toast, which was fine, since I was in a hurry anyway.

Jesse was back in town and only too happy to provide backup. I called Raskin at home and got him to agree to meet us at the lab. The preparations took over an hour, but we were finished before midnight.

We met in the parking lot at seven-thirty the next morning to go over things one last time. I reminded Jesse to try to get Detective Dreyer there before we got rolling, then Jesse helped Raskin rehearse his part. Everything depended on his sounding convincing.

"Oh, hello, Catherine," Raskin said, pretending to speak into a phone. He paused for several beats. "What good news?" Another, longer pause. "Oh my God, that's right, you did put a camera in there. I'd completely forgotten. You think we got him taking the EMS?" A shorter pause, then: "That's terrific. Just what the cops need. They released him, you know, told him he couldn't come near the lab. . . . Yeah, yeah, I agree. I think it sucks."

He paused again but nodded as if silently agreeing, and said, "Well, the tape ought to take care of that. You want me to get it from the recorder in the darkroom? . . . No, sure, you know how to work the equipment. I'll wait for you."

After a final pause, he said, "Okay, see you in an hour or so."

We all grinned at each other. "Showtime," I said.

I was in place in the darkroom at eight o'clock. The knock on the door that told me our quarry had arrived came at nine fifty-five. I checked my watch and waited. Jesse would be placing the call in ten minutes. If all went as expected, I wouldn't have to wait much beyond that.

After ten minutes, I crouched behind a large cabinet that hid me from anyone standing in the doorway. Seven minutes later, I heard the key in the lock. The door opened and closed and the light flicked on. I stood to confront Teri Shaw.

She gasped in surprise.

"Well, well," I said. "And I thought it'd be Paul Raskin. Looking for something?" I held up a blank tape.

She stared at me in amazement, trying to decide how to react.

"You're very bright for a kid," I said. "I never even thought of you as a serious suspect. Why the hell did you do it?"

"Do what?" she asked. "I don't know what you're talking about."

"Kill Raymond and Chuck. Try to kill Julie and me. You know your picture's going to be on this tape. That'll start the police digging, and when they dig deep enough, they'll find something you forgot. They'll certainly find Galen Wells. I wonder what he'll tell them when they threaten him with a murder charge? And I'll bet they'll find papers from Chuck's apartment."

"They'll never prove a thing," she said. Her voice was cold, not even a trace of fear. "No one will believe I could have killed those two. Or you. I'm just a sweet little college girl, the kid next door. You didn't take me seriously. They won't either."

"Why?" I asked. "Why did you do it?"

"You still don't have a clue, do you?" she said, and made a bitter sound that might have been a laugh. "I did it for the same reason Chuck stole the seed. Money. Money and power. I'll bet you thought I was a woman scorned. Well, I was the one who told Chuck to pretend to break up with me so he could get close to Julie and find out more about her work. We could have been rich if the schmuck hadn't freaked out after Raymond died."

"Why did Chuck kill Raymond?"

"Chuck didn't kill Raymond. Raymond just died." She sounded disgusted. Certainly not remorseful.

"But Chuck fed him the appetite suppressant."

"I fed him the stuff. Chuck was too squeamish. He had a fit when he found out. I suppose he was right in the end. It really screwed up everything when fatso died. How was I to know he had a weak heart?"

"Of course," I said. "Chuck wouldn't have tried the corn on a human subject; he knew better than to risk a human trial when you knew so little about it."

"He wasn't so smart," she said. "He just didn't have the balls. He was afraid to take the risk. I was surprised he got it together to go see Wells."

"And because he was afraid, Wells decided to kill him."

"I decided," she said sharply. "Wells was almost as much of a coward as Chuck. He loves to talk about risks, but he was scared to death when he found out we'd stolen that corn."

"I still don't understand why you killed Chuck," I said. "Wells needed him to front for the new company. It would have been so much easier with him alive."

"Except that he freaked out. Once Raymond died, he was afraid to go on with the deal with Wells. Then with you poking around, he really spazzed. He just lost it. Couldn't take the pressure. He'd have cracked and gone running to the cops."

"So you killed him to keep him quiet."

"It was the only way," she said. "I couldn't let him turn me in."

"And the attacks on Julie? You were behind those, too?"

"Chuck took the vials from the refrigerator, but they weren't any good without Julie's notes. I slipped some stuff in her coffee to make her sick and get her out of the lab."

As I talked, I could see her eyes search the room. Letting me talk was her way of stalling, killing time while she decided what to do.

"I've got to give you credit for the cold room scheme," I said. "If it had worked, you'd have been rid of me and Julie. Wells would have been assured of his patent. Dorian would have been arrested, and if there were ever questions about Chuck's death, he'd have been the fall guy. With everyone thinking you were the intended victim, they'd never have suspected you of Chuck's death."

Something shifted in her expression. The uncertainty was gone. "With you dead, they still won't suspect me," she said. She reached behind her and shot the bolt on the door, then hit the light panel, simultaneously switching off the overhead light and turning on the red safe light and the outside IN USE sign that warned against opening the door.

The room was bathed in the silky warmth of red light. It was a bad move on her part. During the seconds it took our eyes to adjust, we were in near-darkness. If she'd been as smart as she thought she was, she might have wondered why I didn't rush her then.

In the red gloom she reached for a bottle on the counter. A bottle marked "Sulfuric Acid, Concentrated" with a skull and crossbones on the label. I could barely see what she did with it until I felt the cold liquid hit my face.

The door burst open and Shaw spun around as Detective Dreyer barked, "Freeze." She dropped the bottle and it shattered on the floor, then after a second she slowly raised her hands over her head.

"You guys sure took your time," I complained. "What were you waiting for, an engraved invitation?"

"The door stuck, the one on our room, not yours," Jesse said. "You okay?"

"I'm fine," I said, reaching for the towel I'd left on the floor in the corner. "Wouldn't you know, we remove the bolt from this lock and the other one sticks. Did you get all that on tape?"

"Sure did. She came through clear as could be."

The hall was rapidly filling with people from the surrounding labs. Detective Dreyer had handcuffed Shaw and was reading her her rights in an officious tone.

"I knew she'd go for the acid," I told Jesse. We'd carefully removed any object that might serve as a weapon, but even when you think you've found everything, it's a good idea to provide a distraction. I figured the bottle of acid would appeal to Shaw; that's why I'd replaced the acid with water.

Dreyer took Shaw back to Crawford's office while Jesse and I checked the tape and gathered up the recording equipment. We'd taken the camera from the greenhouse and hidden it in the darkroom so that when the time came, the DA could do show-and-tell for the jury. That tape should make it considerably harder for Shaw to pull off her innocent schoolgirl facade.

Shaw had retreated into silence as soon as she was read her rights. She sat stonily in Kendra's office, staring at the floor. I was struck by how young she looked, not much older than Molly, really.

How could things go so wrong in one so young? In my college psych course they'd have blamed her parents. Now they'd probably suspect her genes. I wonder if science will ever be able to explain why one kid who's beaten and raised in poverty grows up to become a civic leader and another raised with wealth and privilege ends up a killer. I doubt we'd want it to.

I realized Teri was staring at me intently. "You set me up," she said, her voice more surprised than angry. Then she turned to Dreyer. "I want to talk to Catherine alone. Can I?"

Dreyer didn't like the idea of leaving his prisoner, but I wanted to hear what she had to say. I got him to agree to wait just outside the door by suggesting that I might get information useful to "his" case and pointing out that he could watch us through the window.

Once we were alone, she said, "How did you know?"

"You told me that Ethan Mather had taunted Chuck about his allergies by saying that maybe the universe was trying to tell him something. But Ethan also has allergies. I couldn't see him making that comment."

"That's it?" she said incredulously. "That's all? You decided I was guilty based on that?"

"Once I considered the possibility you might be guilty, I realized that you were the one most likely to know what Chuck was up to," I said. "You'd have seen the rats in his apartment; he'd have discussed his plan with you.

"And I could see how neatly your personality fit the

crimes. Chuck's murder and the cold room scheme were much too subtle and indirect for Dorian. If he'd wanted to kill Chuck, he'd have confronted him with a weapon, probably a gun. But subtlety and indirection, those are the tools of a woman who considers herself very smart, smarter than almost anyone else."

She frowned as I said the last part, and I had the feeling that she wanted to correct me, to object that she *was* smarter than almost anyone.

"I remembered your saying how much your parents valued money," I continued. "And how they assumed only your brothers would be able to become wealthy. Chuck's scheme with its huge payoff would have made you rich long before your brothers made their fortunes. That must have been terribly tempting."

"I'd have showed them," she said bitterly. "They'd have been coming to me for loans." Her face twisted in a nasty pout.

"And that, the ability to prove something to your family, that was worth the lives of two men?" I struggled to keep the anger out of my voice.

The pout never left her face. "You wouldn't understand," she said.

She was right. I wouldn't. And I didn't want to. I was out of the room before I realized that my hands had tightened into fists.

Detective Dreyer had overheard Shaw's confession in the darkroom, and it did wonders for his commitment to nailing Galen Wells and recovering the corn that Chuck had stolen from the greenhouse. Faced with the threat that he could be part of a murder case, Wells would be only too happy to return the corn and bargain for a slap on the wrist.

"And the seed from the corn room," Kendra said as we discussed it. "Make sure he returns that, too."

"He doesn't have it," I said. "I'm picking it up at one o'clock."

"Who has it?" Kendra asked.

"I had to promise not to reveal the identity of the thief. It was the only way I could get it back. I figured you wanted the corn more than you wanted revenge."

Put that way, she had to agree, but she wasn't happy about it.

36

JESSE AND I got down to the Albany greenhouse at a quarter to one. Ethan Mather wasn't there. Not only wasn't Ethan there, most of his grass plants weren't either. His outdoor plot was a patchwork of fresh holes where plants had been dug out.

"Damn," I said. "I never figured he'd be dumb enough to run. He hasn't got the resources to get far."

Vipul and the other bio-control guys claimed they hadn't seen him and knew nothing about his whereabouts, but none of them were very good liars.

"He's going to make it much worse on himself," I told them. "I can't keep his identity a secret now. He's going to turn a misdemeanor into much more serious charges. You'd be doing him a favor by convincing him to give himself up."

"We don't know anything," Vipul said. The others all nodded.

The nurseryman I found in the barn was more helpful.

"Ethan, he's gone," he said, and went back to shoveling soil into the autoclave to sterilize it.

"Any idea where?"

"I don't know, but far. Out of the country. Said he wouldn't be coming back."

"Where would he get the money to do that?" Jesse asked. "I thought you said he lived on the margin."

"Maybe from the guy in the Jag," the nurseryman said.

"Oh, shit," I said. Jesse gave me a look that said he knew what I was thinking and we headed back to get the cell phone in the car.

I found Kyle's number in my book and dialed. His secretary answered. She informed me that Kyle was out of the country for a few days. Would I like to leave a message?

Would I ever. A long list of obscenities came to mind. I decided to save them to deliver in person.

"Kyle's out of the country for a few days," I told Jesse.

"Oh, shit."

"My thoughts exactly. The bastard's taken Mather and the corn and gone to set up his own lab offshore. He's probably starting the patent application as we speak."

"But won't Crawford be able to beat him to it, especially since she has the mutant corn that Nishimura stole?"

"She's got the edge for a U.S. patent, but I'd bet he'll apply for one in England or France. Crawford's got the research, but Kyle's got connections to patent attorneys who make the university lawyers look like preschoolers. And he can fund his lab as generously as he needs to. I'd say it'll be a close race."

Jesse shook his head. "I never realized he was so unscrupulous. I knew he played by his own rules, but I didn't think he was a crook. The greedy bastard."

"Oh, no. It's not greed," I said. "This isn't about money. This is about getting rich consumers to pay for feeding poor people. We're talking Robin Hood, not Rockefeller."

"Robin Hood?" Jesse said.

"The profits for this little scheme will fund a lab to

develop plants that are insect-resistant or grow in sandy soils or need less water. The kind of stuff that's only valuable to people too poor to demand that it be done."

"Sounds good, but you really think Kyle'll go for that? That he won't rip Ethan off and take the profits himself?"

I shook my head. "It's not that Kyle's a closet saint, but money's not as important to him as he pretends. It's just a way of keeping score. And playing Robin Hood is much more fun than playing Rockefeller. No, Kyle will have a ball helping Ethan set up this lab."

Jesse shrugged. "Rich folks feeding poor folks seems like a good idea to me."

"Yeah," I said. I was beginning to cool down a bit. "It does have a certain appeal."

"A lovely twisted morality, I'd say." Jesse grinned as he quoted my own words back to me.

I told myself that I wasn't really responsible for Kyle's scheme, though my poor judgment had made it possible, and that I'd do the ethical thing and not charge Kendra Crawford for the last phase of the case. I still felt guilty. A little.

Crawford was furious, of course. And angrier at me than at Ethan. I accepted the tongue-lashing. I had it coming.

Raskin didn't say much, but an odd half-smile played at the corner of his lips from time to time. He was working as hard at suppressing it as I was at acting repentant.

As I was leaving, he asked if I'd join him at Pat Brown's.

It was too cold to sit outside, so we took a table next to the window.

"So," he said. "Business is over. You up for pleasure?" His sensual grin had the same effect it'd had at our first meeting. My body was not at all interested in monogamy.

I smiled back. "It's tempting," I said. "But I'm already in a relationship. Even if it is long-distance at the moment."

"Too bad," he said. "I'd have liked to get to know you better."

"Me, too," I thought, but I was trying hard to be better behaved than I wanted to be, so I said, "If you'd like, I can look into the status of the charges in Oregon. There's a good chance you can stop running."

"Thank you. I'd like that. I think I'm ready to settle. I'm pretty excited by the possibilities at the lab."

"Kendra's or Ethan's?"

He laughed. "You're a sharp lady," he said. "There was a time I'd have joined Ethan in a minute. But now I think I'll stay here at the university. It's not that I think what we're doing is more important than what he's doing; it's just that I'm more interested in this now."

"So you've chosen Kendra's kind of fire," I said, referring to our discussion over lunch.

"I guess I have," he said. "It's a powerful thing, that sense that you can suddenly understand a little piece of the universe." There was an edge of excitement to his voice, the same excitement I'd heard when he was explaining Julie's discovery. "I didn't realize how much I missed doing science. I guess that after what happened to Jimmy Partlow, I was afraid of it, afraid of feeling that strongly about anything."

"What changed?"

"I don't know. Maybe I realized life's too short to live it halfway." He smiled and it lit his eyes; then the smile faded. "But it's also true that I've lost my taste for living on the edge. This whole thing has really shaken me. To find that an ordinary kid like Teri could kill in cold blood . . ." He shook his head. "I don't know how you do what you do."

He seemed to be waiting for an answer. I didn't have one.

We sat in silence for a few moments, then he said, "I was wrong when I said you were afraid of the fire. You may be afraid, but you also love it. You had a great time setting up the sting; you were juiced when you confronted Teri."

I was. It was true. Maybe I was getting addicted to danger.

37

IT TOOK PETER three weeks to get home, and it'd have taken a lot longer if Kyle hadn't stopped in Guatemala City on his way back to the United States and discovered that Peter and the forensic anthropologist were in jail up-country.

I spent two weeks on the phone to Washington; Kyle spent two weeks talking to Guatemalan officials. My talks went nowhere; Kyle's paid off. More likely, Kyle paid off. He refused to tell us exactly how he managed the prisoners' release, but I was pretty sure it involved large sums of money.

The crisis with Peter drove all thoughts of corn and Ethan Mather from my mind, and by the time Peter, the anthropologist, and Kyle got home, I wasn't about to hassle my lover's rescuer. The closest we ever came to discussing it was one evening when Peter tried to get Kyle to let him contribute to the payoffs. Kyle smiled wickedly and said, "Not to worry. Catherine's already taken care of that."

To Peter's credit and Kyle's disappointment, he didn't rise to the bait. He merely gave me a quizzical look and waited till later for an explanation. When I told him of Kyle's double cross, he was delighted. The idea of wringing weight from the rich to help put pounds on the poor appealed to him as much as it had Kyle.

I've become rather fond of the idea myself.

Molly managed to bring her grades up to B's and is doing almost too well at the office. She's co-opted Amy and Chris and is working on Jesse. I knew things had gone too far when she got Amy to intercede on her behalf during curfew negotiations. On the other hand, Chris has begun advising her on her wardrobe and we haven't had an argument about body pierces in weeks.

Paul Raskin, whose real name is Paul Rawlins, is no longer wanted by the Oregon police. They closed the case years ago. He's stayed at the Crawford lab and seems to be succeeding at making it a happier place. I still don't understand how he can work for Kendra; he must see a side of her that I missed.

And Peter. It took three weeks to get him home, but only one long kiss to convince me that I'd been right to resist Raskin's charms. As for Alicia, since her carelessness was the reason Peter ended up in jail, I don't think we'll be seeing much of her for a while.

I haven't had a nightmare since we caught Teri Shaw. Now it's Peter who wakes up several times a night. But I don't mind. I'd much rather be the one who offers comfort than the one who needs it.

"She may specialize in corporate crime, but Sayler, a black belt in aikido, is no white-collar wimp."
—*Entertainment Weekly*

BLIND TRUST
A Catherine Sayler Mystery

by LINDA GRANT

When Catherine Sayler's biggest client goes broke, she can't be choosy about her cases. So she agrees to help First Central Bank find a missing hacker—to prevent him from using the bank's flawed computer system to steal a huge amount of money.

If he isn't found in fourteen days, millions of dollars will be gone. And as Catherine gets closer, she discovers she's not searching alone.

Mitch Morrison is a loner and a recovering alcoholic—and now he's dead. Catherine Sayler thinks his murder is connected to a respected judge who sexually abused Mitch when he was a child.

As she uncovers evidence against the judge, she learns about the perils children face every day—placing both her reputation and her life on the line.

LOVE NOR MONEY

by LINDA GRANT

"A tense, powerful, sensitive, and even hopeful novel with complex characters."
—*San Francisco Chronicle*

Published by Ivy Books.
Available at your local bookstore.

Private investigator Catherine Sayler's case starts out routinely: Systech Corporation wants her to find out who is sending lewd e-mail messages through the company's computer system.

But the situation worsens when female employees start receiving photographs of women being tortured—and then Catherine discovers a brutal murder. When the perverted killer begins to stalk her, she finds it will take all her strength and intelligence to survive.

A WOMAN'S PLACE

by LINDA GRANT

"A guaranteed pulse-pumper . . . A superb psychological thriller that'll keep you glancing anxiously over your shoulder until the very last body bag is zipped up."

—*The Washington Post*

Murder on the Internet

Ballantine mysteries are on the Web!

Read about your favorite Ballantine authors and upcoming books in our monthly electronic newsletter MURDER ON THE INTERNET, at **www.randomhouse.com/BB/MOTI**.

Including:
- What's new in the stores
- Previews of upcoming books for the next three months
- In-depth interviews with mystery authors and publishers
- Calendars of signings and readings for Ballantine mystery authors
- Bibliographies of mystery authors
- Excerpts from new mysteries

To subscribe to MURDER ON THE INTERNET, send an e-mail to **srandol@randomhouse.com** asking to be added to the subscription list. You will receive the next issue as soon as it's available.